CHAPTER ONE

As he slowly awoke, he found himself staring up into a deep blue sky. It was a cloudless sky, peaceful, with the faintest haze of sunlight coming from behind his head, so scant he was hardly aware of it. A distant refrain echoed through his head repeatedly: 'Something's got a hold on you...something's got a hold on you...' The words meandered about aimlessly and the softly reverberating voice faded away.

As his senses slowly returned, he realised he was lying flat on his back, on what felt like grass. The air was stiflingly warm and he was sweating profusely. Slowly sitting up, he scrunched his watering eyes shut against the invasive bright sunlight. Feeling dizzy, he put his hands to his head. Immediately, he felt a damp sensation spreading throughout his slick hair, down his neck and trickling through his fingers. He looked down at his outspread hands: blood. Both his hands were sticky and dark red. They looked almost alien, as if not his. His head began to throb with a pain that spread from the back to the front, trying to scramble its way out through his burning eyes. He heard no real sounds, just a dull murmur, as if his ears were stuffed with cotton. He frowned, looking down at his hands. He felt as though he was having an out of body experience, as if he was looking at someone else sitting here on the grass and not...what was his name? How could he not remember his own name?

A shrill scream jolted him awake, slashing through his foggy haze like a razor blade, senses bursting awake in a flash. The man looked up from his blood-smeared hands and inches from his feet, saw a dead bird. A huge gull of some sort, cleaved in half, dark blood oozing out of its body, pooling at his feet. Beyond the gull, a few more feet away, the source of the scream, an old woman stood facing him, her dull eyes staring plainly at him. Strangely, the woman's face was expressionless, the mouth open, but no sound coming out. Her screaming had stopped quickly and her mouth was agape. He didn't recognise her and she did not appear to recognise him. She looked old and haggard, dressed in a velour grey tracksuit and white trainers, stained and dirty. Her eyes were looking at him but, somehow, not seeing him. It felt as if she was staring right through him. He watched as the decrepit, pale, woman, abruptly fell forward, face down, her head thudding onto the ground beside the gull. She made no effort to stop herself, her arms hanging limply at her side as she plummeted down.

His brow furrowed in confusion as the woman's head smashed into the ground. The back of the woman was a bloody mess. Her clothing was ripped open exposing nothing but torn tissue, melted skin and muscles dripping with blood. Rays of sunshine bounced off the glistening bones of her exposed spine. The back of her skull was open, pried apart like a coconut and he could see her milky, mushy brain. He started to feel queasy, delirious. Where was he? What had happened? Closing his eyes and drawing breath to concentrate, he tried to remember. Nothing came to him. He tried to remember his name, where he was. He drew a complete blank. He clambered to his feet so he could look around and work out where he was, trying not to look at the dead woman in front of him, hoping he would recognise something, or someone.

Lying to his right was another woman, much younger, perhaps in her thirties he guessed. Behind her, a low, square, sign, reading B77 in bold, black, paint. The yellow sign with black print was cracked and it meant nothing to him. He refocused on the young woman. He didn't know if she was dead or alive, but there were no immediate signs of injury. She was wearing jeans and a green top, but no shoes. Her feet were bare, which struck him as quite odd. Her face, wrapped in curly brown hair, was beautiful but dirty, as though smudged with charcoal. For one fleeting moment, he thought he recognised her, but he couldn't think of a name or where he'd seen her before. It occurred to him that he should see if she was okay, but before he could do anything, he glanced away to his left and panic charged through his body. His heart started pounding faster and faster, as if trying to keep time with the pulsing drumbeat in his head.

He saw a huge aeroplane in front of him, split in half, slumped on a concrete runway like a beached whale, guts and entrails spilling out, snaking their way across the tarmac. The escape chutes were open and there was black smoke billowing from the rear of the plane, hiding its tail. Sunlight skipped off the broken wings and scattered pieces of metal so brightly that he had to shield his eyes from the glare. He estimated the plane was a hundred feet away, maybe two at the most. Between him and the plane, debris was everywhere: suitcases, shards of metal, fabric, clothing...bodies. The runway was awash with dead bodies and people were laid out on the tarmac, as if sunbathing. Parts of them were scattered around unevenly over the runway. He saw severed arms, legs, heads, hands, parts he couldn't even recognise: just hunks of meat and blood. Was he a passenger, a survivor? He couldn't remember being on the plane, but then he couldn't remember anything right now.

He noticed a few people milling around closer to the plane, though they were too far away to see clearly. His hearing was getting better, the low growl in his head fading, and he began to hear shouting, moans, and calls for help. He looked closer around him on the grass verge and realised there were very few people around him, just the old lady and the younger woman, but no one else. Had one of them dragged him free from the wreck? He stooped over the young woman, unsure of what to do. If he had ever known first aid, he had surely forgotten it now. He picked up her arm, which was still warm, and felt for a pulse on her wrist: nothing. He tried her neck but couldn't find a pulse and she didn't appear to be breathing either.

He saw a young boy a few feet away and decided to see if he could help him. As he drew closer, he realised the boy was gone. A deep cut in the boy's face ran through his entire skull from top to bottom. A chunk of metal protruded out the top of the boy's head and pieces of bloody brain dribbled across it onto the ground. He could only have been five or six years old. One hand still fiercely gripped a grinning teddy bear, as if he couldn't let it go, even in death.

A flash of light jumped out at the man from beside the boy on the ground. It was a metal clip holding a photo. The man picked it up and was surprised to find his own face staring back. It was him! The casing of the photo was charred and wrinkled, but he could still make out what it said beneath the photo. It simply read:

EVAN CROW

"Evan Crow," he whispered. He had to say it out loud to himself to make it seem real. He was relieved a little, although, whilst he knew it was he, his head ached and he couldn't remember anything else. Tiny pockets of memories unfolded in his brain erratically, little chinks of history sparkling back into his consciousness, refusing to merge into a single cohesive memory.

Fleeting memories jumped in and out. He recalled that he was thirty-five, of that he was sure. Or was it thirty-four? He hated pizza. He had been on that plane. *Focus, damn it!* He had a vague recollection of sitting by the window, looking out over the flat clouds and drinking beer. Where he was going to, or from, he didn't know. Was he travelling alone? He was wearing a dark brown suit and had a wedding band on his finger. He tried to remember if he had been sitting next to his wife on the plane. He couldn't picture her though and the effort of trying to recall her seemed to make his head hurt worse. Nothing else was coming back to him. His head began to spin as he tried to take it all in, the sound of people around him crying in agony and fear, the burning aeroplane, the smell of blood, the smell of petrol, the poor dead boy at his feet, and the photo of himself staring back blankly. He took a step back and tried to steady his nerves. His hands were shaking. He looked up at the plane and put the ID into his pocket.

Okay, one thing at a time, I've got to help them, he thought. He looked around for fire-trucks, the police, anyone coming to their aid. It looked as if nobody was coming. There were no sirens suggesting that anyone was on their way. He couldn't see much past the plane, just the blue sky filling with black plumes of acrid smoke. Help was not at hand.

Beyond the rear of the plane, he saw a control tower, buildings, hangars, warehouses, and a huge building with more grounded planes encircling it. Evan presumed this was the terminal. The other way, he saw just low trees surrounding the area and a chain-link fence, no doubt marking the airport perimeter. It was impossible to see through the trees, they were too dense. He resolved to help anyone he could and began jogging toward the plane.

"Hey! Anyone need any help?" he called out as he jogged. Stupid question, he thought to himself as soon as he'd said it. It seemed as though almost everyone was dead already. As he jogged, he splashed through dirty pools of blood and oil washing together. The few people standing near the plane apparently heard his shouts and turned toward him. Evan could vaguely make out a man and woman in uniform, probably flight crew, but he wasn't close enough to see their faces. They would surely know what was going on, why there was no help.

As he began to run, an arm reached up from the ground and grabbed his ankle. He stumbled and stopped. He'd thought she was dead, but a young woman, also in uniform, white shirt covered in blood, lay there helplessly.

"Please help me," she said, whimpering, "please?"

Evan knelt down and took her hand in his. She was ashen-faced and had cuts all over her face and body. He was surprised she could see anything. One eye socket appeared to have been smashed completely and was full of a deep red gelatinous mush and broken glass.

"What can I do to help? What's going on?"

The stranger looked at Evan and she opened her mouth to speak again. Blood welled up and over her lips, dripping down her face. Suddenly, her body tensed. The woman's hand lost its grip on his and he watched as she expelled her last breath on Earth. Evan stared, powerless, as the woman died in front of him.

He gently laid the woman's limp arm by her side and stood up. He looked at her. He was certain he'd never seen a dead body before and now he'd seen someone die in front of him. He shook his head in exasperation. Where the hell was everyone? How can an aeroplane crash at an airport in this day and age and there be no one coming to help? A burning anger began to overtake the shock. His thoughts were abruptly cut short when the breast pocket of his suit started vibrating.

His mobile phone! With everything happening so fast, he'd not even thought about checking his pockets. As he hurriedly tried to get the phone out of his pocket, he accidentally pulled a small black wallet out with it too, dropping both onto the grass. He shoved the wallet into his back pocket quickly, but the phone had stopped vibrating. He flipped it open and the first thing he saw was his screensaver, a photo of a small yacht. He read the name on the hull: 'Lemuria.'

The screen also told him he had a message. He clicked it open and followed the prompt through to his voicemail where a man, sounding rather too happy given the circumstances, told him he had two new voicemails. Evan listened as the first one started to play, received ten minutes ago.

"Dad, where are you? It's dark. Dad? Anna's here, but she's trapped in the cabin with me. It's really dark and we can't get out. Grand-dad said we should stay..."

The message ended abruptly. He listened, electrified by what he was hearing. The second message beeped in, received thirty seconds after the first.

"I wish you were here, Dad, Anna's not moving. Please, can you come get us? I'm scared. I'm scared of..." The young voice was hidden by muffled thumps and bangs, and then a few seconds later, cut off.

He looked for the contacts frantically so he could call back to his son. His son! God, he didn't even know his name. Was it Chris? Charlie? The name eluded him. And who was Anna? His wife? A daughter? He hoped that whatever troubles his son was in, that this Grand-dad he'd spoken of was helping. The boat on his mobile seemed familiar too. An image of a blue-eyed young boy, his son, sitting on that yacht streaked through his mind, but was gone as quickly as it had come. Too much information was cascading through Evan's mind, overloading his brain cells as he tried to remember everything.

He started to look through the list of names in his phone, desperately hoping they would jolt his memory. The first two or three names meant nothing to him, but the fourth name set alarm bells off in his head. His hands were trembling so much he could barely hold his phone still. Charlie. His son's name was Charlie!

"Charlie Crow," he whispered, and swallowed hard.

That image of the boy on the boat resurfaced but with more clarity. Charlie was sitting at the wheel, with an old man standing behind, helping him steer, both happy and smiling. Evan started to call Charlie's number. He didn't even get as far as hearing it ring, as a deafening explosion rocketed out from the plane.

Evan felt the outspreading warmth of the fireball envelope him and a split-second later, he was thrown off his feet. He flew backwards, airborne for several feet, finally crashing down hard onto the tarmac, rolling over as he landed. Every roll caused a jarring pain as the rock hard runway smacked into his body. When he came to rest, he was breathless, face down. He was still conscious, and was letting his body catch up with his brain. Cuts and bruises covered his whole body, his suit was shredded and his headache had grown a whole lot worse. He had no idea where his phone had gone, ripped from his clutches when the massive explosion had torn through the plane. Evan lay there panting, coughing, and hearing strange thudding noises around him.

He retched, spitting grimy saliva onto the tarmac, and slowly lifted himself up onto his knees. Various things dropped down around him from above, pieces of metal and lumps of flesh. Wreckage from the explosion was scattering itself around, falling from the sky like heavy snow. A metal seat from the aircraft landed in front of him with a screeching crash, and he jerked instinctively away from it. The seat was charred and smoking. Evan scanned his eyes over the remains of someone still trapped in the seat by the seatbelt, barely recognisable as once a human being. The seatbelt was bizarrely intact, yet the torso it was keeping prisoner was not. The body was black and still smoking. Below the knee, both legs were amputated with such a clean slice; he guessed something in the explosion must have scythed them off. The arm sockets were empty, presumably blown off in the explosion too. He couldn't even tell if it was male or female. The head was torched beyond any hope of recognition. Its cracked skin was pure black, the hair singed away to nothing, the ears completely gone. Its lips were peeled back like overcooked sausages, exposing a mouthful of bloody broken teeth. Where the eyes should be, were two dark, empty holes. Evan felt as if he was looking into the pits of hell. He didn't feel pity or grief. He felt nothing. He couldn't.

He retched again but had nothing to bring up. Evan shook his head and tears came to him. Where were the emergency services? He was shaking, shit-scared and bruised all over. What about his son, his family? He gingerly stood up and composed himself, mentally checking himself over. At least nothing was broken. His body ached and it felt as if his head had been used as a football.

Evan heard a faint metallic clang as the metal seat rolled forward on the concrete. The body seemed to shudder as if it were somehow trying to cling onto the last remnants of life. The charred remains shivered and then stilled. Evan frowned. He, she, whatever it was, had to be dead. He was about to approach the burnt creature when a sharp cry from above stopped him.

A murder of crows circled overhead. One of the crows swooped down and landed at his feet. It pierced a fresh hunk of meat with its beak and greedily tried to swallow it whole. Another landed beside it and began cawing loudly. For a second, its cawing blurred in with the screams of the people around Evan, becoming one terrifying shrill noise, two of God's creatures crying out: one in torment, one in salacious greed for the raw meat it was feasting on.

He turned and saw one of the flight attendants. She was kneeling over the young boy he had seen earlier. The boy's teeth were ripping apart the woman's face with terrifying ferociousness whilst his arms firmly held her head down. The woman was trying to stand but the dead boy wouldn't let go. They were locked together as if in a passionate embrace. Evan heard the metallic clang of the metal seat behind him but was dumbstruck by what he was witnessing. The flight attendant's screams subsided as the boy dragged her down to the ground, a bloody mangled mess where her face used to be. Overawed, Evan was rooted to the spot with shock.

An old man raced past him. As he did so, the old lady in the grey tracksuit who had died in front of Evan a few minutes ago, reached out a hand and sent the old man stumbling to the ground.

"Oh my God, Macy, is that you?"

The old man was wide-eyed at the sight of the old lady next to him in the dirt.

"Thank God! I can't believe it, I thought you were..." As the man reached for his beloved, she responded by grabbing his fingers and biting them off with a surging, powerful snap of her jaws. The old man fell backwards, crying out in pain, and hiding the clang of metal once again behind Evan. Oblivious to the absurdity and danger of what was happening, the old man, clutching his bloodied stump, crawled over the grass toward his wife.

"Shit, what's wrong with you, Macy?" He began, but his question was left hanging in the air as she raised herself up off the ground and towering over him, ripped out her husband's throat. Sinews stretched taut, her sharp fingernails dug into his neck and she greedily shoved her face into the bloody wound, drinking her dying husband's blood and devouring the soft human tissue.

The cawing of the crows behind Evan suddenly silenced. One bird flew past him up into the sky and he turned around as the woman in the green top he had lain next to earlier, snapped a crow's neck with one swift movement. He frowned as she began gnawing at the stump of its neck, blood pouring down through silky, black, matted feathers, stickily dribbling down the woman's chin. The other crows circled overhead, black eyes watching over their deceased comrade.

Evan turned to face the burning plane. Everything seemed to be happening in slow motion. He could not believe the horror spreading out in front of him. The people he had been running toward to help were now in pieces, scattered over the runway, bits of bloodied limbs strewn around like confetti. The dead boy was apparently feasting on the flight attendant. The old lady, resurrected, was now pulverising her dead husband's body, pummelling it into the ground. His mind raced as he remembered his son's phone call.

"I'm scared. I'm scared."

The words flew around inside his head like an angry wasp that demanded escape. He had to get out of here and find that boat. He had to find his family. Incredibly, there were people ahead of him wandering around: survivors? He saw a small black girl in pigtails and a yellow, flowery dress. She reached down to the ground, picked up an arm, and began gnawing at it like a dog with a bone. A man next to her, in a garish Hawaiian shirt and shorts, was smearing something around his face, leaving red trails behind like a disgusting slug. The man's shirt was blowing open, exposing a fat belly. His gut had been slit open and the man's intestines slithered out slowly. Evan saw more people around them: men, women and children, ambling around in a stupor, all acting the same. They were survivors in a sense, but not like Evan.

Some of them were clearly injured, some so badly that they should not be able to move. One young man had no arms, and his head was bent at such an angle that there was no way he could be alive, but he was walking around! His face seemed almost to be grinning. The pigtailed girl noticed Evan and started toward him, arms stretched out. The others too, some carrying body parts, motioned toward him. A girl, barely a teenager, was dragging herself along the ground. Her fists slapped against the blackened tarmac with each heave, whilst she left behind her, a trail of slimy blood where her legs used to be. She was naked, her back criss-crossed with blood splatter and shards of glass protruding like masts. Her eyes were focused on Evan. It was as if she was driven by anger or hatred. Her eyes burned fiercely through him as she advanced upon him.

Overwhelmed, Evan spun around to run, to escape this absurd scene of death and carnage and to find his family, wherever that might be. Amid all the screams and commotion of the explosion, he hadn't noticed the metal clanging behind him getting louder, as the burnt corpse in the seat rocked closer. Evan immediately tripped over it and smacked once more into the filthy runway. Amazingly, the limbless creature was rocking back and forth in the seat, in violent frustration. It was imprisoned by the seatbelt and couldn't free itself. Desperately, Evan got to his feet and stumbling away from the smouldering monster, turned straight into the face of a young child. It was the dead boy with the teddy bear, now covered head to toe in bloody gore and the last straggly remnants of the stewardess.

The boy's brown eyes moved slowly down from Evan's face, over his body, until they reached Evan's legs. The boy grabbed

Evan's leg and thrust forward to bite, eager for more flesh. Evan managed to grab the boy by the neck and hold him back. The boy's grip was firm and surprisingly strong for a dead six-year old. Evan could hear the scraping and shuffling noises of the approaching dead getting closer.

"Help! Help me!" Evan screamed, vociferously.

No one answered his calls. He heard a set of footsteps running close by, but they did not pause and quickly faded away. Evan was sweating, his arms shaking as he kept the boys chomping jaws at bay. With one free hand, he reached over to the edge of the aircraft seat. He pulled on the seatbelt dangling down and the frayed end tore free from the seat. The charred corpse fell out of the seat, inches away from Evan. With a surge of energy, he thrust the boy's face upward and kicked it hard, sending the boy tumbling over backwards. Evan clutched the seatbelt and whirled it in front of him, metal clasp winging through the air. The dead boy, ignoring it, jumped up and began walking toward Evan again. Its eyes were black and soul-less, yet locked onto Evan. The dead boy was unwavering, like a lion stalking its prey.

The metal buckle smacked into the side of the boy's head uselessly. The dead boy didn't even flinch. Evan knew the seatbelt was useless, and scanning around quickly, saw a piece of metal on the ground, an armrest thrown from the plane. He lunged for it just as the dead boy groped for Evan again. Collapsing in a heap together, Evan gripped the armrest and swung it at the boys head as he prepared to take a chunk out of Evan's leg. The blow made the boy pause long enough for Evan to muster enough energy to swing again. The second blow knocked the boy off of him. Evan felt vibrations shoot up his arm as the strong metal whacked into the boys soft skull. Blood and hair flew aside, yet somehow the boy still had one hand clutching Evan's ankle. It was determined to attack. Evan smashed the metal armrest into the boy's skull again and saw it crack open, exposing brain. Blood gushed down the boy's face. Evan's eyes were stinging with salty sweat from his brow. His head was pounding. He raised his arms high and repeatedly brought the armrest down on the boy, caving in its skull until it finally relinquished its deathly grip on him and stayed still. The teddy bear lay on the ground, grinning at Evan.

Evan wanted to spit, to rid himself of the sick taste in his mouth, but his throat was dry and coarse. He stood up. The others were close now, the pigtailed girl mere feet away. He could not face anymore, could not think anymore. Trembling with adrenalin, he ran. He fled down the tarmac, jumping over body parts and debris, away from the plane. He had no idea where he was going, but he knew he had to get away from here and figure out what was happening. Where were the police, the authorities? How could this be happening? Dead people attacking the living just did not happen.

He saw the terminal in the distance and headed in its direction. He desperately needed help and rest. Someone had to know what was going on. Weren't there armed police at airports now? He ran fast and hard, trying to forget the pain blasting into his brain from all over: his arms, his legs, his chest, and his head. Evan was lost. He couldn't remember who he was or where he was. He turned briefly to look behind him. Yellow lines flew around the tarmac like limp spaghetti, and the walking dead were coming directly for him. They seemed too slow to keep pace with him. He saw no one that looked alive and there were no pleas for help. The screams of the dying had been replaced by the silence of the dead. They continued shuffling toward him, enveloped by the blue sky above and the burning plane. He ran.

CHAPTER TWO

As Evan approached the terminal, he began to realise why nobody had come to their aid. Through the glass windows up high, he could make out people fighting and running. Arcs of blood sprayed across walls and windows. Muffled, distant traces of sporadic gunfire came from somewhere deeper inside the terminal. He glanced up at a huge jumbo jet as he ran past it, the undercarriage open, ready for bags to be loaded or unloaded. The windows above were lit up with brilliant sunlight shining through, and yet, he could see no sign of life. It looked as if a bomb had exploded inside. Every single window was smeared blood red. There was no movement from inside the plane.

On the ground, outside the terminal building, there were a few people, but alive or dead was a question he could not answer. Dressed in overalls or luminous hi-visibility jackets, they were evidently all airport workers of some sort. They were shambling about with no evident reason or purpose: their clothes were torn and grubby. Evan slowed to a walking pace. Whether it was the noise of the explosion or his presence, he didn't know, but they were all staggering toward him now. Fuck it, he thought.

"Hey! Anyone alive here? We need help," Evan shouted. No one answered him. From their movements and appearance, it soon became clear that they were all dead. God knows why, but they were still moving. He wasn't sure now what to do. A dead baggage-handler was getting close and Evan noticed the man's neck was broken. His throat was split open and drying blood had turned the yellow jacket a sickly orange. The man's eyes were lifeless, his face blank and pale with the slackness of death. Yet Evan sensed this man was looking at him. It was unnerving. He turned away and ran for an unmarked door that seemed to lead into the terminal. It was heavy and despite pushing and pulling it, he couldn't make it budge. His legs felt as if dead weights and his knees were shaking from the physical punishment his body was taking. He gave up on the door and jogged alongside the building, away from the deadly mob, past plain walls until he eventually reached another door. The door was ajar, spilling light outside onto the tarmac beneath the shadow of another jumbo. Evan pushed the door open and stepped inside.

It was a departure gate and there was a huge number seven on the wall in front of him. It only took a second for him to realise the room was a dead end. Solid blank walls, splattered with hair, gristle, and blood, seemed to mock him for thinking he could escape. A wave of nausea passed over him when he saw the bodies. He was confronted with a shocking sight. There were a hundred people, or more, literally piled up in the corner of the room. He guessed a panic had caused a mass crush. The door at the other end of the waiting room was blocked. He could barely see it and there was certainly no way he could get to it now. A young couple was sitting in the middle of the room, evidently munching on eviscerated limbs. They stood up menacingly when Evan walked in. He turned to leave and found the doorway blocked by a huge figure. He recoiled as a grotesque dead man, arms flailing, reached for Evan. Evan took a step back, aware that he was cornered. He couldn't dig his way out through the mass of corpses, so he had to fight his way back out of the door to the runway. Panicking, he looked around for a weapon.

There was precious little at hand but there were some stanchions tethered together by the ticket desk. He ran to it and lunged for one of the stanchions, grabbing a metal pole and yanking it out of its heavy base, the leathery belt slipping out just as the first of the couple reached him. Evan flinched at the gruesome sight. The approaching man had no eyes, they had been gouged out and eaten along with half the man's face, yet he still knew where Evan was.

Evan swung the heavy pole with both hands, crashing it into the young man's head. The pole struck the man's head with enough force to send him flying backward. Evan saw the lumbering giant from the doorway approaching but the man's dead girlfriend charged Evan; arms outstretched, hands taught, fingers tense and nail sharp, careening toward his face with one aim. He barely had enough time to swing the pole again. Evan managed to hit her arms, shattering both her wrists, making her swerve off course. He ducked as she flew past him, teeth gnashing and biting as she whisked past his head. She landed in a heap and Evan swung around to face the behemoth. Evan could smell the man, the stench of death intermingling with rank body odour.

It crossed Evan's mind at first to warn the man off, but then reality sunk in. He knew it would be pointless. The immense man standing before him was clearly dead. Half of his face had been chewed off, exposing his upper jaw, scraps of pink flesh hanging in shreds between his incisors. His shirt had been slashed open exposing his torso, which was cut to ribbons. Evan could see the man's ribcage and he felt his stomach turn. Sweat beginning to sting his eyes, Evan swung the heavy stanchion as hard as he could. He connected with the man's temple but the towering man only tottered and kept coming. Evan swung again, but the man raised his hands and Evan, growing weak, fumbled and dropped the stanchion, watching it roll away and out of reach. The man's hands grabbed Evan's shoulders. The giant's mouth opened, as if he was going to swallow Evan whole like in a grim fairy tale. Evan tried to repel the man and took hold of his arms, but the man-mountain retained his strength even in death, and Evan knew he was going to lose this fight. He heard the snarl behind him of the woman he had dodged and in the corner of his eye, could see the other young man rapidly bearing down on him.

"I'm scared. I'm scared."

The words pinged back into Evan's head and he knew he couldn't give up, couldn't die like this. He let go of the grasping arms and punched the man's ribs as hard as he could. The man paused just long enough for Evan to grab hold of the man's ribs with both hands. He pulled as hard as he could and one bloody rib snapped, breaking off with a disgusting, wet cracking sound.

Dripping with blood, he thrust the rib into the man's left eye and pushed him back toward the door. The reeling giant tripped over the discarded pole and fell like a redwood. His flailing arms pulled Evan on top of him, which drove the rib deeper through the man's eye-socket and into his brain. Through gritted teeth, Evan kept his grip firm, shoving the rib into the man's face further and further until the monster's grip relinquished and it lay still, occasionally twitching.

Evan felt fingers on his ankles and kicked back. His feet connected with the jaw of the young man just in time to stop him from biting. Jumping up, he grabbed the dropped pole from the ground and charged. Swinging it above him, he brought it crashing down onto the young man's lolling head. There was a solid crunching sound as the dead man's skull split open. Brain tissue spattered Evan's face and blood splattered his jacket. He didn't wait to see if the man was dead, but swung again, not aiming, just swiping through the air frenziedly. The young woman had regained her feet and was inches away. Amazingly, the woman ducked. Evan realised he did not need to fight; he would only end up attracting more of these things and getting stuck in here until they overpowered him. He threw the pole at her, turned, and ran out of the now clear doorway.

He sprinted out of the building, away from the woman and the curious mob of dead outside who were now approaching fast. Evan ran straight into the blinding late-afternoon sunlight. He wiped his brow, plastering sweat and blood across his forehead. Through aching eyes, he spied a small hangar a little way over the runway and ran headlong for the building's door. There was a car parked outside and he prayed someone would be inside the building, or that at least the door would be unlocked. Reaching it, he grappled with the door handle but it stayed shut. He banged rapidly on the hangar door in frustration.

"Hey, anyone in there? Let me in! Hey!"

There were scuffling sounds and muffled voices behind the door. Finally, a faint voice said, "Go away."

Evan continued to beat on the door.

"Let me in, please. I'm on my own. Just let me in!"

A moment or two later, the door suddenly flew open. A male voice said, "Get in, quick."

Evan ran into the gloomy hangar and the door slammed shut behind him. It felt dark and cold after being in the hot sunshine. He heard the door being locked and bolted. There was a jet in front of him, reflecting the sunlight coming in from the only open skylight above. Various boxes and shelves were stacked around the walls. Save some dim light coming into the hangar from one skylight in the ceiling, there were no other windows or doors that he could see. The man who had opened the door approached Evan, cautiously.

"You all right, mate? You look like shit. Here, sit down," and he pulled a wooden crate over, which Evan slumped onto gratefully.

"Thanks," panted Evan, as he took in his surroundings. "I don't know what the fuck is going on out there, but thanks for letting me in."

His head was throbbing and now he could relax to some degree, he felt incredibly weary. Instead of being charged by adrenalin, he felt like curling up into a ball and closing his eyes. He took in the man who had opened the door. A little older than Evan, he was wearing a black suit and shoes. He was paunch and showing a few wrinkles around the eyes but he looked trustworthy, the sort of man who would give you his last dollar.

"I'm Joe. Take it easy for a minute, eh? We didn't think anyone else was out there. Well, not alive anyway."

Almost on cue, there came banging sounds from the door. Not as urgent as Evan's, but insistent. The noise spread around the building. Thumps and moans accompanied by pathetic scraping sounds on the walls, all echoing eerily around the cool hangar. A tall blonde woman in a sharp business suit appeared out of the shadows and strode up to Evan.

"Who are you? You shouldn't be here. You've put me, and my children, in danger."

Her face was stern, her eyes glaring, and she folded her arms as she spoke. Her confidence belied her years. She looked as if she was barely out of her twenties, thought Evan. Too much make-up and aggressiveness plastered over what was actually a pretty face. If these two were a couple, mused Evan, they were an odd fit.

Behind her, Evan could vaguely make out a young boy and girl cowering in a dark corner, presumably her children. He wondered if they were more scared of what was outside the door, or their mother.

"Evan Crow. So I guess it was you who told me to go away? Look, sorry, but I'm not going out there in a hurry. Have you seen what's happening?" he asked her, incredulous.

"Mrs Craven, just calm down," Joe began, "I think we can all wait in here safely until..."

"Until what?" she interrupted. "Just remember who pays your wages, Joe." As she spoke, her face turned crimson.

"Thanks to you, we're stuck in here for God knows how long. Now this stranger wanders by and you just let him in. Perhaps we should open the door for everyone to come in? Should we let all those people banging on the door in? I don't think so.

"Right now, Joe, you need to stop thinking, and start taking care of my family as you're paid to. We don't pay you to *think*, we pay you to *do*. And you haven't done a very good job of late. As for you, Mr Crow," she spat his name out as she said it, "as soon as this mess is sorted out, you can be on your way. And stay away from me and my family."

Speech over, she returned to the young children in the shadows. She disappeared into the corner and Evan could only see their shadows now. Joe sat down beside Evan.

"Sorry about her, mate," he said, sighing. He frowned with concern at Evan's ragged appearance.

"Karyn Craven, my boss. Well, by default. I work for her husband, Pete, really."

Joe looked over the newcomer with curiosity. Looks as if he's been to hell and back, he thought. Evan was covered in blood, his clothes were ripped to pieces, and he smelt strongly of fuel and vomit.

"Nice suit. So where did you come from, the terminal? Do you work here? It's chaos from what we saw. We barely managed to make it in here."

Evan wiped his brow, only making his face even dirtier.

"I'm not really sure, but I think I was on that plane. I just woke up on the runway out there. Then the plane exploded and...I don't know. I just ran and ended up here. There are things out there. People, but, they're dead. Only they're not." Evan felt dizzy. "My head..." he began, trying to hold himself together. "Do you have any water?"

Joe disappeared momentarily and came back with a small bottle. It was warm, but Evan drank it down gratefully.

"Thought you might want these too?" and Joe held out two tablets in his hands. "Aspirin. There's a first aid kit on the wall there. You look pretty banged up, mate."

As Evan swallowed the pills, Joe continued.

"We heard the explosion from in here. Shook the whole bloody building, freaked the kids right out. I thought it must be one of the planes coming down. Did you see anyone else out there?"

"No, nobody alive anyway. There were a couple of people I tried to help but...I don't think anyone else made it. There were bodies everywhere. I don't know how the hell I made it here."

Evan was massaging his temples, the blinding pain in his head only intensifying.

"You should take it easy, mate, you've had a bang on the head. Probably a few by the sound of it," Joe said with genuine concern. He could see a massive bruise forming on Evan's head. There were cuts and grazes all over him and his suit was littered with scorch marks and rips. Joe wasn't sure how it still hung on his body.

Evan felt in his pockets and remembered the lost phone. His wallet was gone too, but there was something in his shirt pocket, a small scrap of paper. It looked like a boarding pass but it was so badly ripped and charred that he couldn't make anything out. There was a number: QF136 or 138? Seat 13A. That was all he could make out.

"Doesn't tell me much, does it?" The numbers meant nothing to him, only serving to confirm that he must have been on that plane. He crumpled it up and threw it on the floor.

"Before the plane blew up, I had a phone in my hand. It's gone now, probably smashed. There was a message from my son, Charlie, saying he was trapped. I had a photo on me of a boat too. I don't remember anything before today, but when I saw that boat, I had a vague memory of him being on it. I feel like there's some connection to that boat, but I can't quite put my finger on it, you know?"

Evan trailed off, lost in his thoughts.

"Well, I hope your family wasn't on that plane. In that suit, you look like you're dressed for business, so maybe you were on a business trip? Look, they're probably safe at home waiting for you. Karyn, Mrs Craven, I told her to stay at home, but she wouldn't listen. Wanted to get away, leave the country, as if we could. There's nowhere safe to go, this is happening all over the world. I don't know where she thought we were going to go to.

"Her house is like a fortress too: security locks, gates, electric fencing, the works. Too late now. She's lucky her kids are here. Shame about Pete, he was a top man."

Evan's head was spinning and he was struggling to focus on Joe's words. He stood up.

"What the hell is going on anyway? Where are the police? Why isn't someone doing something about this? How long are those things going to be out there?" The constant bangs and scraping noises on the hangar walls were beginning to agitate him. "I can't stay here. I have to find my family."

Evan started talking faster and his words slurred together. Spots appeared in front of his eyes and Joe only just managed to catch him as he swayed and collapsed, dropping the water bottle which rolled away into the shadows. Joe slid off his jacket and put it under Evan's head, laying him down carefully. With Evan passed out, Joe walked over to the corner of the hangar, far away from his boss and sat, waiting for the nightmare to end.

* * * *

Evan lay in the dark, listening to his new companions sleeping, faint breathing and coughing breaking the silence. There was practically no sound coming from outside the hangar, just the wind wheezing and whistling around the building. He could hear no sound of life out there, alive or dead. There were no voices or footsteps. The banging on the walls from earlier had ceased. The shuffling and scratching had stopped. He couldn't see much in the dark and wondered how long he'd been out. There was no way of telling the time and he felt into his pocket for his phone. Of course, he remembered, it was gone, lost in the explosion, probably smashed to pieces. So, he thought, I can remember what happened a few hours ago, but nothing of the last thirty years.

He sat up and waited for the head-rush to fade away. The cold, concrete hangar floor was uncomfortable and Evan's back hurt. Truth was, everything hurt. He stood up quietly. He could see Joe lying on a blanket nearby but he couldn't see the others. He sneaked over to the wall and found the first aid kit. Reaching around inside the box, he fished out some more aspirin. He felt around gingerly for some water, but not finding any, swallowed them dry.

Evan walked over to the door and listened. He couldn't hear anything. Maybe they were alone. Maybe all those things, those creatures, had left! He put his hand on the lock and prepared to bring the deadbolt back so he could venture outside, maybe see if that car worked. As he did so, a hand grabbed his shoulder and his heart skipped a beat. Evan whirled around.

"Steady on, mate," whispered Joe, "I wouldn't do that. It sounds quiet, but you don't know what's out there. They could be waiting."

"Sorry, didn't mean to wake you," said Evan, relieved. They spoke in hushed voices like naughty schoolboys. "How long was I out?"

"Six or seven hours or so I think. It's just past midnight now. Seriously, trust me. It's not safe out there. You feeling any better?"

"A little. Where are the others?"

"They took the penthouse suite," said Joe, nodding over to the jet. "Their own private jet. I've been inside it once. I got the grand tour when they bought it a couple of years ago. Decked out with everything you need for a life of luxury I tell you. Reclining leather chairs, mini-bar, wall-to-wall carpet, even a champagne bar. Oh, don't worry about them, mate, they'll be sleeping 'til the sun comes up."

"Look, I'm sorry about before. Things were a bit crazy." Evan offered his hand and the two men shook.

"No worries. Look, Evan, I'm beat. I'll fill you in with what's going on in the morning, but, right now, I've a nice little spot reserved on a concrete floor. If you ask me, you should get some rest too. I know you said you need to get to your family, but you won't get six feet if you go outside now. You can't see for shit. Wait till morning and we can figure this out, okay?"

Evan decided Joe was right. He didn't even know where he was going. His family might be on that boat, but where was it? He didn't even know where he was right now.

"Sure, thanks. Don't suppose there's any more blankets, are there?"

"Yeah, here you go," said Joe, grabbing a fire blanket that was lying beside the door. He brushed it down and handed it to Evan. Joe went back to his makeshift bed, suit jacket and blanket spread out on the ground.

"Hey, Joe," said Evan, "where are we?"

Joe smiled.

"Coffee capital of the world, mate: Melbourne."

Evan watched Joe lay down and then did the same, spreading the blanket out on the floor, using his tatty jacket as a makeshift pillow. It was difficult trying to sleep, but he knew his best hope of finding his son and his family was in the morning, fully rested. He didn't intend to stop for anything, or anyone. He was itching to get on the road already but his whole body still hurt from the crash and subsequent escape earlier. Despite what his mind was telling him, his body was telling him to take a break. His brain just wouldn't shut down so easily. He kept replaying in his head those last frightened words he had heard Charlie say.

"I'm scared. I'm scared."

Evan kept imagining the worst case scenarios. He was sure that Anna was his daughter, though it was just a gut feeling rather than any certain knowledge. What if his children were alone on the boat, out at sea? He couldn't remember his son much, but he was pretty sure he couldn't steer a yacht. What was it his son had said: that they were trapped? What if they were down in the cabin, locked in, unable to get out? Evan concentrated on picturing his children. He tried to let their images come to him. He envisaged them on the boat, and to where they might have sailed. Vague memories began to come to him. He remembered lying on the deck in the sunshine whilst his son fished over the side. He saw the outline of a woman beside him. His wife? Where was she? He wished he could feel something, but this woman was no more than a blurry memory to him at the moment. Was his wife alive or dead? Were they even married anymore? He consciously ran his fingers over his wedding ring. So he was still married then: 'til death us do part.

Another memory struggled to the front of his tired, overworked mind. He could remember being at the tiller. A memory shot through to him of an old man coming to help him steer. A cold sweat sprung out over Evan as the realisation hit him. This Grand-dad that Charlie had mentioned: he was Evan's father! How could he have forgotten his own father? Images of his father, Tom, yes, Tom, came back to him: a strong, tall, well-built man. Evan instinctively knew Tom was a trustworthy man. An image came to him of his father in uniform. Had he been a policeman, a soldier? It disappeared quickly before Evan could pin it down. Evan remembered how they used to take his son fishing together on the yacht. Tom doted on his grandchildren, he would never let any harm come to them! Fatigue finally began to overtake his restless mind, and he yawned. Somewhere out there was his family, and tomorrow he would go to them, somehow.

Evan was not aware when he slipped into sleep. It was a restless one. The yacht, 'Lemuria,' surfaced occasionally in his thoughts, slipping in and out of his consciousness as easily as it skimmed through the ocean waves.

There was only one vivid, pertinent scene. It was his daughter, Anna, in a bright red dress, skipping down an old stony pier toward the boat. She was giggling and running toward him, shouting.

"Daddy, can we stay here forever? Granddad says Tassie is the best place in the whole world! Dolly wants to stay too," she said, embracing a Barbie doll to her chest. Anna beamed up at Evan with big brown eyes.

Tom, behind her, was talking but Evan couldn't make anything out. Charlie was whispering to Evan, his son's mouth only an inch away from his ear. Evan could practically feel his son's breath on his neck.

"We come here every year. Let's just stay, Dad, let's stay. Forever, and ever, and ever..." Evan's nameless wife was nowhere to be seen. The image faded and Evan was powerless as the elusive memories of his family disintegrated into hazy dreams.

* * * *

When Evan woke in the morning, he didn't remember the nightmares. He forgot about the dead reaching for him in his dreams, the clammy fingers clawing at his legs, the dreams where he hadn't made it off the plane, where he'd sat in his seat, burning in agony, until it exploded. He remembered one crucial thing though: his father's boat *was* on Tasmania and they *did* go there every year. He couldn't recall his past, his marriage, where he'd grown up and gone to school. He still couldn't remember his wife or what he did for a living. But he was pretty certain now that Charlie and Anna were on that boat, which meant they were safe. If they were trapped in the boat's cabin, then he prayed and hoped that was true. Better there than out in the world he had seen yesterday. He had to get to that boat.

CHAPTER THREE

What was it Joe had said, that this was happening everywhere? When Evan woke, the first thing he did was wander over to Joe who was trying to sleep, but failing. He had to know what was going on.

"Hey, Joe, how you doin'?" Evan stood over him and forced a tired smile.

"Rough as a bear's you-know-what." Joe stretched and yawned. He gave up on sleep and got up. "Probably better than you though. Not much chance of a coffee this morning I suppose," he said, putting his jacket back on and kicking the blanket to the wall.

"Hey, Joe, yesterday you said this was happening everywhere. I know this might seem like a stupid question to you, but what is?"

"You really have no idea?" Joe looked at the red and brown bruising on Evan's face. He looked as if he had gone ten rounds in the ring and come off a lot worse than the other guy. Joe glanced over to the jet where the Cravens were still sleeping. A solitary beam of light came in from the skylight above, illuminating the jet's sleek shell. His watch read close to eight am. He walked over to a couple of upturned boxes and sat down, beckoning Evan to follow him. As he pulled his shoes back on, Joe began.

"Twenty-four hours ago, I was doing my job like everyone else. The world was shitty, as usual, and then it got a whole lot shittier. I work for Mr Craven, which means, unfortunately, I work for *her* too." Joe pointed to the jet and sighed.

"I'm supposed to be the driver, but in reality I'm the dogsbody. I do a bit of babysitting, pick up the groceries, the dry-cleaning. I even have to clean the bloody pool. I like my driving though. I used to be a driver in a different sense, if you know what I mean." He winked at Evan.

"Anyway, I was working on the car yesterday and Mrs Craven runs into the garage, shouting her head off about some riots going on and that I have to go get the kids from school. Makes it sound like a big emergency. I thought she was exaggerating, of course, acting like she's the boss. She likes to think she is, but I know who and what pays my wages and it ain't her pretty face.

"So on the way to the school, I listened to the radio. It was all a bit muddled but it was true, there *were* riots everywhere. Not just here, but they were saying it was some worldwide event, as if somehow they were connected. Europe, America, China; even our cousins over the ditch were having some trouble in Auckland. The news didn't say why though, just that there was lots of fighting going on and the army was being called in. I thought shit; it must be bad if they're calling the green berets in!

"Anyway, I picked up the kids and it seemed everyone else had the same idea. Nearly everyone else had cleared out; I was last getting to the school. I didn't want to scare the kids so I turned the radio off and told them they just had to go home and speak to their mother. The kids didn't say a word, just ran inside when they got home. I guess they probably heard something at school about it, you know what kids are like. They were probably on their mobiles in class and knew about it before bloody CNN. So anyway, they flew off and I stayed in the car and turned the radio back on. This is when it gets fucking freaky.

"The radio was saying that Melbourne was now in lock-down: that we all had to stay inside, lock the doors, you know? They said that if anyone in the family was injured we had to lock them *outside*."

Joe emphasised the last word. Evan said nothing. He wanted to hear as much as possible. If he was going outside, he needed to know the full picture and he didn't like where this story was going.

"The radio said that the dead were coming back to life, that if anyone you knew had died, that you had to either lock them outside or kill them by...by severing the head. *Severing the head? Can you believe this shit? I swear I've done some things in my past I'm not proud of, and I've seen some weird stuff, but this? This was insane. I tried a few different stations but it was the same on every one. They were talking about zombies, running around the streets, our streets!"

Joe paused and shook his head as though he still couldn't believe it.

"I haven't got any family myself, so I called Dan, a mate of mine, he lives in Sydney. Now you've got to remember, this bloke can handle himself. Built like a brick shithouse he is. Never started a fight, but never lost one neither. *Never*. We used to call him Dangerous Dan. Yet when I called him, he sounded like a little boy again, like when we used to hang out at school. He lives up in the hills and you can see Sydney, beautiful from his place. He made a lot of money back in the day and built himself a sweet pad. He told me he was looking out of his window and Sydney was burning. He said the whole city was on fire. He said the police, army, or someone, had just been down his street, shouting and waving guns around. Reckoned they'd shot his flat-mate, Sammy, for no reason except Sammy was unlucky enough to be in their way. Dan said that Sammy took it and just got back up! Evan, you're not supposed to get back up when you've a chest full of lead.

"Next thing I know, there's a load of banging and stuff in the background and he's telling me that Sammy's back in the house. Last thing I heard before we got cut off, Dan said he'd barricaded himself in his bedroom and Sammy, full of bullet-holes remember, is banging on the door, trying to get in. What is that about? I've never heard Dan sound that scared in my whole life."

Joe watched Evan taking it all in. "I need a drink."

"Me too, mate. Look in that box over there; I think there might be some water left. You find anything stronger, let me know," said Joe.

Evan found a solitary, dusty, bottle and brought it back to share with Joe. Evan realised that his headache was only going to get worse as Joe went on, and he gently rubbed the bruising on his face.

"Well, two seconds later, and there's this banging on the car window and it's Mrs Craven, back in my face, telling me I need to go get Pete, now. He was working in the city. I didn't really fancy going out there, but he's not like her, he treats you right. He was more than a boss; he stood by me in the past when I had a bit of trouble, so I couldn't just leave him. I figured I could get there and back fine, I'm pretty good behind the wheel. So off I go again, errand number two." Joe stopped abruptly. The jet's door swung open and its steps cascaded down onto the floor with an echoing clang. A pair of feet shuffled forward and appeared in the doorway.

* * * *

"What's that light?" grumbled Karyn, as she woke. A small but bright glint of sunlight was striped across her face. Her son, George, was wide-awake, lying in the doorway of the jet, tapping away with obvious concentration on something.

"I'm just writing my diary, Mum." George was absorbed and had opened the door to let some light in. He didn't turn to look at his mother when he spoke.

"George, for God's sake, that diary is pointless. If you want to be doing something, you should be studying. Just put it down."

George indignantly turned off his iPad, shoved it into his back pocket, and sullenly walked down the steps into the hangar. His sister, Lucy, stirred from her slumber and Karyn watched her follow him. Both children trotted over to Joe, and Karyn went to the small on-board bathroom, clapping her cheeks awake. She turned the tap on and nothing came out.

"Cheap bastard," she muttered.

She straightened herself out, brushing down her suit, flattening her unkempt hair. Looking in the mirror, she admired herself. A widower at twenty-nine but still, she looked good. Sure, Pete not being around would be a pain, but he was well insured. They had made sure their wills were set up. Karyn smiled. Soon she'd be able to get all the things he had denied her. Like a decent fuck for starters. The jet needed a makeover and she'd be able to afford a proper nanny now. Joe had his uses, but she had no doubt as to where his allegiances lay.

"I suppose I will have to take charge of the situation, as usual." She strode out of the bathroom purposefully, out of the jet, heels clacking loudly in the hangar, and headed toward Joe and Evan.

"George, Lucy, stop pestering Joe, please."

"It's all right, Mrs Craven, they weren't bothering us," he said, defensively.

She crossed her arms and spoke directly to Joe, ignoring Evan completely.

"So what have you managed to sort out so far, Joe? Have you called the authorities? What's it looking like outside now?"

"Phones are down, Mrs Craven, no signal at all. Don't suppose you can get internet on that thing can you, George?"

"Nah." George and Lucy were sitting on the floor playing a game on his iPad.

"Nah, it's broke," said Lucy. At five, she was a few years younger than her brother. She was cute, thought Evan, not much like her mother.

"So," said Karyn, ignoring her children, "have we enough petrol to get back home? I'm not wasting any more time in here. It's cold and it stinks. I need to feed the children and there's a lot to do. Mr Crow, do you know how to fly a plane?"

"Er, no, I..." Evan was stopped mid-sentence as Karyn interrupted him.

"Didn't think so, somehow," came the patronising response. At no point did she break eye contact with Joe. She waved her hands dismissively.

"Well, Joe, bring the car around, I'd like you to take us home now. You can find you own way home now, Mr Crow, I'm sure." She gathered up her handbag and sat down expectantly, looking at Joe who let out an exasperated sigh.

"Mrs Craven, I'll go check on the car, but I am *not* going out there alone. You saw what it was like yesterday. You lose me, and you don't have a driver no more."

She was not used to being talked back to, certainly not by her employees.

"Now look here." She started raising her voice, asserting her authority. She had gotten used to the power struggle between her and Joe over the years, but with Pete gone, it seemed different now.

"Mrs Craven, Karyn, I can go with Joe. I can help. If you can perhaps just give me a ride out to the city with you, I can find my own way from there." Evan didn't know how on earth he was going to find his way to Tasmania, but sitting around here wasn't helping any.

"I'm not leaving Evan on his own. There's no way we're leaving anyone behind." It was Joe's turn to fold his arms. Karyn quietly seemed to think it over for a minute. She had never bothered learning to drive. There had always been someone to do it for her, like most things.

"Fine. I've decided you can come with us, Mr Crow. If you two can actually make yourselves useful and get the car, we'll be on our way. Sometime today would be nice?"

Evan and Joe headed for the door, pleased to be leaving Karyn behind. Under his breath, Joe said, "Thanks, mate."

Standing by the door, Evan paused. He needed to talk to Joe for a minute.

"Never mind the battle-axe, Joe, I'm more worried about going back out there. I don't know what we're going to find out there so let's be careful, eh? Those things I saw yesterday didn't seem like they were going to give up and go away. There could be none, or there could be a thousand of them waiting outside.

"Look, when we get out of here, maybe you can drop me near the airport terminal. If it's clear, I can probably find a car I can use. I've got to get to my family. That boat I told you about yesterday? Well it's on Tasmania. That's where I've got to get to. My son, Charlie, I'm sure he's there with my father and my daughter, Anna. At least I think so."

"Sure. Evan, if it's no good, just sit tight with us. If we can make it to the house, I'll see you right. Don't worry about her. With Pete not here to back her up, she's all mouth. Look, I can drop her and the kids off and then take you down to the harbour. Maybe it won't be so bad. You can take a boat and be with them by tomorrow. I'd come with you, but I can't leave George and Lucy. Not now."

Joe was optimistic. Evan felt determined but didn't have Joe's confidence. He felt like a rabbit in the headlights, not knowing which way to turn.

"Right, let's see what the damage is," said Evan, opening the door carefully. It squeaked slightly, but they heard no other noise outside.

Joe slipped out of the door first and glanced around. It was dark and gloomy. A blanket of fog had covered the airport like a shroud. He spotted a few bodies sprinkled over the tarmac, but none was moving. He cleared his throat softly, hoping the noise might stir any into life whilst they still had time to run back inside the hangar. Nothing moved. He trod softly toward the car and discreetly motioned for Evan to follow him.

Evan slunk out of the doorway and shivered as the fresh, cool morning air wafted over his face. It brought a unique array of smells, not least of which was the sweet burning smell of aircraft fuel. Evan didn't want to think about what the other smells were. Through the murkiness, he too noticed the bodies on the ground, looking like piles of dirty washing. He couldn't see to the terminal or any planes. The fog was too thick.

Joe reached the car and opened the driver's door quietly. He started the car and the engine hummed into life immediately. Evan got in beside him. Joe gripped the wheel and pulled the car up to the hangar door.

"I don't like this. The sun should clear it away soon, but it's gonna be hard to drive through this fog," said Joe.

"I'll go get the others." Evan feared they were going to delay. He knew it was a risk, but he chose to ignore Joe's words. He wanted to get going as soon as possible.

Evan slipped through the hangar door and a moment later, came back out with the Cravens in tow. Karyn fussily strapped George and Lucy in the back seat before climbing in next to them. George started humming which made Lucy do the same. She was always copying her elder brother, acting like him, following him everywhere. George often complained to his mother about Lucy, but secretly liked the fact that she looked up to him. He glanced over and gave her a wink. Lucy smiled and tried winking back, failing miserably, scrunching up both eyes together. George smirked and kept humming away.

"Quiet."

One short, stern word from their mother was enough for them both to know that they had to be quiet, and quickly. George stared out of the car window. There was an undeniable tension in the car as Joe pulled them slowly away from the hangar.

"Can't see much," he said quietly to Evan. The car lights stretched out a short distance but just hit the dense wall of fog. Joe kept the car creeping forward.

As they continued on, the car's headlights picked out eerie images: an abandoned loader, suitcases strewn around it lazily, the belly of a small plane splashed with blood, a man's cadaver bizarrely sat upright, as if in meditation. As they inched past it, Evan looked in the wing-mirror, back at the man. His head was empty, hollowed out like a pumpkin. Evan shivered.

The fog cleared a little and Joe realised he was on the right track, the terminal building just barely in sight now to their left. A lone figure stumbled in the distance in their direction, just a grey figure thrashing along in the fog.

"Nearly there," Joe said confidently, speeding up some more, leaving the figure behind.

"Don't go too fast, Joe, we don't want to hit anything," said Evan. Moments later and the car bounced over something causing them all to jump. Everyone was privately hoping it was just a discarded suitcase that they had run over.

George pressed his face up against the glass straining to see.

"Hey, Mum, there's someone out there."

"I know, dear, just ignore them please," said Mrs Craven, taking her son's hand. She was nervous but didn't want to show it. She had to project the strength she knew everyone else was expecting from her. Her mind cast back to yesterday. On the way to the airport, she'd made George and Lucy close their eyes. Such horrible images she could not forget. Joe had earned his dues yesterday, she had to admit. He had gotten them here. It wasn't his fault there were no pilots. God knows where their regular one had gone. She could see the zombies now, remembering how Joe had swerved around them like on an obstacle course. Bloodied corpses everywhere, people pleading for help, arms reaching for the car. She shuddered and put it out of her mind.

"I've got a rough idea where I'm headed, but...shit." Joe was cut short as he pulled the car dramatically to the left, dodging a zombie that appeared out of the gloom. As it brushed the side of the car, Mrs Craven shrieked in surprise. The children recoiled in terror as the lurching zombie's hands slithered off the windows and it retreated into the mist. Evan saw a brief glimpse of green flash by his window, a flash of flowing hair, and the figure was gone, fading away as the fog swallowed it up as fast as it had appeared. Joe sped up.

"Mum, someone's waving at us. There's two of them," said George.

"All right, George, that's enough!" Mrs Craven squeezed her son's hand tightly. She did not want to see any more zombies waving around in her face. George spoke no more.

"I believe you, George," said Evan. "Once we've found some help, we'll try to go back for them, okay?" The taste of fear in the car was palpable.

Evan glanced in the mirror, but all he could see now was a lone figure running away. He felt guilty for not asking Joe to stop and see if someone needed help, but he had to put his own needs first. He rubbed his temples, trying to ignore his growing headache. He had to find his family.

They drove on in silence for a minute, the awkwardness slowly dissipating as painfully as the fog. It was Lucy who saw it first.

"Look, Mum, there's the airport. Is that where dad is?" She said it so cheerfully and hopefully that Karyn had to bite her lip from saying anything. It was better they didn't know.

They all looked at the building that loomed out of the fog and said nothing. Yesterday it was a busy airport with thousands of people scurrying around, today it was desolate, no sign of life anywhere. There was a row of taxis at the front, all crashed into the back of each other like fallen dominoes. Dozens upon dozens of bodies littered the pavement. Two abandoned police cars blocked the road and Joe had to drive over the pavement to get past. The terminal doors were open and the windows shattered. Joe kept his eyes fixed on the road ahead.

"We get past the building, take the next left, and we're home free."

Joe relaxed a little and turned around to give Lucy and George a quick reassuring smile. He didn't see the woman run out in front of him. Evan called out, but Joe was going too fast and ploughed straight into her, sending her tumbling over the bonnet with a sickening thud. Joe swerved and the car rammed headfirst into the line of taxi's, coming to a sudden stop. Lucy and George were crying and Karyn was groaning, rubbing her neck.

"Tell me that was one of those things!" shouted Joe as he jumped out of the car.

"Stay here," said Evan, ignoring Mrs Craven's glare. Smoke was coming from the car's engine as Evan leapt out and he saw Joe standing over a figure on the road. He heard the screams before he could see where they were coming from. Evan took a step back toward the car.

"If she's dead, Joe, she's dead. We've got to get out of here."

Through the fog curtaining the airport, two figures came running straight toward him. A young woman was screaming something unintelligible. An older man ran beside her, grim-faced and breathing heavily. The woman's face was fraught with worry, but she looked otherwise uninjured. She ran straight to Evan and he grabbed her shoulders.

"Help us, please; we have to get out of here!" She took in the scene and looked at Joe standing over the body. She left Evan and raced over to the body.

"I'm sorry," began Joe, "she just ran out in front of me." He tailed off and watched the young woman bend over the body, sobbing. He trudged back to Evan wiping his brow.

"What's done is done; we've got to go, Joe. It was an accident," said Evan.

The second figure finally made it to them. An older man, dressed in overalls, overweight, and struggling for breath.

"Tell me your car works. We need to get out of here, fast. I'm Miguel," he said, offering a sweaty hand.

Shaking it, Evan asked, "Who are you two? Who was that who ran out in front of us?" Joe looked down ashen-faced.

"I don't know them really, I'm just a cleaner. I don't know anything. Although I know we'd have been all right if she'd kept her mouth shut. We were fine, then this morning that stupid old woman starts mouthing off, getting all panicked and shouting something about Kyonshi, whatever that is. Don't ask me. All I know is, we've got a heap of trouble coming. I'm serious, can we go? *Now?*"

Another figure came stumbling through the fog toward them. Only this one was not shouting or screaming. Evan swallowed. The figure came toward them, swaying like a drunkard.

"Get in the car. Let's go," Evan said urgently. Another figure appeared behind the first one. Then more and more shapes came out of the shifting fog: moaning, crawling, wheezing, and stumbling. Joe and Miguel jumped in the car as Evan ran over to the crying woman.

"We have to leave now, come on," he said gently, but insistently. She looked up at him through tears and nodded. He led her by the arm to the car as she stumbled alongside Evan. He opened the back door and she got in next to Miguel. Lucy was now on her mother's lap and George was squashed in the middle. Mrs Craven glared at the newcomers, but there was no time for introductions or explanations. The young woman sat in the back seat sniffling, and Evan jumped in beside Joe.

Joe was trying to start the car but the engine just spluttered and died. Joe punched the steering wheel in frustration.

"Oh come on, I can't fucking believe this." The engine twinkled into life and died for the last time.

"It's gone. We've got to run for it."

"Right," said Evan, "stick to the plan, let's get to the main road, we'll try to find a car there. Everyone follow Joe and keep up, we don't want anyone getting lost in the fog. We can out-run those things." He didn't know if he believed what he was saying but they had to try.

Everyone jumped out and Joe raced to the boot.

"Here," he said to Evan, and handed him a nine-iron. "They're Mr Craven's golf clubs. I've got a feeling we might need them."

He took one for himself and scooped up Lucy. She held on piggyback style as they jogged off into the distance. Karyn grabbed George's hand and Miguel, taking a club too, ran after them. The mysterious young woman followed on autopilot and Evan brought up the rear. As they ran, Evan glanced back over his shoulder. The zombies were following but they weren't gaining. Joe kept barking out where he was and they managed to keep each other in sight as they ran through the foggy street. They passed scattered broken cars and stuck to the middle of the road. At an intersection, Joe stopped, waiting for everyone to catch up.

"Over there," he said pointing. There was a car rental yard, its big red sign sticking out of the fog like a beacon. They all trotted over to it. There was a small building in front of the yard. The office was open, glass and keys littering the floor like a sparkling welcome mat. Evan called out, but there was no reply and he ventured inside, brandishing the golf club above his head. There was nobody around and everyone followed Evan in.

"Looks like someone else had the same idea," said Miguel, looking around at the mess.

As they all sheltered briefly inside, Evan looked at Joe.

"You can drive anything, right?"

"If you can find some keys..." Joe was resting on the golf club, getting his breath back. There were a few keys left scattered on the floor, and Evan picked them up.

"Follow me, everyone." He took the handful of keys outside and they all followed him out into the car park, nervously looking around.

"Karyn, stay here with George and Lucy. Everyone else, look for the reg. First one to find a car, shout out." Evan handed the tearful woman, Miguel, and Joe, a few keys each. He could hear the zombies getting louder. A few moans carried over the wind, the pounding of scurrying feet on the dewy road with them.

Karyn held onto George and Lucy and watched the others spread out into the fog, gradually disappearing from sight. She shivered. George and Lucy clung to her in silence.

Joe approached a large saloon in the corner of the yard. The driver's door was open and the headlights shone weakly. The keys were dangling in the ignition but as he reached the door, he heard a muffled scraping sound from inside. It was still dark and he couldn't see anything moving. Gripping the golf club tighter, he went to the back and pulled the handle. The door clicked open and Joe braced himself, but nothing stirred. He was sure he hadn't imagined it. The boot was full of coats, bags, and suitcases. He pulled out a large case and heard it again, a scratching sound accompanied by shallow breathing. If he got into the car to try the keys, he didn't want to be jumped by anything with teeth so he pulled aside a second case.

Joe sprang back in shock. A small dog, yipping with excitement, jumped out past him. The dog ran off instantly, barrelling under cars and through legs, out into the road where it quickly disappeared into the fog. Relieved, Joe went to the driver's door and tried the engine. It whined pathetically and the headlights died. The car had been left on all night and the battery was dead. He gave up and carried on searching.

"Hey," said Miguel, anxiously, "this one. This one!" He was standing outside of a people carrier that would easily take them all. He had started the engine and honked the horn, once, so they could all find it.

As one, they all swooped to it clambering in. "Not very quick on its feet," said Joe, "but it'll do for now."

The young woman approached Evan. "I'm Amane. Thank you for helping me."

Her words were genuine, but spoken in a hushed soft tone. She was slightly younger than Evan was. Her eyes were a deep brown, matching her long hair. She looked Japanese, although she had an Australian accent and Evan thought she looked pretty, yet very sad. She had seemed to know the old woman that Joe had knocked down and he thought he would ask her about it later. The sound of the advancing zombies was growing louder every second, so the priority was to get away.

"That's all right. I'm Evan. Let's get out of here, okay?" He nudged her to the van. There was no time for chatting now. Joe got behind the wheel and then, making sure everyone was in, Evan leant through the passenger door.

"Joe, that gate is blocking the way. I'm going to move it, and then we'd better step on it." Joe peered through and saw what Evan was talking about. The chain-link fence around the rental park was bent and smashed open, probably torn down in desperation by people fleeing in stolen cars. A large flat section was hanging off the post, blocking the exit.

Evan ran over and began dragging it back so the car could get through, out onto the open road. The metal scraped on the concrete; the screeching, scratching sound jarred horribly in Evan's thudding head.

Joe watched open mouthed in horror as a figure emerged from the gloom beside Evan. The shadowy zombie rose up from the ground between two cars silently, advancing on Evan who was looking in the opposite direction. Joe hit the horn to alert Evan and put the car into drive.

Evan looked up, confused and startled by the horn. He saw the crowd of dead advancing down the road toward them and then bristled, as clawing fingers clutched his arm. He whirled round and came face to face with a walking corpse. It was dressed in uniform, its shirt in pieces exposing flaps of shredded skin. The zombie's face had been sheared of its skin. Its bulging, staring eyes locked onto Evan and bearing sharp teeth, the zombie suddenly bore down on him. Its grotesque face appeared in front of him with alarming speed and Evan, startled, swung at the creature. He barrelled into it, both of them ploughing into the chain-link fence. As the zombie reeled, Evan grabbed the golf club from the ground and aimed a blow at the thing's head. He missed as the zombie jerked toward Evan, only connecting softly with its shoulder. They both tripped over the fencing and fell down onto the cold, hard road.

Lying on his back but still holding onto the club, Evan forced it horizontally above his face just as the zombie's jaws descended, snapping onto the metal club inches from Evans' face, splashing him with gore and blood. Teeth smashed free of the zombie's mouth as it bit the club and they bounced off Evan's cheeks onto the ground. Drool and blood sprayed Evan's face and the stench emanating from the zombies rotten mouth made Evan gag. With trembling arms, Evan could barely keep the zombie at bay, its hunger to kill seemingly providing it with never-ending energy. It was like a berserk animal, intent on eating Evan alive.

Just as his grip on the club was weakening, Evan heard an engine and headlights flashed on his face. Joe drove his nine-iron full force into the zombies head, sending it tumbling off Evan who scrambled to his feet. The zombie staggered upright and Joe stabbed the blunt end of the club into its mouth and through the other side, pinning it against the chain-link fence. Barbwire caught on the zombie's head, sinking into rotting flesh and digging in with tiny vicious claws. It was enough to hold the zombie back briefly and Evan and Joe ran back to the car. The dead horde on the road was now close enough to smell.

They tore out, tires screeching, as hundreds of zombies reached the car yard. Some of the zombies at the front of the pack managed to reach the car as it pulled out. Arms, hands, and bodies all ran full pelt into the side of the car. Karyn and the children screamed in the back as hideous faces of dead men and women slammed up against the windows.

"Move it, move it!" shouted Miguel. A one-armed soldier caught on a back door handle and the door flew open. The soldier lunged and grabbed Miguel's arm as he tried to pull the door closed. The soldier lost its grip on Miguel as the weight of the zombies behind knocked it down and it rolled under the car. Miguel yanked the door shut and recoiled further into the back of the car, staring in terror as the wave of zombies swept toward them. Evan pushed the lock down on his side, securing all the doors.

Joe struggled to keep the car level as the force of dozens of zombies ploughing into one side threatened to knock them over. For a few feet, Joe thought they were going to succeed. He kept his foot down, barely flinching as he swept over and through the mass of dead funnelling into the front of the car. Heads rolled and crushed under the wheels. Blood sprayed over the windows and Joe had to turn the wipers on so he could see. As the zombie's thinned out, he got enough grip back on the road to pull away. Joe was grateful the road was empty, as at this speed in fog, anything blocking the way would bring them to a very quick, and painful, stop.

A moment later and they were clear, the ravenous horde behind them swallowed up by the dense fog. Joe slowed down slightly, reluctant to go so fast but desperate to put some distance between themselves and the airport. The fog was clearing, but still. Evan turned around and looked at the pale faces staring back at him. Miguel had his eyes closed and seemed to be praying. Karyn and her children were hugging, silent, and Amane looked like she was in shock, her eyes glazed and vacant. He turned back to Joe.

"How far is the house? Can you make it?" Evan was tenderly feeling his head. The attack had opened yesterday's wounds, which were now seeping. He dabbed at the open wounds with a rag from the car floor. Joe was hunched over the wheel, straining to see.

"On a good day, it's a thirty minute drive. Today? I don't know," he said, shaking his head. "Plus we have to go through a pretty big built up area to get there. If the airport's anything to go by, I don't think we'll be on our own."

Joe swung the car around an abandoned limo. The driver was draped out of the open door, intestines splayed out as if on show for a museum. The man's face was battered beyond recognition and a large pool of blood had collected beneath his mangled head. Joe turned away in disgust and pity.

Evan watched the houses and shops drift by. The fog gradually lifted to a thin haze and the sun began poking through in patches. He was struck by how lifeless it was. A summer's day in the city and there wasn't a soul to be seen: no children playing, no shoppers, no traffic or music to fill the quiet air. As Joe weaved in and out of crashed cars, Evan looked closer at the houses and shops. Through broken windows, he saw figures moving around. When they drove past, frequently one would peer out at them. He wasn't sure if they were alive or dead.

Sporadic fires were burning on the side of the road. A block of flats they passed had smoke pouring out of every window. At the base, a dozen or so zombies were milling around as if waiting for something. When the car went past, they started chasing it but they didn't have the strength to run, and as they lurched along on unsteady legs and brittle bones, the pack of zombies receded along with the burning buildings. Evan found himself praying again, only this time he was not alone.

CHAPTER FOUR

"Hey, where are we going? We should go to my house. It's just around the corner. My wife will be there." Miguel had stopped praying and began to take more notice in where they were headed. "Hey, hey, come on, we're nearly there."

Joe looked around at the endless houses and shops. "I don't think it's safe, Miguel. We're going to Mrs Craven's house, it'll be safer there." Joe continued driving and focused on getting the children back to their home.

Miguel reached forward and put his hand on Joe's shoulder.

"Come on, mate, you can stop here for a minute."

"I don't think we have a choice, Joe. Look," said Evan, pointing out of the window ahead of them.

The road ahead was blocked. An army blockade had cut off the road completely. Tanks, trucks, and vans were lined up, parked from house to house. Civilian cars sat three or four deep either side too, ensuring there was no way of moving any vehicle out of the way quickly and quietly. There was no way through.

"Maybe they can help us? Maybe there's someone here?" said Amane, leaning forward. She had been so quiet that Evan had almost forgotten her. Karyn snorted and said something derisory under her breath.

"We'll stop for a second and see, okay? But if there were any soldiers here, I think we would've seen them by now." Evan rolled down his window and looked at the blank windows of the houses past the blockade. It was worryingly quiet.

Joe slowed the car down and pulled up in front of a barrier. No official personnel came out to see them. No armed soldiers greeted them. The blockade was deserted.

"We can't drive around it, they've rammed those trucks right up to the side of the buildings," said Joe, exasperated. "Fine. Miguel, can you find your house on foot from here?"

"Sure, easy, I've grown up here all my life! When we get there, you can relax, okay? We'll be safe there. You can borrow my car if you really need but it's okay, take it easy, you'll see." He seemed happy to be almost home, unaware of the potential dangers outside. They all got out of the car. Amane went to pick up Lucy.

"I can carry her for you," she said to Karyn, offering Lucy a hand.

"No, she's fine." Karyn disregarded Amane's offer of help and scooped Lucy up into her arms. "George, stick by my side. Follow Joe and me. When we get to this man's house, we'll borrow his car and go home. Just us."

"Just trying to help," said Amane, shrugging her shoulders.

Karyn walked up to Amane and looked her up and down.

"If it wasn't for you, we would have been halfway home by now. I don't need to know you. Or who that stupid fuckwit was who ran out in front of us. Just stay away from me."

Amane was too shocked to reply. Evan offered Amane a club as Karyn walked away.

"Sorry. Here, take this."

"Thanks. I just thought..." Amane fought back tears and took the club. Evan could see she was fragile right now.

"Look, ignore her, her bark's worse than her bite. Stick by Joe and me." He gave her a reassuring smile.

Miguel started jogging off down a side street. "Come on, follow me!" They all followed him, Joe just behind.

"Hey, Miguel, don't go shouting too loud okay, we don't want to attract any attention."

Miguel ignored him and jogged further down the deserted side street, flanked on both sides by old wooden houses and high picket fences. The only sound came from the disparate group running for the safety of Miguel's house. The sun had burnt off the morning haze and despite a few vanishing clouds, the sun shone from a rich, blue sky, heating the city up.

Up ahead, Miguel had stopped and waved at the others to join him.

"Here, you see, my house. Easy!"

Evan winced as Miguel shouted out again a little too loudly, worrying who or what, the noise might attract. Maybe he was being too cautious. Maybe it would be safe. If Miguel had a car, he could borrow it and get to the harbour. Joe would help him. Seeing Karyn holding her children close only made Evan think more about his own children. He longed to be able to hold them close like her. Miguel's talk of his wife also made Evan wonder if he would ever get to see his wife again. He picked up the pace and watched as Miguel opened a side gate and disappeared through. Joe followed behind into a back garden cluttered with games.

The group gathered in the garden and Amane, last through, bolted the gate behind her. It felt relatively safe in the garden, surrounded as it was by a tall fence. Still, thought Evan, if a hundred zombies came calling, it would be torn down in a minute. They all watched, catching their breath, as Miguel approached the back door and knocked.

"My keys are at work, but don't worry, my wife, Alma, she'll be at home. She looks after my mother so she's always home."

Karyn put Lucy down and she and George found a football to kick around. Evan took a step forward. "So your mother lives here too?"

"Of course, she's not well. She's too old to live on her own now." He knocked again and peered through the dirty glass in the door. It was dark inside and no one came to answer.

"Hmm." Miguel frowned and tapped on the door again. "Maybe she's in the bathroom."

Evan turned to Joe. "I'm not sure about this. It's not safe to stay out here. We need to get inside or find a car or..."

He was cut off by the sound of breaking glass. Karyn had gone down the side of the house, and using one of the golf clubs, smashed open a window.

"Come on kids," she called, "in here." She brushed away the glass as George and Lucy ran up to her. She helped them through the open window into a small bedroom.

Evan and Joe exchanged looks as Miguel ran up to Karyn. "Hey lady, you gonna pay for that?" Miguel brandished his club, angry. Karyn looked at him, unable to bring herself to think that this poor man was worth speaking to, and with a dismissive cursory glance, she turned away and climbed through the window. Shaking his head, Evan walked down the side of the house toward them. Amane and Joe hung back in the overgrown garden. They heard Karyn call out from inside the house.

"George? Lucy? Don't run off, come back here."

Evan followed Miguel through the window and was struck by how dark it was. The air was stuffy. It tasted foul and warm. Evan was thirsty and vowed to find the kitchen first. Miguel had wandered off to look for his wife. The room they were in was quite bare, but comfy. Evan tried the switch on the wall and clicked it a few times, but the light did not come on.

"Miguel? You all right?" The words hung in the air without response. He knew something was going wrong. Goosebumps spread down Evan's arms as he heard a crash and a scream. A short guttural cry followed by a high-pitched shriek from opposite ends of the house. He raced out of the bedroom. Miguel stood to his left in the kitchen doorway, unmoving. Evan heard Miguel say, "Alma?" but the crashing noises were away to his right, and growing louder. Evan ran down the dingy corridor and pushed open the door at the end.

Karyn was grappling with an old woman, who was dressed in a nightgown, stained almost black with blood. George was silent, kneeling over his sister. Lucy was dead. She was splayed out, arms outspread, one hand still holding her rag-doll, whilst blood poured from her throat and soaked into the floral carpet beneath her. Her lifeless eyes were staring accusingly at Evan.

"Miguel!" called Evan, as he rushed to Karyn's aid. At the sound of his voice, the old lady ferociously pushed Karyn away and sprung toward Evan. Her snarling mouth was smeared with fresh blood from Lucy's throat. Evan had no time to use his club. He dropped it and charged, the two clashing like rutting stags. Evan outweighed his opponent though and the force of their collision sent the old woman flying back, tripping over a small coffee table. Evan picked the table up and crashed it down over the zombie's head.

"Karyn, help, hand me the club!" He turned around, only to see Karyn chasing George out of the room, club in hand, slamming the door behind her. Miguel's dead mother was getting to her feet. Evan spied a drinks cabinet and grabbed the first bottle at hand. He flung it at the approaching zombie and it shattered, spilling its sweet contents all over her. He did it again and whisky spilled down the nightgown. The glass shattered over the zombie's head, its own blood pouring down its face and mingling with Lucy's. The old woman was close now and sprang off her feet to attack.

Joe and Amane had heard the commotion and come in. Out in the corridor, Karyn stood guarding the lounge door, brandishing her club.

"Mrs Craven, let me in there right now!" shouted Joe.

"No! We need to get out of here. Lucy's fucking dead and you're our driver, Joe, I can't afford to lose you! We need to get out of here." Her eyes were wild. Her hair was matted with bright red blood and she was shaking. Joe wasn't sure if she was more interested in protecting George or herself. They heard a moaning sound behind them and whirled round.

Miguel stood in the kitchen doorway facing them. His wife had him in a bear hug, teeth sunk deep into his neck. Miguel was gripping the doorframe, eyes shut, unable to move, as his wife's teeth sliced through his jugular, spraying his blood over the dusty walls. He crumpled, weak, and his wife shoved her fist through his open neck. She repeatedly pulverised his dying body, beating it down to the floor. In a frenzied blood lust, she tore at his clothes, his skin, ripping off anything and everything: fingers, toes, ears. Like a rabid dog, she savaged her husband's face, sharp incisor's tearing out his eyes, fingernails slashing and hacking without mercy. Amane threw up and Miguel's wife turned around. Dead, black eyes fixed on Joe and Amane.

In the lounge, Evan was struggling to hold off Miguel's mother. Behind the dead pale eyes, he could see a hunger, a fiery, burning passion to kill. He had grabbed a leg from the shattered table and brandished it like a sword, but the zombie paid no heed and kept swiping at Evan. There was a fireplace behind the zombie and Evan saw the sunlight glint off the coal shuttle. He lunged for it and the old woman fell on top of him. Evan's hand pulled at the first thing it found, and he drove the copper poker into the zombie's face, straight through her old brittle skull. Miguel's mother stopped clawing at Evan and he pushed the sinking, stinking dead woman off him and got up. The zombie was not dead though, merely incapacitated. Its mouth was gasping like a fish out of water, making blood-curdling gurgling noises. Its arms floundered and caught the dying embers of the fire. Latching onto the alcohol, the fire suddenly swept down Miguel's mother's body.

Evan recoiled as the burning body unsteadily got to its feet. With the poker still sticking out of her head, Miguel's mother began lumbering toward him, flaming, flailing arms outstretched. The bloody nightgown had shrivelled up exposing the old woman's crackling, saggy body. Drops of flaming skin fell to the floor, her drooping breasts charred, swinging limply. Evan tried the door but it wouldn't open.

"Open it!" Evan shouted, "Now!" He pushed and pulled on the handle.

Karyn, shocked by the sight of Miguel's wife approaching them, loosened her grip on the door handle and backtracked down the corridor with George. Evan flung the door open, ready to unleash his vitriol onto Karyn, when he saw Miguel's prostrate body. Joe and Amane were backing slowly away from the dead woman approaching them. Miguel's wife, whilst covered in her husband's blood, looked otherwise almost unharmed. Evan saw bite marks all down her exposed arms. She was shuffling slowly toward them down the narrow corridor, looking at them from one to another, as if choosing her next victim.

Evan pushed Karyn aside and tried the front door. It rattled in its frame and Evan heaved, throwing it wide-open, sunlight bursting in. Miguel's advancing dead wife was silhouetted against a backdrop of billowing dust. Behind her, Miguel was clambering to his feet, his head hanging to one side, barely clinging to his lifeless body.

"Out, now!"

Needing no further invitation, they all tripped down the front steps after Evan. Evan looked over his shoulder to see Miguel and his wife following them. Outside were more zombies, heading toward them from both ends of the road. Evan didn't know if they had been alerted by the noise or the scent of fresh blood. Either way, they were here now and had to be dealt with. They were being closed in on from all sides.

"What the hell do we do now?" Joe was fighting the urge to vomit, adrenalin pumping through his body. Evan quickly scanned around for an escape route. The houses around them looked no safer than the one they had just been in, just broken windows and doors, masses of zombies pouring out. He saw what looked like a large warehouse nearby.

"Follow me!"

They ran after him, not knowing where they were going, not caring, just glad to be going somewhere. A policeman appeared from behind a car next to Joe and briefly, Joe dropped his guard, thankful that help was at hand. Then he noticed the policeman was limping. One leg had been brutalised down to the bone and the face wasn't right either, it looked almost lop-sided. The policeman opened his mouth, showing a limp, swollen, purple, tongue and blood-stained teeth. It lunged and Joe swung his club, knocking the zombie off balance and toppling it over. The policeman's hands narrowly missed Joe as it fell.

"Hurry up, they're getting closer!" George was lagging behind, agog at the advancing dead, his mother running ahead of him now. Joe grabbed George's hand and dragged him along. George's feet barely touched the ground.

"There!" called Amane, pointing to the warehouse. They ran through the car park, past empty trucks and vans, squeezing between the zombies. A metal grill was rolled half-up, leading into a loading bay. It looked quiet, dark, and cool out of the sunlight. As they all ran in under the metal grill, Evan shouted to Joe, "How do we close it?"

Karyn took George's hand and hugged him against her chest whilst the others scanned the walls. After what felt like an eternity, Joe found the switch and the metal door began rolling down to the rough concrete floor. The mass of zombies were close, and inches from the bottom, hands appeared, groping, feeling for life. Evan and Amane pounded on them with the golf clubs, breaking bones, mushing deadly hands into the ground whilst Joe held the switch down until the door finally closed, sealing them in. Decapitated fingers lay strewn over the dirty ground and Evan kicked them to a corner, disgusted. Joe flicked another switch, fluorescent lights flickering to life above them, lighting the room in a yellow glow.

"Where are we?" said Amane, looking round. The bay was largely empty. A truck was to their right, a couple of empty refuse bins and boxes to the side and in front of them, a tall, windowless, brick wall with a solitary door. The metal grill was rattling and shaking as more zombies continued to pile up against it, eager to get in.

"You okay?" said Evan to Amane. Her face was flushed with colour now and he was relieved to see she seemed more alert and alive. She nodded and flashed him a quick smile.

Joe went to investigate the truck whilst Evan and Amane sat down, gathering themselves. Karyn sat too, holding George close, thinking her own private thoughts, feeling the warmth of her son's body against hers. She smelled his boyish hair and was grateful he was still with her. George said nothing.

Evan and Amane sat in silence, listening to Joe start the truck. Evan had propitious thoughts of escaping. Take the truck, crash through the metal barrier and get everyone away from this prison. Get himself back to his family. Joe turned the engine off and climbed down from the cab.

"No good. The gas tank's empty." He sat down beside the truck and looked around at the faces staring back at him. He felt guilty for bringing such bad news, as if it was his fault the truck was useless.

Karyn cast fierce, teary eyes around the group and stood up. "How secure are those doors, Joe?"

"Not secure enough," was his reply. It was not what she wanted to hear.

"I would suggest we try that way," said Joe, looking at the door into the warehouse. The metal grill holding back the zombie horde was rattling back and forth violently. The sounds of murmuring and groaning outside grew louder with every second.

Evan and Amane got up and approached the door leading into the warehouse. Evan put his ear to it and listened.

"I can't hear anything. I'll go in first."

Evan exhaled and turned the door-handle with a measured, steady hand. Amane gripped the golf club, knuckles white, sweat beading on her forehead. Casting it open, Evan ventured in a few feet. The warehouse was lit up by more overhead fluorescent lights that only exacerbated Evan's headache. It was lined with rows and rows of boxes stacked on metal shelves. To the right, there was a small office: empty.

"Looks safe. I can't see any other doors." Evan came back to the doorway. "There doesn't seem to be anyone here, but me and Amane will sweep around and check, see if there's anyone else in here."

Evan wasn't worried about who they might find inside, just whether they were alive or dead: or both. He and Amane disappeared inside, leaving Joe waiting with Karyn and George in the loading bay. Locked in silence with nothing but the sounds of the undead just feet away, it was a painful five minutes for both of them. Joe could think of nothing useful to say to Karyn, nor she him. They were both thinking about Lucy. After a few minutes, Evan appeared back in the doorway.

"It's clear. We should be safe. Come on." Angry, Evan looked intently at Karyn who was avoiding his searching eyes. She would have to wait. Evan went back into the warehouse followed by a weary Joe.

"Go on George." Karyn ushered her son through the doorway and looked back at the metal pull-down grill that was keeping the zombies at bay. As George disappeared inside, leaving her alone, she listened to the moaning and growling sounds outside. How had it come to this? Rolling back her sleeve, she looked at the teeth marks where Miguel's mother had bitten her during their fight. The bleeding had stopped and she gathered herself together and pulled her sleeve back down, covering up the wound.

"Right."

She strode purposefully through the door and shut it behind her.

CHAPTER FIVE

In the cool warehouse, they splintered off. Karyn had taken George and was rummaging through boxes. Amane had gone exploring down a different aisle to Karyn. Joe needed some space; he was devoid of spirit and sat on the chair in the manager's office, half-heartedly examining some pointless paper work on the desk. Evan thought it best he kept clear of Karyn for now. She had jeopardised his life and her selfishness was a real threat, not just to him, but his family. He pulled a couple of boxes in front of the door to make sure they were safe and went to find Amane. He trod carefully: the overhead lights cast suspicious shadows everywhere.

"Found anything useful?" he said, approaching her. She held up tins of fruit and beans.

"Hungry?" she said, tossing him a can. He pulled back the opener and took the apricots out, swallowing them greedily. He literally couldn't remember the last time he had eaten and didn't realise just how hungry he actually was.

"Just what I wanted without even knowing it," he said through a mouthful of fruit.

Amane sat down cross-legged on the floor and delved into a tin of peaches. Evan ate, watching with curiosity. He couldn't figure her out. She wore skinny jeans and a simple red singlet. Apart from the sadness in her eyes, she was good-looking, slim, and healthy. Innocent, he thought. He sat down opposite her, leaning back against a crate. As much as he wanted to talk to her, Evan was quite happy sitting in her company without forcing conversation. They ate their fruit until Amane's slender fingers plucked the last peach from her tin and she sucked it down noisily. She looked up at Evan and he averted his eyes, realising he had been staring at her.

"We should take some of this to the others, they must be hungry too."

"Uh-huh," she mumbled in agreement. "You know these people well? Are they your family?" she asked him. She wiped her sticky fingers on her jeans before running them through her long dark hair, tying it behind her head.

"No, I only met them yesterday. My family is...lost. Well, I'm the one who's lost really. I was in an accident at the airport and hit my head. I can't remember anything before yesterday. When I say it out loud like this, it sounds bloody nuts."

"You have some nasty looking cuts on your head. We should see if we can find some medical supplies in these boxes. There's bound to be some somewhere." Amane reached out to him but stopped short of touching him as Evan stood up and grabbed some more tins from the box.

"Later. Let's go talk to Joe. We need to figure a way out of here."

Amane stood up, grabbed some tins, and followed Evan. From afar, Karyn watched them. Joe was still sitting in the office chair, rifling through papers. Evan dropped a couple of cans on the desk.

"Eat. Think of it as part of your five a day," Evan said, leaning back against the wall alongside Amane.

Joe thanked him and tucked in, relishing the sweet taste, the sugary food arousing his senses.

"Find anything useful?" asked Evan looking at the papers spread out over the desk.

"Nah. Found a nice calendar though. I present Miss WA 2038." Joe held it up, grinning at the blonde woman in the bikini, draped over a rock on a glorious sun-drenched beach.

Amane raised her eyebrows. "I guess she won't be joining us for the celebrations next week. We'll be lucky if there's any Australia left to celebrate."

Joe finished off the fruit and sat back. "Look, Evan, things didn't go exactly to plan out there. Poor Miguel. And I can't believe Lucy's gone. She was such a good kid...I'm not sure what to do now to be honest, mate. I'm through with Mrs Craven. It's her bloody fault Lucy's dead, rushing off into the house like that. You know she would've left you behind to die in that house? She's a piece of work I tell ya. If Pete knew what had happened to his Lucy..." Joe slapped the desk in frustration.

"She'd never admit it, but she only married Pete for the money. He always was a sucker for the ladies. God rest his soul."

"I know I only just met her, but I don't trust her," declared Amane.

"Believe me, there's nothing I would like to do more than throw her to the wolves, but we have to think about George. He just lost his sister and I'm not confident Karyn has his best interests at heart," said Evan.

They were silent, thinking about their situation. The zombies outside were very faint now, locked outside the building.

"Amane, isn't it?" said Joe. "Where's home? Where are you headed?"

"I have a flat in the city. I was just at the airport collecting my parents. They'd flown in from Tokyo." She closed her eyes and clasped her hands before continuing.

"They're dead now: still at the airport. I could go home, but what's the point? There's nothing there for me apart from boring textbooks. I don't even know how I'd get there. I reckon there are a million zombies between here and my place."

"And you Joe?" asked Evan.

"Similar story actually. I've got a small place south of the city, close to Pete's place, but there's no chance of making it there through those things. Unless you found an armoured bulldozer? I thought Mrs Craven's might be a good hideout until this shit is sorted out, but we'd never make it. You'd basically have to go into the city to get there. That's *not* going to happen."

"You think this *can* be sorted out, Joe? I don't think so." Amane was shaking her head. A dark cloud of fear and depression hovered over her like a summer thunderstorm brooding over a cornfield.

"When I met my parents at the airport, they said they were pleased to see me, all the usual you know, but they said that back home in Tokyo, it wasn't safe anymore. I hadn't honestly followed the news, I'd been studying so much, but they said fights and riots had broken out all over the city and was spreading to the rest of the country. Apparently, Fukuoka was a no-go zone, the military had cut if off completely. It was the same in China, Korea, everywhere. They left just as things were getting out of control. They said they were pleased to be in a safe country. Look how that turned out.

"The Kannushi were saying it was a curse and that our 'Kami,' our souls, were facing a day of reckoning: that mankind had brought this on itself. I'm not a believer in that anymore but my parents are. Were," she corrected herself and went on.

"At the airport, we went to look at the television screens and the things they were showing, my God. This isn't some terrorist attack that we can send the army in to fight. This is unnatural: un-Godly. Dead people are walking around, killing us: killing the living. I'm starting to wonder if my parents were right. I mean look outside, right now, and you will see a hundred zombies just waiting to get in here and rip us apart. It only takes a second and we'd be dead. At the airport, my parents and me were leaving, when all of a sudden, it was happening right around us. It took just a few minutes and it was chaos. It was so quick. My father..."

Amane welled up and bit her lip. She felt at ease with Evan and Joe, but still, she didn't want to cry in front of these relative strangers. It wasn't right.

"From what I've seen, Joe, she's right," said Evan. "No one is going to come and save us. There is no police, army, or government. Law and order is fucked. I think the only thing we can do now is look after ourselves. Outside of this room, and George, that means I need to find my family."

"Well," said Joe, "if you have any bright ideas let me know. Otherwise, we could be stuck in here for a while. You go out there now, it's suicide. And it will not be quick and painless."

Joe opened the desk drawers and found a mobile phone. Whilst he spoke, he held it up, trying to find a signal. He threw it down on the desk.

"Nothing. Mind you, who would I call?" He pursed his lips, thinking. Evan put his hand on Amane's shoulder as she dabbed at her eyes.

"Remember last night, Joe?" Evan said. "Those things had us surrounded out at the airport, but we stayed quiet all night and they disappeared. When we went out this morning, we only saw a couple. At least until we got to the terminal, anyway."

"So we wait this out," said Joe. It was more of a statement than a question. "Kind of makes sense."

"How long? Hours, days?" Amane wiped her nose. "I spent all of last night stuck in a closet. We thought they had gone this morning too. But then..."

"In a couple of hours it'll be midday. No matter how determined those things are, with the sun beating down on them, they're gonna start to flake out. Surely?" Evan was feeling more confident about his plan now.

"The sun will sap the strength right out of them. They might not be human anymore as we know it, but they're human bodies. I don't think they've got the intelligence to shelter, so that should help us. Maybe they'll get distracted? If we're quiet enough, they might forget we're in here and fuck off to find some other poor bastards."

"That's a fairly sound plan. Even if they don't all piss off, they should thin out enough for us," said Joe, getting up out of the creaking black desk chair. "But then what?"

"Look, I can't ask you to come with me, but I have to find my children. I need to get a ride to the docks or a harbour somewhere and find a boat." Evan turned to Amane. "They're on Tasmania. My father has a boat and I think they're in trouble. I *have* to go."

"I think it's safer if we stick together," she replied. "My parents are gone. I've nothing here. Look, if it's okay with you, I'll tag along?"

Evan held out his hand and she took it with both hands.

"Sure, thanks," he said.

"Me too," said Joe, decisively. "If we wait until it's quieter, we should be able to get to one of those trucks out in the car park we ran past on the way in. They'll be tanked up, ready to go, and I know how to handle them. We're the other side of that blockade now, so provided we don't hit anymore, we should be able to make the docks all right. No need to go through the city either, we can skirt right around it on the ring road. Besides," he said, smiling, "I've always fancied visiting Tassie."

"Only one problem," Evan said, shoving his hands into his pockets. He nodded out into the warehouse. They all looked through the doorway at Karyn. She was sitting down with George, both with their heads stuck in boxes. She had stacked some around them as if making a fort.

"I'll try and talk to her in a bit, see where her head's at," said Evan. "Meantime, let's make use of our time. Rest if you want, but I'm going to see what's in these boxes. Even if we get an easy ride to the docks, with the boat trip over there it's going to take us a while to reach my family. We should find supplies: water, weapons, food, whatever you think is useful and easy to carry. Bring it back to the office here and we'll see what we've got."

"I know where I'm starting," said Joe, striding out, "cigarettes and alcohol."

Evan laughed as they left the small office and took their own paths around the warehouse, walking up and down the aisles, examining any box that looked like it might offer up some token of help. Karyn and George kept to themselves.

* * * *

As Evan looked around, he saw above the office a small empty space, only dimly lit by the flickering neon above them. He found a small ladder propped against the sidewall and clambered up. He left large footprints behind on the floor, which was covered in thick dust and grime. A few mouldy pieces of cardboard lay scattered around, some empty boxes and various items that were clearly broken and had been discarded; many were coated in bird-droppings and dirt. Evan was about to climb down when he noticed a pull-down hatch in the roof. Trying to avoid breathing in the cloggy, gritty air, he went over to it and pulled on the latch. Brilliant sunlight burst through as the door swung on its hinges, the sunshine highlighting every droplet of dust hovering in the air. He pulled over a rickety three-legged stool and hauled himself up. It wasn't easy, the roof was flat and hot, and there was nothing to grip onto. Grunting and sweating, he eased himself over the ledge and lay on his back staring up at the blue sky. What the hell am I doing, he thought to himself as he lay there quite still, listening to the decayed army below.

Evan rolled over onto his front, and achingly slowly, crawled over the hot, harsh concrete to the edge of the roof. He surveyed the scene below him. There must have been at least a hundred, maybe two, banging on the warehouse door, trying to push past each other to get inside. As he peered over the edge, the noises grew louder and the putrid stench of the dead floated up to him, making his eyes water. He had to put his hand in front of his mouth to stop himself from gagging.

This affliction, this curse or whatever it was, thought Evan, it truly spared no one. A splintered slice of society shambled beneath him: young and old, male and female. They were surrounded by a plague of people who had been planning their futures, only to find the future was both painful, and painfully short. Evan was surprised at the colours. He couldn't deny the sickening blood that sheathed most of them was at the forefront. But these were people who, until about two days ago, were living their life as normal, wearing their everyday clothes. There were young men wearing bright football shirts, kids wearing clothes of great blues and bright greens, young women wearing skimpy tops and tiny shorts of all colours: yellow vests, bright pinks and vivid ambers. Who knew death would be so vivid?

There was an absence of life though, sorely missing from the city. He heard no birdsong or barking. No voices or music. Even the grass seemed to be browner, as if it too were dying. He saw a dead dog in the street, a retriever, its tongue hanging out, glassy-eyed, guts ripped out. Its hind legs had been chewed off. It seemed these abhorrent monsters, once human that they so frivolously called 'zombies,' were intent on destroying life. Perhaps not just human life, thought Evan, but life on earth. He subconsciously shook his head to get rid of the encroaching dark thoughts from entering his mind.

The more he looked on, the sadder he felt. These un-human beings, he observed, were utterly devoid of life. Sure they were moving, but why? Were they aware of their own existence? Some of them stuttered along aimlessly, joining in the banging on the door even though they couldn't possibly know why. Some of them moved quicker, not as injured as others, and so were able to roam the streets, swiping past their counterparts, apparently unaware of them. Their spiritless faces were as one: disjointed, soul-less, ambivalent. Except when they made eye contact...Evan remembered back to the airport and the eyes that had looked at him with such strange energy. It wasn't like looking at another person. He couldn't recall ever looking at someone else the way they looked at him with such anger, envy: a soul-sapping hatred.

Evan felt despair. Despair for himself and his children who he feared in that moment, he might never see again. Despair for Joe who he had come to rely on, and George, so young to experience such death at close hand. Despair for Amane, such a captivating young woman whose future weighed on his shoulders now. Could he ask them to come with him? Was it fair on any of them?

He looked up to the horizon, surveying his surroundings and the city. He was shocked by what he saw – polluting black smoke hung heavy over the city skyline. He could see the tops of skyscrapers poking through like beacons. There were menacing, fiery fire-clouds billowing through the city. Closer to home he noticed a few shops, but mostly just row after row of houses. On the street corner, a church was blazing away merrily. It was a new-build design, ordered by an architect rather than inspired by a creator. The shining cross on the spire sparkled strongly, lit up by the sun from above and the roaring flames from beneath. The glass windows had shattered and an inferno raged; tendrils of grey smoke escaping the churches interior furnace, rising up to the heavens.

Evan noticed the fractured gravestones and furrowed graveyard. The consecrated earth was churned over as if ready for harvesting. Deathly pits surrounded the church from where bodies, once consigned to the ground, had emerged. For what purpose, wondered Evan. Zombies were staggering around the church, some alight, clothes smouldering, hair blazing and eyes crying droplets of fire. Yet they sensed no pain or anger at their situation. Evan watched, bemused, as one blindly fell into a freshly dug crater. With clearly broken legs, it still scrabbled to get out, clawing at the mud to no avail. How long would it burn, Evan speculated, before it burnt itself out? How much skin and bone did it still need to be able to walk around before it truly died? Sever the head, that's what Joe had said. Maybe it was as simple as that. With no brain function, perhaps the zombies would fall, their shells useless.

Reluctant to stay any longer for fear of being noticed by the zombies below, Evan stealthily moved back away and into the centre of the roof. Ponderously, he levered himself back through the rooftop opening and dropped back onto the office roof, causing more dust to shake itself free and float through the musty air of the warehouse.

* * * *

Time passed unnoticed as Evan discovered backpacks, torches and matches. He managed to find some bandaging and a first aid kit, and tried to tend to the wounds on his face. In the end, he gave up and just dropped everything in the office on the desk. The pile grew, bit by bit. Amane had found more food. Just tins, some of it useless, but some of it more than adequate: tins of fruit, beans, even vegetables. There were cans of coke and lemonade, but no one had found any water. Evan saw a couple of bottles of vodka on the office desk and smiled wryly, imagining the look on Joe's face when he'd found them. He turned to leave the office and bumped into Amane. She was carrying a plastic bag.

"Look," she said with glee, and opened the bag. Inside was an assortment of kitchen knives. She'd picked out the smaller ones, rejecting them for the more useful larger ones: boning knives, Santokus, carving and paring knives, cleavers. There was even one hefty axe.

"That one's mine," she said as Evan traced his fingers over it.

"Impressive. Slightly disturbing that you're so happy about your new knife collection, but impressive," he said looking at her.

"Come with me, there's something else I want to show you." She dropped the bag in the office and took Evan by the arm, leading him to the furthest corner of the warehouse where it was damp and cold.

"Hockey sticks. Not bad," said Evan surveying the pile Amane had amassed.

"I know. Pretty solid too," she said, holding one aloft. Evan picked up a roll of masking tape.

"They'll be even better when I've finished with them. Take one hockey stick, one butcher's knife and hey, presto." He lunged with a hockey stick at the air.

"Zombie kebab."

Amane laughed, her giggle echoing off the wall around the warehouse.

"You're a little crazy," she said. Amane pulled a large box out from under a shelf, swept the dust off and sat down.

"Evan, I'm grateful you helped me, I really am. You didn't have to. Back at the airport, if you hadn't come by when you did...Well, I probably wouldn't be here now."

Evan sat down beside her, resting the hockey stick between his legs.

"Well, I'm pleased you're here. I'm sorry about your parents. What happened back there? Who was that woman who ran into us?"

"That was my mother." Amane's voice became softer.

"Shit, I'm sorry. Look you don't have to..."

"No, it's okay. I need to talk about it. The last twenty fours have been unlike anything I've ever known. It's incredible. I came out here from Tokyo to study a few years ago. After I got my nursing degree last year, I stayed on to keep my studies going. I'm training to be a doctor. I love it here but I missed my parents. This was only the second time they'd visited me. Neither of them were very keen on flying. Understandable at their age I suppose.

"Anyway, like I was saying earlier, they were trying to tell me how things were back home. The airport had the news channels on and there was a huge crowd gathered around watching the screens. One of the channels obviously had a helicopter and there were amazing pictures of Sydney burning. The harbour bridge was a like a stream of fire. All the cars were burning and the cables and steel were melting. It was hard to believe it was real. When they zoomed into the streets, you could see the people. There were thousands and thousands of them running for their lives. It was awful.

"It was only a minute or two, when all of a sudden, people were shoving and jostling around us. I don't know what started it. Then I heard gunfire. People panicked. *I* panicked. I grabbed mum and dads' hands and we ran outside. It was pandemonium. The police were shooting at us; cars were running people over, crashing into each other. A man next to me got hit by a bullet and fell over. I swear it hit him square in the head and yet seconds later, he was up on his feet. He grabbed my dad and started biting him! His hands and arms, his face...I tried to hold on, but I couldn't. Dad was old and weak; he had no fight left in him. He fell to the floor and the last I saw of him, this crazy man was biting him and others were piling on top of them.

I kept hold of mum and we ran back inside. There was no way we could get to my car, what with the bullets flying and people running around attacking each other. Back in the building, it was just as chaotic. I thought maybe we could hide somewhere. The toilets were close by and just as we were running in, Miguel was going into his cleaning room. I just barged in past him and pushed mum inside. He wasn't too pleased. I pleaded with him to let us stay. He was okay, you know, he helped us. He let us stay in there with him. He didn't deserve what happened to him." Amane wiped her eyes again before continuing.

"He locked the door and we waited for the commotion to die down. It didn't. It went on for hours and when the shouts and cries faded away, we could still hear things moving around out there, slithering and sliding over the floor, groaning and moaning. We just about had room to sit down but we dare not go outside. The room smelt like chemicals too, it wasn't very nice. All night we waited. I tried calling the police on my mobile but the number was just permanently engaged. I tried a couple of friends but got no answer from them, and in the end, I gave up.

Mum seemed to fall asleep eventually and I supposed Miguel and I did too. Curled up on the floor next to a bucket and mop though, I didn't sleep much. I kept seeing dad in my dreams, being dragged off into the crowd.

When mum woke, she was hysterical. I tried calling for help again but the phone was dead, I couldn't get any signal at all. My mother kept saying we had to find Kagami, my father.

She wouldn't be quiet so we thought we may as well try our luck outside, see if we could maybe make it to my car. Miguel helped me calm her down a little bit, so we left the closet. The airport seemed quiet. I thought everyone had gone. But we'd only gone from the closet a few feet before we heard them. My mother ran ahead and was pointing, shouting. 'Kyonshi' she kept saying. A second later, I heard her calling for my dad: 'Kagami! Kagami!'

"Before I could catch up with her it was too late. She'd found my father, or rather he'd found her, but he wasn't the same. He looked terrible. There was no way he was alive, yet there he was walking around, staring at my mother. He grabbed her and...I wish he had killed her outright. He bit her all over. He tore her ear off first, and then he bit her hands and arms as she tried to protect herself. She tried to stop him but couldn't. He wasn't a weak old man anymore.

"Miguel had a broom or something with him, I don't remember what, and hit my father round the head with it. It was enough to stop him briefly and I grabbed my mother. There were hundreds of those things. They just appeared out of nowhere. My mother screamed and ran out the door into the fog. I think she was so scared she didn't really know what she was doing. She was bleeding badly, and well, next minute, you appeared. It isn't anyone's fault what happened to her but her own. She was dying before she ran out in front of you."

Evan stopped spinning the hockey stick around.

"I'm sorry, Amane."

They sat in silence for a minute.

"So what's your story? You..." Amane was cut short by the shouting.

"Are you fucking joking, Joe?"

Karyn was screaming at Joe, hands on her hips. Through gaps in the shelving, Evan saw her jabbing her finger into Joe's shoulder.

"I think we'd better get over there," he said. Amane followed Evan down the row of dusty shelves to the argument.

"Karyn, keep it down. We're supposed to be hiding in here, not alerting the whole city to where we are," said Evan, marching up to her.

"Is that right, Mr Crow? I suppose this was your idea was it? Thought we'd have a nice little drive down to the ocean did we?

Perhaps stop off for an ice cream on the way? You are out of your fucking mind." She took a step up to Evan and stared at him.

"Joe works for me and he is taking me and George home. You and that Asian cunt cowering behind you can..."

Evan slapped her, hard. Karyn stumbled back, shocked, and put a hand to her stinging cheek.

"If you don't watch your mouth and your temper...say anything like that again and I'll personally throw you outside into hell. Don't think I haven't forgotten what you did back there at Miguel's either. Listen, you're not the boss now. We are in this together and you need to start working with us, not against us."

"Joe," said Karyn in a low voice, "I demand that you take me and George home now."

"Hell no." Joe folded his arms. Karyn's face was burning red.

"In five years, you have never said no to me, Joe. What would Pete think? What about my Lucy? Are you going to abandon us now, just when we need you?"

"This has got nothing to do with them," he said, gruffly. "Listen up bitch, you need to start thinking straight, start thinking about what's best for George. Despite what I think about you, he's lost his dad, and his sister, and he needs his mum right now. You've seen what it's like out there. We simply cannot get to the house, Mrs Craven. Our best bet is the ocean and to get to Tassie. We'll get on a boat with Evan and Amane, and get the hell out of here."

"Where is George?" said Amane, glaring at Karyn.

Karyn, nursing her red cheek, eyes glistening, said, "Exploring, playing, I don't know. Doing whatever it is little boys should be doing." She sat down looking defeated.

"I'll go look for him," said Amane, shaking her head in disbelief as she walked away. Joe and Evan stared at Karyn who looked defeated.

"Fine," Karyn muttered, looking at the grimy concrete floor, "we'll come with you to the boat."

Evan and Joe exchanged looks.

"Just so as we're clear," Evan said, "if you ever come between me and getting to my family again, I will not hesitate. You are this close, Karyn. From now on, you do what we say. Clear?" He turned and walked away.

Joe shuffled off awkwardly as Karyn began sobbing into her hands.

"This isn't fair," she said between sobs. "This isn't fair."

Joe started to feel sorry for her. She might be a queen-bitch but she had just lost her husband and daughter. Maybe they should cut her some slack. If Pete could find some good in her, shouldn't he try? She probably wasn't thinking straight. He left her alone, and started rummaging through more boxes, looking for those elusive cigarettes.

* * * *

Amane found George curled up on a beanbag, still in its polystyrene cover. He was clutching a rag-doll similar to the one Lucy had. She let him sleep. Looking at him sleeping so peacefully made her realise how physically exhausted she was. She found another beanbag, and pulling it up beside him, slumped down into it, able to relax at last. She curled up listening to George's gentle breathing and let herself relax. The lack of sleep from last night and the loss of her parents were catching up with her.

Evan meandered down the rows of boxes, looking for anything useful. He needed to refocus and forget the argument with Karyn. He began rifling through one box and grabbed a couple of blankets that might be handy later. He opened another box, full of clothes. He sorted through it, past t-shirts with 'I love Melbourne' on them, and at the bottom of the box, found an olive-green jumper. Picking it up, he swooned and grabbed the shelf to stop himself from falling. A memory jolted through him of his wife, wearing a jumper just like this one.

He slid to the floor holding the jumper to his chest and closed his eyes. He and his wife were standing side by side on a pier. He could almost smell the sea-salt air. They were waving. He saw the boat, 'Lemuria,' again in front of them. The picture gradually came into focus. His children, Charlie and Anna were waving, standing tall and proud on the boat's deck. They were shouting goodbyes. Evan smothered his face with the jumper. He had left them on that boat for their usual summer holiday. He vaguely remembered turning to his wife, kissing her, and saying it was okay, that they would be back in a week to pick them up. Then what? His mind went blank again and the picture faded. Damn it, why couldn't he remember?

Evan pressed his palms against his eyes, pushing down on them, patches of light fading in and out of the black-red mist, swirling around. He screwed his eyes shut tighter and the orange circles were replaced by pools of deeper black: bursts of magenta and crisp dark blue shimmering in and out of focus. Opening his eyes again, Evan's head felt lighter. The horrible fluorescent lights were still there but the pain that had been building in him had subsided. He took a deep breath and clutched the green jumper to his chest closer, trying to remember anything else useful, hoping he could kick-start his brain.

Another memory flowed through his mind and sent shivers down his body; the woman on the tarmac lying beside him had been wearing a green jumper too. That familiar face, so pale in death, was his wife. So he had known her. It was his wife, his poor wife. She must have been on the plane with him. Evan began crying for his lost wife, muffling his sobs into the jumper. As he lamented his wife, his tears dried up. He found he was grieving the idea of her but could remember little about her in reality. What was her name? When was her birthday? What was her favourite food? How long had they even been married? All he had to hold onto was this memory of them together waving at their children.

It struck him that this particular memory must be important, such as it was being the only one he really had of her. Or maybe it was a recent memory. Waving at their children on the boat...he mused and tried to recollect when it was. What was it Charlie had said in his dreams?

"We come here every year."

'Every year.' He and his wife took the children to their granddads yacht on Tasmania every year for a holiday. Another piece of the puzzle fell into place. What was the date today? He pictured the calendar that Joe had been waving around earlier. Was it January 23, 24? That would mean it was school holidays now. 'Every year.'

Evan was overcome with emotion. Grief for his wife weaved uneasily through him alongside relief. His children *had* to be on that boat: that was where they were trapped. He and his wife had dropped them off as usual and were headed back home, as they did every year, but then their plane had crashed. He tried to picture home. Was it in Melbourne? His head hurt as much as it had that day on the tarmac. He could not envisage the street or the house where they lived. He buried his head in the jumper, remembering his wife, and hoping he would find a way to his children soon.

* * * *

As the afternoon dragged by, Evan busied himself exploring the warehouse and regularly checked the loading bay. He needed to keep his mind focused. He had lost his wife; he did not want to lose his children. Each time he went out to the loading bay, it seemed quieter. The grill wasn't shaking as much and the moaning noises outside had lessened. He was sure the zombies were losing interest. Eventually, the grill didn't move at all anymore. Just the very occasional knocking sound as if someone half-heartedly wanted to come in but wasn't quite sure or was just brushing past it.

Evan had found Amane sleeping beside George, but finally, desperate to talk to her, he woke her, unable to wait any longer. He put a hand on her shoulder, gently shaking her until she woke. Kneeling down beside her, he whispered in her ear, putting his finger to his lips.

"Hey, I didn't want to wake George, but I need to show you something."

Amane rolled her head on her shoulders, waking herself up, and traipsed behind him. By the ladder outside the office, she paused, noticing he seemed distracted.

"Are you okay?" she said, touching his arm warmly, "You look a bit pale. Has something happened?"

"No, it's fine." He ushered her up the ladder but she knew something wasn't right. His words had a distinct lack of conviction, yet before, he had been so direct and confident.

They padded across the grimy storage area above the office, and she followed him up through the rooftop doorway. He intimated to her that they should be quiet. Once up on the roof in the sunshine, she kept low and sat down next to Joe. The murmurs from below were un-nerving.

"Over there," Joe said to her, as quietly as he could in his gravelly voice.

She shielded her eyes from the sun and looked to where Joe was pointing whilst Evan sat down next to her. It was a house, over the road from the warehouse, looking like every other house in its row, except for one thing. Beneath an upstairs window, someone had hung out a sheet and painted on it in deep crimson letters:

HELP – ALIVE

Amane looked worriedly from Joe to Evan. "Have you seen them? Who's in there?"

"We don't know. I didn't see it at first," said Evan in a hushed voice. "I showed Joe up here and he saw it."

"I've not seen anyone," admitted Joe, "and I've been out here quite a while now." There were discarded cigarette butts littering the rooftop around his feet. "Look at the front door."

A dozen or so zombies were pressed against it, scratching at the wooden door, pounding at the brickwork, leaving bloody handprints behind.

"Fuck," she said. "We can't just leave them."

"We agree on that, but," said Joe, gravely, "to play devil's advocate for a minute, we don't know who is in there or in what state. When we get out of here, it's going to be risky trying to get in there and we don't know what we're going to find. Is it worth taking a chance on something that could be nothing?"

Amane scanned the house. She couldn't tell if there were any lights on due to the glare from the sun's rays hitting the windows. The road between the warehouse and the house was empty, save a few decrepit corpses straggling behind the rest on the road to nowhere.

"Come down, I want to talk about it inside where it's safer." Evan led the way down and they filed down after him, congregating back in the office.

"Look, when we do go, we can't just leave them. I'm sure someone is in there or those zombies wouldn't be so keen to get in, would they? We have to at least try," said Evan. He was glad to be able to talk about this. He didn't want the responsibility squarely on his shoulders.

"Nearly four o'clock. We should go soon. I don't want to try doing this in the dark. You know, no matter how long we wait, there's always going to be some of those things out there," Joe countered.

"I know," agreed Evan, "we're going to have to move quickly."

"That truck out there is running on fumes, but it'll get us to one of the other trucks in the lot. Be safer than running for it." said Joe.

Evan was filling backpacks with their abundant bounty: medicine, blankets, food, cans of drink, matches.

"Okay, stick with me here, I've got an idea" Evan said. "I'll run for it to the house. The back garden looked empty. I can smash the window and get in there in two seconds. You two get another truck, swing back here to pick Karyn and George up, then get me and whoever I find in that house."

Joe began stuffing his backpack with his essentials: cigarettes, lighters, booze.

"I don't know," said Amane, "for all we know, they're dead, or dying in there and we could be risking ourselves for nothing. What if you get hurt, Evan?"

"I have no intention of being eaten thank you, I'll be careful. I just couldn't live with myself knowing we left someone who might need our help. Look, you take the backpacks into the truck. I need to be quick on my feet, so all I'm taking with me is a weapon. I'll grab one of those hockey sticks."

Evan picked one up and examined it. One end had a carving knife wrapped around it, securely held in place by thick layers of masking tape.

"Let's do this now," he said. "This waiting's killing me."

Joe and Amane nodded in silent agreement. He stuck his head out of the office.

"Ten minutes, Karyn. Get George and pack up, we're leaving."

* * * *

As Joe helped Karyn gather together the few measly things she had managed to muster up, and explain to her and George what was going on, Amane walked with Evan to the metal grill.

"Just give me a five minute head start, okay?" he said, brandishing the homemade weapon.

"Sure." Amane looked at him seriously. "Evan, what's wrong. I mean, more than the obvious, there's something wrong, I can tell."

Evan sat down on the cold steps in the loading bay and glanced over his shoulder at the door behind them. As she sat down too, he explained to her in a few words how he had woken up on the tarmac, met Joe and Karyn in the hangar, and eventually met with her and Miguel. She listened intently, not interrupting or hurrying him.

"I told you I couldn't remember anything before that day and that's true. But earlier I found a jumper. Nothing special, but it reminded me of my wife. I remembered her from the airport. She's dead."

Amane rubbed his back as Evan choked up. He wiped his eyes and continued.

"I also remembered my children. They're on that boat, Amane. My wife is gone, but my kids, Charlie and Anna, I have to find them, I have to."

He stood up, hearing footsteps approaching. Amane gave Evan a hug.

"They'll be okay, Evan," she whispered in his ear. He held her, the presence of her warm body against his reassuring him as much as her words.

Joe came through the door as they released each other.

"Ready?"

"As I'll ever be," said Evan. "You talk to her and George? They know what the plan is?"

Joe nodded.

"All sorted, mate. Good luck." Joe shook Evan's hand firmly. "We'll pick you up in five minutes."

"Don't be late," said Evan, giving Joe and Amane one last look. He hit the button to roll the grill up and slid out quickly when it was a few feet over the ground. Joe rolled it down, listening to Evan's footsteps diminishing as he ran.

CHAPTER SIX

Evan's race across the car park was surprisingly easy. Most of the zombies had indeed left, leaving him to dodge through the few standing easily. He sprinted around the warehouse and down the road unhindered, ignoring the feeble arms and hands reaching for him. Jumping over a low wooden fence, he landed in the back garden of the house. One large window showed him it was dark and quiet inside. Evan wasted no time and smashed the window with the hockey stick. The noise instantly alerted inquisitive zombies and Evan rushed through the big bay window he had knocked out.

The room was dim, but clean, and he could make out two open doorways flanking a huge flat-screen television. One door led to a small kitchen, the other to a hallway. He could hear the sounds of the approaching dead and had to take a chance.

"Hey, anyone here?" he called out loudly.

He heard movement upstairs and went to the foot of the stairs in the hallway. At the top were closed doors and Evan called out again.

"I'm here to help! Hello?"

He heard more movement and tensed, preparing to run. A door opened and a young girl walked out. A pale face looked down at Evan.

"Are you alone?" she said, timidly, sizing Evan up.

"No, my friends are outside. We've got a truck and we're getting out of the city. We saw your sign. Are your parents here? Are you hurt?"

She relaxed, realising Evan evidently wasn't going to harm her.

"I'm okay. My dad's in Canberra and my mum went to church yesterday to pray, but I haven't seen her since. I put the sign up this morning but you're the first person I've seen: other than those things out there."

She walked down the stairs and Evan was glad she was alone. He wasn't sure what he'd have done if a whole family had appeared. The girl was about fifteen or sixteen, dressed in black jeans and a skin-tight black top that looked like it had been sprayed on.

"I'm Lily," she said, "Um, look, can you take me with you? I can't stay here anymore. I'm not stupid, I know my mum's not coming back." She precociously swung a tiny handbag over her shoulder.

Evan could see her clearer as she got to the bottom of the stairs. Her hair was tied back in a thick ponytail and she'd caked the make-up on a little too thick.

"Sure, but we need to hurry, okay?" Evan heard the moaning and groaning of the dead worryingly close now. A few zombies had gotten into the house through the broken window and were stumbling around in the lounge. One of them, an old Chinese man in a tatty, torn bath-gown, suddenly appeared in the doorway beside Evan. Lily screamed.

Evan instinctively sliced the bladed hockey stick through the air, tearing the zombie's throat out in one swoop. It reeled backwards and stumbled into three more zombies, all converging on the doorway.

"Come on!"

Evan grabbed Lily's hand and they ran down the hallway into the kitchen. Through the tiny window, Evan saw the front yard was swarming with zombies, thrashing and gnashing, desperate to get into the house. He saw a white van screech to a halt on the road.

"That'll be our ride," he said to Lily. "Look, I know this is crazy, but our best bet is the way I came in. Just follow me and run to the van. Don't stop for anything, all right?"

"Okay," she said, trembling. Lily's bright red fingernails were digging into Evan's hands. He let go and charged back down the hallway into the lounge. Using the hockey stick like a battering ram, he speared the first zombie that lunged for him, knocking it over. He pulled his makeshift spear out and swinging it over his head, sent it smashing into another's head. Another zombie grabbed his arm and he shook it free. He rammed the hockey stick upwards, the blade entering through the chin and penetrating its brain. The zombie tottered backward unsteadily with the tip of the knife sticking out of its head. As Evan yanked the hockey stick back, the knife refused to budge and tore free from the stick, permanently lodged in the zombie's head.

"Run!"

Evan jumped through the bay window with a terrified Lily in tow. In the garden were more zombies: lots of them. He couldn't possibly fight them all in such close proximity. Head down, he charged through them like a bowling ball, hoping that the snapping teeth wouldn't catch him. The zombies flailed and failed to get a decent hold on him or Lily. He jumped the fence and Lily followed in his wake. She saw the van and raced ahead of him. Evan saw the back door was open and Amane was swiping at anything coming close, knives slicing through skin, shaving off fingers, keeping the clamouring zombies at bay. Lily jumped up and Karyn helped pull her into the safety of the van.

Evan suddenly slipped and fell. His hockey stick flew out of his hands and he felt fingers curl around his leg as he fell to the ground. He lashed out, trying to kick free but the grip was too strong. The zombie's other hand grabbed him at the knee. Evan saw the remains of the dead dog he had slipped in and thought how stupid he was. Trying to wriggle himself free, he began punching the zombie on the head so it could not get a stronghold. It was another old man: larger though and a lot less fragile than the one in the house.

Evan rapidly brought his fist down, again and again, on the man's bald head, feeling his knuckles strike bone through blanched, leathery skin. The zombie could not bite Evan being jostled about and it looked up at its prey. Evan landed a left-hook that broke the zombies jaw, but did not dislodge its grip. He saw a dozen more zombies only feet away and felt almost overwhelmed by the futility of what he was trying to beat. He frantically felt around for his hockey stick, but it had fallen frustratingly out of reach.

Just as the zombie was preparing to take a chunk out of Evan's leg, an axe butchered its way through its head, smashing onto the tarmac road, taking the old man's face off in one clean slice. The death grip on his legs disappeared, and with nothing holding him down, Evan scrambled to his feet. Amane grabbed him and with the axe in her other hand, ran to the van dragging Evan along with her.

"Come on, hurry!"

With no time to thank her, they both jumped into the van that roared off, leaving a trail of bloodthirsty, dissatisfied zombies stumbling after them. From the safety of the van, George watched the crowd of zombies. One little girl, throat ripped out, stumbled after them on stiff legs, her arms outstretched. One hand still held tightly onto a ragged doll and George watched her until she disappeared from sight.

Joe drove as fast as he could, knocking down anyone, or anything that got in his way. Zombies bounced off the van, spinning and bouncing away onto the verge, sometimes careening right under the van. Joe felt them crunch satisfactorily.

Leaving the hungry zombies behind him, Joe picked his way carefully through the city. George was strapped into the passenger seat beside him staring at the foot-well, purposefully avoiding looking at what was in front of him through the windshield. The others rolled around in the back of the van, trying to steady themselves as Joe lurched and swerved down the road. It was a small van with small seats and even smaller windows on the side. It did not offer much of a view.

He stuck to the ring road as planned and the roads gradually became clearer. As they drove, the crashed cars and wrecks became less frequent. Occasionally, they would pass an abandoned car or truck on the side of the road, doors open, and no sign of life.

Initially Joe saw zombies wandering around aimlessly, some on the side of the road, some farther afield. Many of them appeared to be young people who should be fit and healthy. Presumably, other zombies had killed them. Despite their young appearance, most had a leg or arm missing, torn clothes and clawed torsos. The further they went, the more the zombies thinned out.

Joe kept driving past the poor damned souls. He was in a hurry and pretty sure the police had more on their minds than speeding tickets. In fact, he was sure there weren't even any police left. They had seen no sign of law enforcement at all in the last few days. Civilisation had taken a break from the world. He put his foot down. It was hard to generate much speed though. Invariably, he had to swerve past a vehicle or a body on the road.

He sped through Heidelberg and down Manningham Road. Everyone crammed in the van was stressed and exhausted from the situation they had inexplicably found themselves in. Nervous, unsettled stomachs were not being helped by being cooped up in the back of an increasingly hot van.

Karyn was staring out of the window at nothing, eyes vacant, lost in her own thoughts. George was now staring out of the window into space, Joe noticed. If he was looking for answers in the heavens, he thought, he wasn't going to find any. Evan watched as normality flew past them into the past. He read advertising hoardings and billboards offering cold beer and new cars, prime real estate and cheap cremations. Shops displayed their perfect pizzas and crunchy chicken, all surplus to requirements now; there was nobody to buy them. Joe pulled up on a bridge.

"We need five minutes," he announced, and got out. Cars littered the suburbs, but the bridge was deserted. Everyone gratefully got out and stretched their legs.

"I feel sick," said Lily. Amane, feeling queasy too, put an arm around her and took her aside for some much needed fresh air. Evan walked over to Joe, who had lit up a cigarette and was leaning over the railing, looking at the river below. The Yarra was sluggish and murky. A small dinghy drifted past, unmoored and free. There was nobody on board to guide it as it slipped away toward the city. The trees should have been vibrant and green but looked limp and sad. The leaves were brown as if it were autumn, not summer.

"Seemed like the best place to stop," he said, "nothing around for fucking zombies to be hiding in and surprise us."

"Good point." Evan cracked open a warm can of coke from a backpack and downed it. Karyn was preening herself in the sun whilst George was casually dropping leaves onto the river below, watching them float slowly away.

"So who's the stray?" said Joe. Lily and Amane were walking down the bridge, stretching their legs and their voices, any conversation inaudible from anyone else.

"Her name's Lily. She said her mother had gone to church and she's not seen her since, most likely dead. Her father's in Canberra. She asked if she could tag along. Couldn't leave her, could I?"

Joe took a long drag on his cigarette.

"I was thinking we should take the Eastlink, head to Mornington, try our luck there for a boat. I'm not saying it'll be easy, but I reckon it's our best bet."

The names meant nothing to Evan, but he trusted Joe. They'd come this far together, unscathed.

"Sounds good. How long do you think it'll take us?" Evan was squinting against the sun. It was low in the sky now and the evening was drawing in. He was hoping they would make it to a boat before nightfall.

"Probably a couple of hours," guessed Joe, "depends how the roads are or if we run into any more road blocks." He finished his cigarette and lit up another one.

"If other people had the same idea about getting out of the city, then chances are the roads are going to get a hell of a lot busier. Plus it'll be dark in an hour or so. You want to try finding a boat in the dark? Can you even remember how to sail one because I sure don't know how to. I'm wondering if we shouldn't try to find somewhere to bed down for the night. Carry on in the morning?"

Evan thought Joe was probably right, but didn't want to admit it. In the back of the van, he had been imagining his children, how they would be when he found them. He had assumed they would just jump onto the first boat they found and be in Tasmania by tomorrow. Could he remember how to sail? He trusted that it would just come back to him when he got on board. Suddenly, Charlie and Anna seemed a very long way away.

"What do you say we carry on for a bit, see how far we get in the next hour or so. If we're not getting anywhere, we should try to find a quiet house or a motel to stay in. Find one that looks empty and hope no one's home."

Joe agreed and asked, "Can you sit up front? I could do with a second pair of eyes."

"Yeah. Rolling around in the back ain't much fun anyway. Look, I'll go fill the others in. When you're ready we'll head off."

Evan walked back to the van and told Amane and Lily what they were planning. While they were talking, Joe filled in Karyn. Her pacified demeanour surprised him. He had expected a fight, but she just went along with everything he said. It was like she had given up. She didn't look well, Joe mused. Her face was drawn and her eyes sunken. He put it down to stress and thought no more about it. He reminded her that she had George to look after now, that grieving for Lucy and Pete would have to be saved for another time.

They drove through small suburbs, once a hive of activity, now ghost towns. They drove past a small rail station and Evan noticed a stationary train, waiting by the platform expectantly. The driver's door was open and the carriages behind were pregnant with zombies. The driver had apparently escaped and left his passengers to their own fate. Through the doors and windows Evan watched them slowly moving, bloody fingers sliding down the glass, faces pressed up against the doors, frustrated in their permanent tomb. It must have been a hundred degrees inside that carriage. Dead eyes stared back at him, oblivious to the incredible heat that was slowly cooking them.

Beyond the rail-tracks was a field full of dead cattle, swarming with buzzing flies hovering greedily over bloated carcasses. Evan wondered if the cows' demise was natural, if the farmer had simply been unable to attend to them anymore. From the van, he couldn't see the animal's bodies that had been ripped apart, stomachs carved open by carnivorous dead humans.

The drive was becoming tedious. Joe had to start going slower as he weaved in and out of more traffic on congested roads.

"So, Evan, did you get on well with your parents?" asked Amane, breaking the silence. She was restless and needed the distraction of conversation.

After a pause Evan replied, "I don't know. I don't remember much. My father, Tom, yes, I'm sure, but I can't remember my mother. She..." Evan broke off. He didn't know what to say.

"I'm sorry about your parents," he said, looking over to her. Amane was leaning toward the window, a faint wind blowing her brown hair back out of her face. She shook her head in disbelief.

"I can't believe this. I just can't believe what's going on. My parents had come over to visit me, have a nice holiday, and now... Jesus."

Evan realised he wasn't the only one with problems. It occurred to him he had been selfish in his actions. But wasn't it better that they stuck together? There was more chance of fighting those things off in a group. Maybe he just wanted some company. Being apart from his family, not knowing where they were, he felt very alone. He reached behind and she squeezed his hand. Evan tried to give her a smile over his shoulder.

"Thanks," she said. She meant it but her eyes betrayed her inner sadness. She was grieving for her parents they'd left behind at the airport.

It was slow going, despite Joe's best efforts at manoeuvring around the vehicles on the road. At times, it was a crawl, as they had to negotiate multiple crashes and mangled bodies.

"Mr Crow," said Karyn from the back after a while, "I know where you are heading, but I have to ask you to take a detour. I need to take George home." She leaned forward so she knew he would hear her.

"Let's get real here. My son does not need to go on some wild goose chase with you. I am going to take him home where we'll be safe. Take the next left and I'll give you directions. If we keep going like this, we'll be home in less than an hour. You can keep the car once we're home, I don't care about that. You've already cost me one child. I do not intend to let you murder my son, too."

Evan sighed. He had hoped that her silence had meant she had accepted the situation but suddenly she had burst back into life. The old Karyn was back.

"Look, I'm sorry about your daughter, but don't try to pin that on me. You should have..." Evan broke off as Karyn punched the back of his seat causing everyone in the van to spring awake.

Karyn shouted, "If it wasn't for you, we would be fine. *I* would be fine. You brought those fucking zombies with you. We could've found a pilot and been long gone. But you had to fuck it all up didn't you." She was apoplectic with rage. George started crying. Lily cowered in the corner, snuggling up to the side of the van as far away from Karyn as she could.

"Mrs Craven, hang on," began Joe.

"Oh please, you're just as useless as him! Where is my husband, Joe? Tell me. Oh yes, you let him die didn't you. Instead of bringing him home safely, you got him killed. Bet you didn't tell George that story, did you?" She was screaming at him, George's crying getting louder.

"For Christ's sake, Mrs Craven, this is not helping. I'm trying to drive here. If we can get to the coast, we can find a boat. Your house won't be safe anymore, think about it. Those things are all over the city. We can't risk going there."

Karyn sat back, exasperated. Joe beat his hand against the wheel, accidentally blaring the horn.

"Mrs Craven, I did not *let* your husband die. I was trying to save him, to get him home to you. We had barely got five minutes away from the office and there was a riot going on right in front of us. People were fighting and running around. It was crazy. Some guy ran in front of us and I had to stop so I wouldn't run him over. Your husband said he recognised this guy, worked with him or something, and then he just jumped out of the car.

"I ran after him, shouted it wasn't safe, but he wouldn't listen. Pete had a hold of this guy and when I caught up with him, this guy was going mental. He punched me and then Tom, sending us flying, and then he ran off. Next thing I know, a couple of young kids are on top of Pete. They were covered in blood and they were just ripping him apart. He was dead pretty quick. I'm sorry, but George should hear this. He should know his father didn't just die in a stupid fight or go out with a whimper. And I certainly didn't kill him. He was trying to help someone and so was I."

The car was overwhelmed by a bloated silence. George was sniffling, sat between his mother and Amane. Karyn looked over, her eyes wild. "What are you looking at?"

Amane turned away, not wanting to get into a fight, and stared out of the window.

"Fucking chinks," muttered Karyn. She spat on Amane's face and lunged forward between the front seats to grab the wheel. Joe tried to keep the van straight as Evan grabbed Karyn's arms. Amane was stunned. She wiped the saliva off her blossoming cheek.

The commotion caused Joe to lose control and they collided with a truck that was half blocking the road. The van smashed into the delivery truck's side and came to an abrupt halt, the windshield shattering, showering Joe with tiny shards of glass, grating his face. The bonnet crumpled and steam began pouring out. A minute ago, the van had been a maelstrom of chaos, a cacophony of screaming and shouting. Now it was silent.

"Everyone okay?" asked Evan, touching his forehead, tenderly feeling the grazes from the airport. His head was throbbing again and his chest hurt from where the seatbelt had dug into him. He looked round and everyone seemed uninjured, but 'okay,' they were not. Karyn was getting out leaving George screaming in the van. He was curled up in a ball, eye screwed tightly shut, crying for his father, ignoring his mother who was shouting at him to get out.

Unhurt, Amane got out and helped Lily who had injured her ankle. She was crying and hobbling over to the pavement where they sat down together. Evan raced around the car and watched as Joe jumped out of his seat and punched Karyn square on the jaw, knocking her out cold. Joe caught her as she fell so she didn't hit her head on the road. He lay her down, leant into the car to tend to George, and began trying to calm him down.

Evan stood over Karyn and quickly took in their surroundings. The truck obscured some of his view, and their immediate vicinity seemed to be full of houses. They were still in a residential area and Evan had no idea how far they'd gone. The sky was darkening fast and he knew the crash would bring trouble. They had to find a safe refuge and fast. He could hear noise from behind the truck already: hidden feet scuffed on the road. Evan grabbed a bag from the car.

"Everyone, we need to go now, grab a bag if you can." Joe appeared, holding George who was catatonic.

"He's passed out." He looked down at little George protectively. "Probably for the best. So what are we going to do now? The van's fucked."

"Amane, Lily, come on!" They were hobbling back to the van when the first zombie appeared. It came around from the delivery truck and headed straight for Joe.

Evan grabbed a hockey stick from the van and slashed at it. A moment later and the zombie's face had been hacked off. The body lay on the ground, twitching.

"Over there," said Evan, waving his blood-splattered hockey stick, "see that building? The coffee shop? The front windows broken. We can get in, try to find shelter or something. We can't stay here."

Evan barked orders whilst Amane grabbed her axe from the van and then, with one arm supporting Lily, headed off in the direction of the shopping centre, looking for safety.

"What about her?" said Joe, looking at Karyn. He no longer felt guilt or sympathy. He was largely ambivalent about her right now.

"Put her in the van, we can't carry her and George. She should be okay in there for now. The zombies will follow us. To be honest, I'm past caring about that witch."

Together they lifted her into the back of the van. Joe scooped up George as more zombies appeared steadily. The sight of the rotting flesh and dripping blood made Joe's stomach turn. Back in the van it hadn't seemed so real, so in your face.

"Come on!" called Evan as he headed toward the coffee shop, lashing out with a hockey stick at anything that got too close. He slashed at faces, hacked off hands and flayed fingers to the bone. Finally, they reached the coffee-shop window and Joe followed Evan through, carrying George.

"Over here!"

Amane was signalling to them from a doorway, beckoning them through. Avoiding turned over tables and chairs they dodged the obstacle course successfully. All the while, Evan could hear the cracking of glass behind and the incessant moans of the zombies. Their numbers were increasing, drawn by the crash and the noise. Perhaps they can smell fresh blood too, thought Evan.

Through the door, they went into a kitchen, the aroma of coffee still hanging in the air, permeating the very fabric of the walls. Evan ran past stainless steel worktops to where Lily stood in front of the only other door, hammering on it furiously.

"I can't open it!" she cried.

Amane pushed her aside and swung the axe, snapping the wooden door down the middle, splinters sailing through the air. She heaved on the axe, bringing it back out of the door to strike again.

"Wait!" shouted Evan. "We're going to need to close that behind us."

He charged at the weakened door and it shuddered on its hinges. He gritted his teeth and charged again, his right shoulder bearing the brunt of the clash. This time the door flew open. He stumbled through, not knowing what he would find on the other side, as the zombies poured through the doorway behind them into the kitchen.

CHAPTER SEVEN

Evan nearly slipped over as his feet landed on cold, hard tiles. He was in a small shopping centre, illuminated only by a little natural light coming through a glass atrium. There was no immediate sign of anyone else inside and before he could say anything, the others swiftly poured in after him.

He could vaguely make out a post office, a newsagent, a drycleaners and a hairdresser. It looked like the place had been ransacked; the windows were broken and glass and rubbish lay everywhere: papers, magazines, chocolate bars, even money. All lay forgotten on the floor where they'd been left and trampled over. Evan took a few steps forward into the silent foyer. A tremendous bang made him jump as Amane slammed the coffee-shop door shut, its echoes ringing around the morgue-like mall. She dragged a rubbish bin in front of it.

"We can't stay here, Evan," said Amane, grabbing his arm. Her face was sweaty and grimy.

They all jumped again as the coffee shop door started rattling as the zombies began launching themselves at it, knowing their prey was on the other side. The bin wobbled and the door barely held together under their weight.

"That door's not going to last long," said Evan. "There's got to be another way out."

He didn't know where to turn, but everyone was looking at him now. Their pleading eyes told him everything he needed to know.

He crept past the empty shops, alert and ready. Leaving the door splintering behind them, the group followed him to the other end of the shopping centre where they found the exit blocked. The iron gates had been shut and locked. It was a dead-end. Evan was contemplating telling the others they might have to fight their way back out the way they had come, even though he knew it would be near suicidal, when all of a sudden a faint voice spoke up.

"Exit," said George. Joe hadn't noticed when he had woken from his stupor and put him down.

"There." George pointed to a small door almost hidden by a huge six-foot advertisement for bargain mortgages. Behind it was an unlit, green 'exit' sign.

"Nice one, George," said Joe, enthusiastically, greasy hands ruffling George's dirty brown hair. "You all right, mate?"

"Yeah, I'm okay. I feel better now. Where's mum?" he said, looking round.

"She's safe, Georgie. She just had to do something but we'll get her soon, don't worry," answered Joe. He took his hand and they all went to the fire exit. As they approached it, they heard another bang. Lily screamed as the coffee shop door gave way. Evan turned back to see a hundred zombies pour through it into the shopping centre. He pushed the exit door and said a small prayer when it opened easily.

They stepped out into an alley. Left or right, it made no difference. It was dark now and Evan could not see much. A tall graffiti-covered fence obscured his view of anything useful. He was about to tell everyone to go left, for no reason other than he had to say something, when a figure appeared at the other end of the alley.

"Oi, over here. Follow me, quick." The dark figure shouted brazenly in the open and waved them toward him.

"Let's go," said Evan, after barely a moment's pause.

"Are you sure it's safe?" said Joe, standing beside Evan.

"No. But it's got to be safer than staying here. We can't keep running around in the dark. Look at Lily, she can't run anywhere."

Joe shrugged, resigned to the obvious fact that they had little choice but to trust a stranger. Evan took off, the two packs on his back now weighing more than ever, whilst the rest of them followed him, Amane helping Lily once again, and Joe gripping George's hand for dear life. As they neared the end of the tiny alley, Evan saw a body at the stranger's feet.

"Don't worry, it can't hurt you now," said a grinning mouth from beneath a black hood. The man held a large, bloodied knife in his hand. He turned and walked past the fence out of sight. Rounding the end of the alley, Evan was relieved to see the hooded man still there, waiting for them, wiping the knife on his trousers. He was standing by a wrought-iron gate that was inching open automatically. The man slipped through it quickly.

"Come on then," he said breezily. There was no fear in the man's voice at all. Evan couldn't tell much but the voice was certainly mature and deep. He hoped the man beneath the hood was only using his cover to hide from the zombies, and not using it as a disguise for more sinister purposes.

They followed the mystery-man down a driveway, flanked on both sides by tall, withering trees. Evan saw black blobs at the bases. Looking closer in the dark, he could make out feathers and wings: dead birds or bats. It felt strange being out in the open like this. Evan couldn't help but feeling he was still being watched, phantom eyes staring at him from the canopy above and tree trunks either side of him.

The gate clanged shut behind them and Amane only just managed to squeeze herself and Lily through in time. Stones crunched underfoot, obscuring the menacing moans of the zombies now stranded behind the fence and gate, as they proceeded down the driveway to a small bungalow. It was also surrounded by a tall fence and a lone candle flickered in the doorway. The rest of the house was unlit, encased by the encroaching night and oppressive, whispering trees. There were no cars outside, but Evan noticed a garage door, closed, and wondered if the man had transport.

The man unlocked the front door and threw back his hood. The candle cast a shaky light over him and Evan saw that their saviour was a lean man, tall and spindly, with a pockmarked bony face and a rugged, wild beard. Evan watched as old, skeletal fingers twisted the key and pushed open the front door. They were led down a corridor lined with unambitious paintings of lush landscapes and flowering fields. A bureau was decked out with a huge vase full of flowers, the sweet aroma filling the air. It felt homely and comfortable.

Through another doorway, the man ushered them to sit down and rest. He told them he'd be back in a moment and slipped back into the hallway, leaving them alone. Joe sat George down on an armchair covered with an unnecessary amount of doylies. The room was small and cosy, the curtains drawn, and a large solitary candle lit up the room from a side table. Amane and Lily sunk into an old mushy sofa with relief. Evan dropped the backpacks in the middle of the room.

"Seems pretty safe. Maybe we should try to crash here for the night?" he said. This stranger had taken them in and they were too exhausted to argue or discuss it. The world where dead people attacked the living was safely locked away outside of the house, outside of the grounds. It already seemed a long way off now. The old man came back in carrying a couple of torches that he handed to Evan and Joe.

"Right, come on, follow me," he said walking back to the doorway.

"Oh hey, thanks, but look, can we maybe stay here for a bit?" asked Evan, cautiously. "We just need to rest for a while. Lily here is hurt. She can barely walk. We're very grateful Mr..."

Beady eyes blinked back at Evan. A moment's silence passed, but to Evan it felt like a year, as the man's eyes looked him up and down.

"That's not a good idea." He took a step closer to Evan, who smelt alcohol on the man's breath.

"There are things that go *bump* in the night. It's much safer next door with me and Thomas." The man grimaced, exposing brown, crooked teeth and flicked a torch on, illuminating the hallway.

"Evan, Lily's dead on her feet. She's knackered. She's only a kid." Amane stopped as they heard a series of muffled bangs. There was a pause and then it started again.

"Ready now?" The old man licked his lips, casting furtive eyes about impatiently. Amane looked at Evan concerned. He held up a palm asking for her patience.

"Lily, can you go a little further?" said Evan, kneeling down to talk to her. "Things will get better. We'll take care of you, I promise." She looked so fragile he wanted to pick her up and tell her everything would be okay, but he knew he couldn't do that. Not yet.

Through sniffs, she muttered a yes and looked at Evan with tear-streaked eyes, mascara staining her cheeks. She grabbed her handbag and stood up unsteadily. Amane put an arm around her shoulder. George grabbed Joe's hand and together they all followed warily after the old man.

Their torches picked out furniture in the gloom: chairs and stacks of magazines, vivid floral tapestries and old black and white photos hanging crookedly on the walls.

They were taken through a small, old-fashioned kitchen and the old man unlocked another door at the end of it. Single file, they went through it compliantly, down a narrow stairwell. The air was cooler down here and Evan thought he could smell something medicinal. It was like a hospital. The sickly air left a bad taste in his mouth.

Their feet clattered loudly on the steps making them all uneasy. The knocking they'd heard before was louder now and joined by crashing and banging. They filed through a corridor, past a large metal door, glistening in the light of the torches. The erratic noises were coming from behind it, and as they passed it, Evan brushed his fingers against it. It was remarkably cool to the touch. The door was locked by large slide-bolts at the top and bottom. They carried on and turned a corner, the corridor becoming narrower: plain, stripped down wooden floors sweeping up to bare walls. The torchlight bounced off the whitewashed concrete casting their leader's body into shadow, his hunched bony old body illuminated as a hideous shadow ahead of them. George felt calm now. He knew he'd freaked out earlier but something in his head had clicked. Lucy was gone. His father wouldn't be coming back. He saw things more pragmatically now: logically.

At the conclusion of the cold damp corridor, the old man opened another door into a cellar. He pulled a cord and instantly bathed it in an amber glow, a single bare bulb hanging in the centre of the room, dazzling them all. Evan saw a huge wine rack running the length of the wall. He estimated it must have been holding at least seventy bottles. The old man was heading up the stairs and the door at the top opened out into yet another dim hallway. Looking around, Evan was wondering when this little jaunt was going to end. The ceilings were higher and the décor was different: simpler. His torch picked out a staircase in the dark and he knew they were in another house now. Through a large double-door, they entered a room that finally felt truly welcoming.

There was a roaring fire and another man drawing heavy velvety curtains together. Over the fireplace hung a magnificent painting of the last supper, sat in an ornate gold frame. Bookcases adorned the walls, stuffed with thick books, papers and manuscripts. A large round table was laid out with food and drink: chicken, dishes of vegetables, cakes, biscuits, beer, and wine. The mystery-man sat down in a cushioned armchair and picked up a half-empty glass of whisky, carrying on where he had left off.

"Come in, come in, please, sit down. My poor dears." The second man approached them. He had close-cropped white hair and in contrast to his friend, had a round face to match his round belly. He wore a blue-collared shirt and high above his expansive waist, brown trousers held up by braces. He helped Amane set Lily down onto a chair by the table.

"Please, feel free! Help yourselves," he said eagerly. "I'm Father Thomas."

"Evan," he said, holding out his hand. The Father shook it vigorously. Evan pointed out the others. "This is Joe, George, Amane, and Lily."

"Thrilled to meet you all, you are most welcome in my house. I'm sorry we couldn't meet under better circumstances but we must face each day as the Lord provides. Eat and drink my friends. Honestly, there is far too much for me and Nathaniel here."

The mystery-man, Nathaniel, raised his glass, acknowledging them, and swirled the whisky in its glass, ice-cubes chinking against the crystal glass, before drawing down a large gulp. As the group offered their thanks and eagerly began on the feast spread out before them, Evan walked to the fireplace and warmed himself. Father Thomas joined him.

"It's Evan, right? We saw the crash, young man. It was lucky we did or you would have been in terrible trouble. We're the only residents left around here. Everyone else has left or, well, you know." He spoke in a hushed, sombre voice.

"Uh-huh,' said Evan. "How did you manage to see the crash from here though?" Something seemed a little bit odd about these two men though he couldn't put his finger on it.

"Oh, from upstairs. I'll show you. Right now, you must get something to eat. Replenish your energy my dear boy. I'll go fetch a bandage for the young lady's leg." With that, he strode out of the room and Evan went back to the table. Joe's face was flushed already.

"Second or third, Joe?" said Evan smiling, watching him take large mouthfuls from a glass of red wine.

"Yep." Joe winked and poured himself another. Evan sat down beside Amane.

"What do you think?" he asked her, taking a handful of peanuts.

"I think we're lucky they found us. I know this is an odd situation, but they seem harmless. We've got a roof over our heads. Food and drink. We should be happy right now." Amane shrugged and filled two glasses of wine.

"Lily, you can have one glass, no more, okay?"

"Fine by me. Mum never let me have *any*. I mean, I'm fifteen, does she think I've never had a drink!"

Evan and Amane smiled at each other picking at the food.

Nathaniel had been sitting quietly in the chair, observing everything, saying nothing. He filled his glass and stood, watching them.

"Do you believe?" he asked, to no one in particular.

"What's that, mate?" said Joe through a mouthful of potato.

"In Him. The Lord. Blessed are thee that follow in His footsteps."

"Not me. I believe in what's in front of me. This Shiraz for starters." Joe took a big gulp. "I believe I'll never get to the MCG again. And I believe the world is royally screwed. Thus endeth the sermon. Cheers." He chinked his glass against the half-empty bottle on the table, oblivious to the atmosphere developing around him.

Nathaniel said nothing. He just stood there staring at them. Amane and Evan cast sideways glances at each other. Before they could speak, Father Thomas came back in with some bandages. He bent down at Lily's feet and began examining her leg.

"Lily was it? Here, let me look at you," he said kindly. Father Thomas studied Lily, and when he rested his hand on her knee, Amane could see Lily growing uncomfortable.

"Thanks, Father," said Amane taking them from him. "Come on, Lily, let's get you sorted."

Nathaniel wandered out into the corridor taking the bottle of whisky with him, muttering through his beard.

"I must say you are lucky we found you," said the Father, standing back up again. "Outside of these four walls is a world that none of us are used to. 'The earth shall cast out the dead.'" He paused, hoping his words would be taken with the seriousness he wanted them to be.

"It's hard to believe, but there's no denying what you can see with your own eyes. The prophets foretold all of this, you know? If I may be so bold, Evan, have you all prepared? With the approaching Armageddon, all our houses must be in order." The Father remained standing over them whilst Amane tended to Lily's swelling ankle. He was getting a little too preachy for Evan's liking.

"I don't think we are really thinking much further than the next day to be honest with you. It's hard enough finding water to drink, and food to eat, let alone contemplating the Apocalypse, or whatever this is." Evan carried on munching on some chips hoping the Father would take the hint to drop the conversation.

"Zombies. That's all they are," said Joe, looking thoughtfully into his glass of wine. "No more, no less. Just dead bodies that have forgotten they're dead. I haven't seen the four horse-men riding around, and I certainly haven't seen God. Just stinking dead bodies everywhere."

"I think the dead are walking because they have no place else to go," said Amane. "Think how many people have died since mankind has been around. For every one that went to Heaven, how many have gone to Hell? What if the gates to Hell were locked? What if they all got kicked out? It's like a dam that's full and the water has to go somewhere. Hell is overflowing if you ask me.

Maybe the souls of the damned have to go somewhere, so they're back here, inhabiting dead bodies."

She looked at George who, if he was listening to their conversation, was paying no heed. He was slurping orange juice down, pretending not to listen, soaking in every word.

"But then, maybe my wine glass is overflowing and I'm talking crap." Amane raised a fake smile; feeling very tired all of a sudden.

"My dear, you may have something there," interjected the Father. "If I may quote once more: 'And death and Hell delivered up the dead who were in them; and they were judged by every man.'

"Man has for too long ignored the signs: murder, deviant sexual practises, greed, and sloth. Common people die in abject poverty while the businessmen of this world grow rich from unrestrained lust. It is all there plain as day! The earth is ripe for harvest my friends. You can't argue with what you see, with what you've seen with your own eyes out there."

"Okay, Father." Evan stood up, reluctant to let this go on any longer. "Look, thank you for taking us in, but can we perhaps talk about this some other time? George is a bit young for all this and I think we are all in desperate need of some rest right now."

"Evan, I wonder if I might take you on a short tour of the house?" The Father belched loudly.

"Yeah, sure. Would be good to know where we are: doors, exits, all that. Joe, can you keep an eye on George?"

Joe looked over at George who was now gorging himself on chocolate. "No problem, mate. We're not going anywhere."

"Oh and everyone, it goes without saying that we should be quiet at all times," said the Father like a teacher speaking to his pupils. "In particular, please do not go anywhere near the front door. You are fine in here, or upstairs. If you stray beyond that, then I'm afraid I cannot vouch for your safety."

Evan left the warm lounge, following behind the Father who whipped a small flashlight out of his pocket. The hallway was quiet, dark, and cold.

"You must be curious, I suppose, about the tunnel?" said the Father, eager to talk. "I'm afraid it's the only way in or out now.

Next door is the mortuary and the old chap who used to live here built the tunnel back in the sixties. Probably thought there was going to be World War Three or something." He gave a little laugh and his big belly wobbled unflatteringly.

"Well, Nathaniel runs it now. Anyway, you must keep quiet. I'll show you why it's so handy now." He led Evan through a door, into a small vestibule. He flicked the torchlight off and motioned for Evan to look through the spyhole in the huge, wooden front door.

Evan looked and gasped. The garden was completely full of zombies, staggering around like drunks. From the front door back to the gate, they filled the garden. The zombies were stuck between the house and the tall fencing ringing it, squashed like canned sardines. Their heads bobbed up and down like seals peering over the ocean waves. Evan broke out in a cold sweat. He felt trapped. Charlie's voice rang through his head again.

"I'm scared, I'm scared..."

Father Thomas pulled Evan away and back through the doorway, flicking the torch back on.

"What the hell is that?" said Evan when they were safely out of earshot.

"Sadly, those poor souls have been there for a couple of days," said the Father. "They get agitated when the sun comes up. I think they can hear Nathaniel when he goes out, but they can't get past the fences. They're stuck in there like sheep in a pen. I wonder if they've developed into some kind of herd or if they're still as individual and selfish as they were in life. We've thought about trying to move them, but it's impossible. Lord knows how long they will be there. Still, as long as they are out there and we're in here, I think it's best to let sleeping dogs lie, don't you? Come on."

He began trudging up the stairs, pausing on the final step to catch breath. Evan reluctantly followed. The house seemed secure but he wasn't comfortable knowing there were so many of the dead out there, so close. At the top of the stairs, he counted at least six doors and deliberated how big the house must be. As they walked, Evan noticed the crosses on the walls: large and small, all depicting Jesus spread-eagled in pain and torment. Through the end door, Father Thomas led him into a bedroom.

"Careful son, it's a little messy in here."

The room was clearly not used. The bed was covered in old magazines and the room was strewn with clothes and boxes. There was hardly any free space to walk on and Evan trampled over old suits and shirts on the floor.

"See? Down there." The Father pointed out through a small window, criss-crossed by elaborate ironwork.

Evan looked through it. To the left he saw the edge of the shopping centre they had passed through earlier. However, the window mostly looked out over the road and he could see their van that had ploughed into the truck. There were a couple of zombies wallowing around, but no activity of note. He wondered if the Father had seen what had happened to Karyn. Surely if he had, he would have said something? Was she still in the van? It was dark and there was no way of seeing inside now. The doors were shut and he could see nothing useful that would indicate if she had left the van or not. For all the trouble she'd caused, he had to admit he felt a little remorseful now. She was out there alone, inside the van or not, probably scared witless, not even knowing where her son was. Evan vowed that tomorrow they would fetch her. He hoped she'd stayed in the van. If not, there was a good chance George would never see his mother again.

"When we heard the crash we raced up here to see what was happening. We hadn't seen anyone alive for at least twenty four hours before you. Nathaniel's a good, stout man. I knew he would find you."

"I'm grateful, Father. We were in trouble, I know." They continued their conversation in the dark. Father Thomas turned the torch off to avoid it shining through the window and attracting any unwanted attention.

"So, Father, is it okay if we stay here tonight? We'll be on our way in the morning."

"Oh goodness yes, of course. Take your time. There are plenty of bedrooms up here, plenty of space for all of you. But tell me, where do you intend to go tomorrow?"

"Well, my family is on Tasmania. We were heading to the harbour to get a boat before we crashed." Evan paused, unsure of whether he should say anymore. Perhaps he should offer to take these men with them? His question was answered without the need to ask it.

"Tasmania!" Father Thomas sat down on the bed, springs creaking under the weight.

"Madness. Oh, of course you must do what you need to but...Evan I have a mission to complete here and I need all the help I can get. I am but a lamb in His service, and I am only one. With more followers, comes more power, and...Nathaniel is a devout believer; he'll stand by me, but...

"Evan you have seen what has become of our world? We are haunted by demons and unclean spirits. It is clear the Armageddon is coming. It is all written in the scriptures. This day has been foretold for generations. I'll show you down stairs in the library!" He was getting worked up again, enthusiastic to bring Evan into his world.

Evan interrupted before he was subjected to any more unwanted lectures. "Father, I'm sorry, but *my* mission is to find my family. That is all. I don't want to interfere with your plan, your calling, or whatever it is. You must do what you need to. I'm sorry, I appreciate your help, we all do, but our paths are only going to cross tonight. We'll be on our way tomorrow."

Father Thomas sat silently on the bed. Evan could hear his wheezing breath and was glad it was dark so he didn't have to look at him. It was a full minute before Evan get a reply.

"And you're not a believer, Evan. None of you?" The Father stood up. Evan could not see the flaring nostrils, or the anger burning the Father's cheeks.

"No."

It occurred to Evan that maybe before all this, he had believed in God. He couldn't remember that life anymore. But he knew he didn't believe now.

"Very well," said the Father despondently, yet firmly. The torch flashed back into life and Evan followed him back down to the library. They did not speak on the way back.

As they entered the warm library, Evan saw Joe had fallen asleep and kicked his chair. Joe stirred and shifted his weight before going straight back to sleep. Amane was chatting to Lily and George had found a book to read.

"The Father has kindly offered us a room for the night. Upstairs, take your pick, plenty of room. Be quiet when you go about the house though. And avoid the front door, okay? I'm serious. You stick to here and the rooms upstairs." Evan felt uncomfortable. He knew he had offended the Father, but just because he had offered them sojourn in this house, didn't mean they had to convert.

"Bathroom's upstairs too," Father Thomas said, walking over to the dying fire and extinguishing it with a jug of water. The hiss of steam broke the awkward silence and the room was plunged into a darkness illuminated only by the torch he carried.

Amane realised that this was their cue to move, and picked up the flashlights on the table. She blinked one on and handed the other to Evan. "I'll take Lily with me. See you in the morning, yeah?"

"Yeah. I'll take George up. May as well leave Joe to sleep it off, I think he'll be out for the night. Take care, okay?"

She could tell something wasn't right, but knew now was not the time to ask. George rubbed his tired eyes and took Evan's hand. They left Joe sleeping, whilst the Father busied himself tidying away the leftovers, crockery, and cutlery.

Evan led the way up the stairs and found an uncluttered room. There was a single bed in the centre of the room but little else by way of furnishings. It was cold and Evan tucked George in, still fully clothed.

"Evan? When is mum coming back?" he asked as he got beneath the covers.

"Tomorrow. She'll be back tomorrow, okay buddy?"

"Why didn't she come with us?"

Evan's cheeks flushed red in the dark room.

"You get to sleep now. She wasn't well so she had to stay behind, but we'll get her in the morning mate. If you need anything tonight, I'll be right next door."

George didn't answer. He seemed so tired now that Evan was convinced he'd fallen asleep almost immediately. He tiptoed out and shut the door gently behind him. He found the bathroom opposite and then headed to the room next to George. He got into the single bed waiting for him. He took his shoes off but it was so cold, he decided to keep his clothes on too. It was a relief to be lying down in a bed. It was old and lumpy but it was a bed nonetheless. The conversation earlier with the Father had worried him, but he put it out of his mind. The Father could be forgiven for wanting to save people. He had a kind heart though; he had taken them in, complete strangers, and given them food and shelter.

He thought again about Charlie and Anna. What must they be going through now? Did they have a bed to sleep in? He was too tired to think like this. Why ask questions that couldn't be answered? He forced himself to clear his mind. They would be fine. He would get a boat tomorrow and see them soon and they would be reunited. He closed his eyes and drifted off to sleep. He dreamt more of his children, playing and laughing on the boat that he would surely be seeing soon.

* * * *

Amane and Lily clambered beneath the covers, thankful for finding a room with a large, king-size bed.

"Thanks for staying with me, Amane. I don't want to be alone. This house is weird. Those men are weird too."

"Yeah, they're a little odd, I agree. We'll get out of here tomorrow, all right? We'll find a way," Amane bristled against the cold and pulled the duvet up to her chin.

"I wish my dad was here. He'd know what to do. I want to come with you but...I wonder if I should go to Canberra. Dad works at parliament. He's not a cleaner or anything, he's a proper politician, he's quite important. He always said if any terrorists attacked them, they'd be safe. I told you about that bunker they built underneath the parliament building? He might be okay."

Amane yawned and thought about Lily. It could be true she supposed. But there was no way she'd get to Canberra on her own, not with only one good leg and not in this world. Without a car, she had no idea how they would even get to the harbour tomorrow.

"Look, if you come with us to Tassie, we'll get Evan's kids and then maybe we'll check out Canberra okay? We can regroup, get a plan properly sorted. Look how difficult it is just trying to get through the city."

"Okay, thanks, Amane, you're right. If dad's safe, then he'll still be there in a couple more days' time. I wish I could text him and tell him I'm okay. It's weird not seeing him." Lily yawned. "Thank God you're here." She gave Amane a quick peck on the cheek and turned over onto her side.

"Good night."

"Good night, Lily." Amane lay staring up at the ceiling listening to Lily's faint breathing. How on earth was she going to sleep? So many thoughts were jumping around her head. She lay on her side and hugged the pillow beside her. She had seen what had happened to Karyn but said nothing. Soon they would have to explain to George where his mother was and that would not be easy. There was a good chance Karyn wouldn't be there in the morning, Amane thought. She'd probably take off and leave George behind.

She thought about her parents, picturing them back at home in Japan. She thought about her friends and if any of them were still alive. She wondered if Evan had ever been to Japan. And as she lay dreaming of home, sleep crept up on her. In the middle of the night, she didn't even stir when the bedroom door squeaked open. Nor did she wake as a dark figure stealthily crept up on her and Lily unawares.

CHAPTER EIGHT

Evan woke and couldn't recall where he was. The room was strange and unrecognisable, the air cold and harsh. He waited a moment and then it all came back to him: the crash, the mortuary, the priest. It was still dark and quiet outside. The early rays of sunlight were pinching through tight-knit clouds, peaking over the horizon, casting just enough light to see by. What had woken him? He listened intently and heard a faint crying. It sounded like it was coming from next door. He padded across the frigid floorboards into the hallway and tried the door to George's room, but it wouldn't open.

"George, you awake?" Evan rapped lightly on the door. "It's me, Evan." He heard soft footsteps approach the door.

"I can't get out. I want mum. I want to go see mum now," came the feeble reply.

"Did you lock this door, George? Have you got the key?" said Evan, worried, pulling on the doorknob.

"No, I think that old man with the beard locked it. I heard him messing about with the keys. He's stupid. I just want my mum!" Evan heard him run back to the bed. George buried his head in the pillows and began crying louder.

Evan rattled the door but it wouldn't budge. He was annoyed. They had no right to do this. What reason could they have for locking George away?

"Sit tight, George. I'll go find the key and then we'll go find your mum, okay?" There was no reply, just muffled sobbing.

Evan looked around the dim landing at the closed doors and pondered where Nathaniel or the Father might be sleeping. There was no way of knowing, he would just have to try them all.

The first door was just a linen cupboard and the next a large bedroom, empty and undisturbed. He skipped the bathroom door, and as he put his hand on the next door knob, he heard more muffled crying. This wasn't George though, this was different. It sounded more like a cry of pain than sorrow. He went to the far door where it seemed to be coming from and listened. The crying was joined by banging noises. Tentatively, he opened the door to what appeared to be a disused nursery. Black, dead eyes stared back at him from stuffed dolls and dog-eared teddy bears. The muted sounds were coming from above and he spied a doorway in the darkest corner of the room. He navigated past an old wooden cot, ignoring the mocking laughing clowns on the wall, and opened the door leading to a staircase. His bare feet were quiet as he climbed up, the noises increasing louder with each step. He grew concerned the further he got; it sounded like someone in a lot of trouble. At the top, he pushed open the door.

Evan couldn't believe what he saw. His chest felt tight, like he was having a heart-attack. Lily was lying on a bed, hands tied to the headboard with a dirty cloth jammed in her mouth. Her feet were tied to the bedposts and her swollen ankle was painfully twisted, causing her obvious agony. Her eyes were screwed shut and tears were pouring down her pale face. Father Thomas' trousers were around his ankles, his disgusting fat thighs jiggling as he thrust himself into poor Lily over and over. Before Evan could shout out or act, there was a click from behind the door and a voice.

"Don't move." Nathaniel appeared with a gun in his hand pointed right at Evan.

"What the fuck are you doing? Leave her alone!" Evan wanted nothing more than to wipe that smirk off Nathaniel's face, grab the gun, and beat the two of them to within an inch of their lives. He felt responsible for Lily and a complete failure that he hadn't been able to protect her. Evan's fists were clenched, ready to strike. Nathaniel guided Evan over to a rocking chair and made him sit with his hands on his head. Evan refused to watch the terrible abuse going on and stared at the floor in silent fury.

A moment later, Father Thomas grunted and slid off the bed. His fat belly hung low over his trousers as he slowly pulled them back up. Zipping himself up, he walked over to Evan.

"Delicious," he said, smiling maliciously.

"You fucking bastard. She's just a kid!" Evan's stomach churned as he looked over and saw Lily on the bed, whimpering like an injured dog.

"This little whore?" Father Thomas walked around to the side of the bed and took the rag from her mouth. He punched her face, breaking her nose, and she cried out as blood poured down her face. He cupped her chin, bringing her around to face him again. He punched her again, harder, this time knocking her out cold. The seeping blood from her nose curdled into the bedspread. Evan curled his hands into tight fists. He was infuriated yet helpless. Nathaniel just continued to stare at him, the gun pointed at Evan's head.

"I'm going to fucking kill you. Where's Amane? And Joe?" said Evan.

"Oh please, Evan. You've brought this on yourselves. Your avarice is your downfall, young man," said Father Thomas. "Your lack of humility and compassion is your downfall. My goodness, the sheer arrogance of you and your kind is breath taking. Do you not think that we didn't see you strike and abandon that boy's mother yesterday? You and your friends are culpable for your sins, Evan. It was evident last night that you are Godless: you, Joe, Amane, even this little bitch. She was desperate for me to fuck her, all that make up and flashing her legs at me. I could see the way she was looking at me last night. She practically begged me.

"As for George, well he's just about young enough to be saved. His soul has not had time to be corrupted by you, yet. We have plans for him." The Father spoke confidently and clearly.

"So why not lock me in?"

"Unfortunately, because you picked a room without a lock." snorted Father Thomas. "I was quite sure that you would find us though. Would you like to join your friends now?"

Nathaniel handed the gun to Father Thomas and picked up some rope from the floor. He bound Evan's hands together tightly.

"Move."

Nathaniel led the way back through the house, down the stairs, followed by Evan. Father Thomas kept the gun shoved into Evan's back at all times. They left Lily unconscious, and tied to the bed.

Back down in the lounge, where the roaring fire had been the night before, Evan saw Amane and Joe tied up. Nathaniel shoved Evan onto a chair and strapped him in, binding his feet like he had done the others. The Father shook his head as he looked at them, keeping the gun pointed at Evan.

"I know you cannot be saved. Quite frankly, I don't think I would waste my time on any of you. But you can be useful."

Father Thomas followed Nathaniel out, closing the door behind him. Evan looked over at his friends. Their hands and feet were bound behind the dining chairs and Amane had clearly been crying. Her face was puffed and Joe was sporting a black eye.

"Sorry, Evan," said Joe, "they jumped me when I was asleep. So fucking stupid." He twisted his wrists but couldn't escape the thick rope.

"Where's Lily?" Amane looked at Evan, her voice close to breaking. Evan couldn't bring himself to look at her and stared into the cold fireplace.

"Upstairs. They tied her to a bed." He gritted his teeth.

"Did they..?" Amane trailed off, horrified, eyes filling up. Evan merely nodded and hung his head. He had promised to look after her and failed. He had broken his promise. Amane began crying and they sat in silence. Not one of them actually thought about what may be in store for them. They felt only remorse for George, for Lily. Even for Karyn.

* * * *

They sat in the dark for an hour or more whilst the sun slowly rose higher, not speaking, and unable to move. With no clock, they couldn't tell how much time was actually passing. It was agonising. Their thoughts perpetually about what might be happening upstairs. Finally, they heard movement and the Father entered the room. Ignoring them, he drew the curtains back letting the light in. The windows overlooked an enclosed private courtyard, separate from the rest of the garden, clear of zombies.

"Where do you preach, Father? Where is your flock? I think you're a fraud. How can you call yourself a man of the cloth?" Joe spat the words out and only stopped when a hand slapped his cheek.

"Shut up," said Father Thomas. "My flock is everywhere. The church did not want me, they were too stupid to realise the truth. We had a parting of the ways. Look where they are now, scrambling around in the dirt with the rest of them. Me? I'm alive. One's soul cannot be compromised. We must bathe in his virtue and shine. They sit in their offices, counting their money, doing nothing. I pursue knowledge. That is why I know the way. What do you know, Joe? I'll tell you what, fuck all. So why don't you just shut the fuck up before I shut you up for good." The Father walked over to Evan and began untying the knot binding his hands together.

"Now don't try and do anything stupid, Evan." He waved the gun in his face as if to prove a point. "You're going on a little trip with Nathaniel."

Ignoring the questions from the others, Father Thomas closed the door on them and pushed Evan into the hallway. Handing the gun to Nathaniel, he walked off upstairs saying no more. Nathaniel led Evan back to the cellar, pushing him along with the gun in his back, down the corridor, and finally back into the hallway of the mortuary they had entered yesterday. As they stopped in front of the front door, Evan spoke.

"Where are we going then?"

"The boy's mother. We're going to fetch her. If we can get her, we can use the boy. What's her name?" Nathaniel zipped up his hood.

"Karyn. She won't help you though. She's only out for herself. You'll be lucky if she's still there."

"I saw what you did to her, you and your friend. You must really hate her to leave her like that."

Evan refused to take the bait. "And what if she's not there?"

"She will be. And if not," Nathaniel sneered, "then I'll be coming back, *alone*. Now, move." He flicked the gun from Evan to the front door. Outside on the driveway the warm, morning sun trickled down through the canopy above and Nathaniel explained the crude plan.

"We took a look; it's pretty deserted right now. When we get out the gates, we run round the centre, straight to the van. Anything gets too close I'll drop them. If Karyn can walk, fine. If not, you're carrying her. Then it's straight back here to the Father. Got it?"

Evan nodded. Nathaniel opened the gates and they slid through. There was little else Evan could do but go along with this madman and hope Karyn was still in the van.

* * * *

After what felt like hours, Amane heard the door creak open and Evan came in carrying Karyn.

"Evan! What's going on?" she said.

"Shut up," said Nathaniel, irritated. Evan put her down on the couch in the study. They had found her in the van, unconscious. Nathaniel had been right about the lack of zombies. It had been relatively easy getting to her, Evan pausing only occasionally whilst Nathaniel shot a few that got in their way. It had been harder getting back to the house. The gunshots had alerted more zombies to the area and they had been cornered in the alley. Nathaniel had to take several out which only brought more. Eventually, they had fought their way back to the gate and left a growing crowd outside. Evan had carried Karyn all the way back over his shoulder to the house, and after laying her down, he sat back in the chair, exhausted. Nathaniel tied Evan back up, the bonds seeming even tighter than before.

"How is she?" said Joe.

"Not good. She's pale and dehydrated. Her breathing is really shallow. She doesn't look well at all. I couldn't wake her up," said Evan feeling nauseous. Events were spinning out of control. Part of him had wished she wasn't there. He wasn't sure now if it was a good thing they had found her or not.

"Look, this is stupid, she can't help you. She clearly needs medical help. We can't help you either. We won't. Just let us go!" said Amane, struggling valiantly, yet unsuccessfully, against her restraints. "Why are you doing this?"

"Why?" Nathaniel aimed the gun at the three of them in turn, finally stopping on Amane. He walked up to her and slapped her, stinging her face and bringing tears to her eyes.

"Because God told me to. I don't expect a heathen, an unbeliever like you, to understand." He went back to Karyn, looking her up and down. "And you certainly *will* help us. Our food supply isn't endless you know, and I'm not risking my neck all the time out there. Young George will be a great asset to our cause when he sees we rescued his mother. As for you Amane, well we still need our...entertainment. Father likes 'em young but I prefer mine a bit older." Nathaniel cleared his throat and licked his lips.

"How do you like fishing, Joe?" said Nathaniel, smirking.

He just looked at Nathaniel with disgust and didn't answer.

"No? No matter. You see we've got a lot of fishing to do. You may have noticed we have a bit of an infestation outside and we need to get rid of it. We need to lure them away, flush them out and I think you'll be perfect as bait."

Evan swore under his breath and vowed to kill this man if he got the chance. Suddenly the door flew open and Father Thomas strode in rolling down his shirtsleeves, his face red and sweaty.

"How is she?" he asked.

"She'll be fine," said Nathaniel, "just needs a bit of TLC. I'll take her upstairs and let the boy know he's got a visitor."

"Good, good," nodded the Father. "Make sure our guest here gets to bed for some rest. See if you can get her to drink some water or something though, she looks terrible. Make sure George knows we saved her from these clowns. He'll be on our side in a heartbeat."

"You underestimate him," said Joe, as Nathaniel handed the gun to the Father and lifted Karyn up, dropping her over his shoulder. Father Thomas went to the fireplace and got a small fire going. He had no desire to make them warm or comfortable but he knew the smoke from the chimney might draw more survivors.

"I'm going up to keep watch for a while. You kids be good now." Father Thomas winked at Evan and smirked. Evan, Amane and Joe were left bound to the chairs, helpless, as the door swung shut on them. At the top of the stairs, the Father stopped, panting for breath. He went into the room where Nathaniel had lugged Karyn to; the same room where Nathaniel had stolen Amane and Lily from the night before. He handed Nathaniel the gun.

"Nathaniel, I'm going to rest for a while." He left Nathaniel trying to get Karyn to sip some water and walked down the hallway into the end bedroom, shutting the door behind him.

"Rest? Yeah, right," muttered Nathaniel. He knew his old friend better than that. He lay Karyn down on the bed and stroked his unkempt beard, looking at her.

Karyn was muttering incomprehensibly, the way people whisper and talk in their sleep. She was trembling and sweating; her eyes were sunken and her skin looked anaemic. Nathaniel went out and unlocked George's room.

"Come here, kid," he said, pointing the gun at George, who was curled up on the bedspread forlornly. George looked at him with burning hatred and didn't move.

"Why should I?"

Nathaniel leered. "Mummy's home. Me and the Father fetched her. Your so-called friends abandoned you, and her, but we saved her, George. For you. Come on."

Uncertain, George jumped off the bed and followed Nathaniel, running over to his mother when he saw her. He took hold of her hand. It was cold and clammy.

"Mum? Mum?" George shook her but she didn't wake up.

"She's sleeping kiddo. Had a rough night. But don't worry; we'll take care of her now."

George felt confused. Maybe these men were okay after all.

"Thanks," he said timidly. He was aware that Nathaniel still had a gun in his hands.

"Look, George, you go rest in your room, I won't lock you in anymore if you promise to be good and stay there, all right? Then when it's lunchtime, I'll come get you and we'll talk to your mum together."

George dropped his mother's limp arm and gave her a kiss.

"Love you, Mum."

Nathaniel watched, smiling, as George reluctantly trudged back to his room. With the boy on their side, there was nothing to do now but wait. Nathaniel sat down to watch over Karyn. The Father would want to speak to her but not yet. Nathaniel knew him better than to believe he was going upstairs to rest. He wouldn't be back down for hours. Or at least until his fat belly grew hungry.

* * * *

Father Thomas sat on the bed stroking Lily's hair. She faced away from him, staring at the walls. He sighed.

"I'm going to ask you one last time. Do you repent all your sins? Do you give yourself willingly to me? Will you sacrifice yourself for our Lord?"

Lily didn't speak. She thought back to a few days ago when her life had been normal, her mum always fussing over her like she was still a little kid. Her dad was always lecturing her about how she wore too much make-up and too few clothes. Her heart ached. She missed them both so much now.

Father Thomas sighed. "I had hope for you, you know?" He took a large knife out from his boots and cut the ties holding her captive on the bed. She was still naked and shivering with cold and fear. He grabbed her by the neck and pulled her up to stand before him.

"Answer me, cunt!" He shouted at her, inches away, saliva spraying her face.

"Let me go, please!" Lily sobbed, her arms folded around herself. She tried to turn away from him but was too weak. With one hand holding the blade to her throat, he forced her over to the window and opened it. He flung it open and shoved her over, face down, so she was dangling dangerously over the precipice. She yelped as the rough brickwork scraped her breasts like sandpaper, grating skin and drawing blood. Beneath her, from the front garden, a thousand hungry zombies looked up and reached for her, a thousand dead people groaning, arms straining to rip her apart. Their appetite for death and destruction was unsatisfied and this young girl before them, dripping blood, sweat and tears, only enflamed their ceaseless appetite.

"Shall I let you go now?" said Father Thomas. He laughed as her tears dripped down her face onto the agitated zombies below. They couldn't reach her, but they tasted her salty tears like an appetiser. She believed that right then, he was going to slit her throat and let her topple over.

Holding the knife at her throat, aroused by the girl's fear, he unzipped his trousers and positioned himself behind her, kicking her feet apart with his. Her ankle was red and swollen and she had to put all her weight onto her body to stop herself from collapsing. Lily cried out in agony as he forced himself inside her, laughing heartily, whilst she looked down on the frenzied mob below her, caught between the devil and the deep blue sea. She howled and cried above the zombies, trying to block out the pain, praying for a quick death.

* * * *

Nathaniel was getting bored watching their prisoner, waiting for the Father. He laid the gun down on the cabinet. He felt Karyn's forehead. He had expected her to be running a high fever but she felt cool. Despite her sickness, she was pretty. Greasy blonde hair lay around her face and beneath the suit; he could tell she was in good shape. Nathaniel licked his lips again. There was no reason why Father Thomas should have all the fun. He slipped his hand beneath her blouse and his warm hand felt ice-cold breasts beneath a silky bra.

"Karyn?" he said quietly.

She did not respond to his voice. She just lay there on the bed, her whole body quivering, her eyes closed. He unzipped her skirt and pulled it down roughly, exposing vanilla underwear and white thighs. He ripped off her panties revealing the intimate area he eagerly wanted. He dropped his trousers round his ankles and clambered onto the bed between her, fumbling to get his erection out. Holding himself above her, he penetrated her, marvelling that she didn't stir as he pushed himself in. Within seconds, he had come. Satisfied, he withdrew, got off the bed, and pulled his trousers up. He pulled her skirt back up, not wanting the Father to know he had not been able to wait. Nathaniel sat down in the chair and closed his eyes, relaxing. He preferred it when they didn't thrash around. Satiated, he started to doze.

He didn't notice when Karyn finally stopped breathing. He was caught up in his own dreams and thoughts. It had been only a couple of days ago when he'd finished with the last one. That one he had got to finish off properly, just how he liked. He had strangled her when he came. He couldn't touch Karyn yet though, he knew if he did, the Father would kill him.

Karyn's body froze and sank into death as Nathaniel sank lower into the chair. He didn't notice when her body was released from the grip of death and her hands clenched the sheets. He failed to open his eyes when she slowly sat up. He was dreaming about what he would do to her tomorrow. Who knows, maybe she would give herself willingly? He had saved her after all.

He failed to notice when her eyes opened and her neck turned awkwardly toward him. Her legs swung off the bed and her shoes suddenly landed on the floorboards. The unexpected noise invaded his morbid dreams and Nathaniel opened his eyes. He was flabbergasted by what he saw.

"Karyn? Are you okay?" Surely she couldn't be one of them? She was alive but just minutes ago. She was fine, wasn't she?

Her red-rimmed eyes stared back at him unblinking and her open mouth made pitiful gurgling noises. He could see her chest was not moving; she wasn't breathing. He stood up and she lunged for him. Her teeth gnashed together, unable to sink into the inviting flesh as he held her back at arms' length. Her rubbery brown tongue lolled uselessly from the side of her drooling mouth. They grappled and he forced her backwards. As she fell back onto the bed, he escaped her clutches and raced for the pistol. He shot wildly as she sprang up again, missing her and blowing the window out, breaking glass shattering onto the empty courtyard below.

"Mum?" George opened the door and saw his mother swaying on her feet. He had never seen her look so ill. When she looked at him, he was reminded of the old lady in Miguel's house. He saw Nathaniel raise his gun and point it at his mother.

"No!" He hit Nathaniel in the kidney, causing another missed shot, the bullet disappearing out the open window. Nathaniel grabbed George's shirt.

"She's dead, you idiot!" George kicked him in the shins and ran just as Karyn jumped and landed on Nathaniel. He pushed her up, blocking her biting jaw with his forearm.

Father Thomas rushed in and kicked Karyn's head. She rolled off Nathaniel who stood up quickly.

"Get after the kid! I'll take care of this, you fucking moron."
Father Thomas walked toward Karyn.

"Get back here, you little shit!" called Nathaniel. That boy had
humiliated him and nearly gotten him killed. Angry and scared,
Nathaniel ran out of the room after George with the gun in his
hand.

CHAPTER NINE

George ran, petrified. He heard Nathaniel's heavy footsteps behind him and ran as fast as he could. He pounded down the stairs two at a time. At the bottom, he jumped the last few steps onto the floor and slipped on a rug, sprawling out into the corridor. He looked back up and saw Nathaniel at the top taking aim. The shot rang out, whistling over George's shoulder, splintering wood as it pierced the wall.

George jumped up and ran down the hallway, stopping at the door to the cellar. He descended the steps carefully, groping in the dark for the handrail. He couldn't find the cord for the light and felt his way along the cool wall for the exit. His hands ran over cold, damp walls, through cobwebs, over dusty wine bottles, until finally he felt a smooth surface. He found the door handle and opened the door to the corridor back to the funeral home. As he did so, Nathaniel entered the cellar.

"Hey, boy, get back here! You little fucker."

George did not stop. His eyes were growing accustomed to the dark gradually and he gingerly felt his way along the narrow corridor. Halfway down he heard the door behind him open and light flooded out from the cellar. George turned to see Nathaniel step out and steadily raise the gun.

"Last chance." Nathaniel was staring, unblinking, both hands on the gun pointed directly at him.

George froze. There was nowhere to run to down here. He stepped back slowly, fingers brushing the walls, the chill air sending shivers down his spine. He thought of Lucy and how much he missed her. He thought of his father and wished he were here with him. His fingers brushed against cold metal and he paused. The door they had passed on their way in! He whirled round and reached up, pulling back the top bolt. A bullet fizzed past his head and winged off the door.

"Stop that, you fucking idiot! Don't open that door!" Nathaniel strode toward him re-aiming the gun.

George bent down and pulled back the bolt at the base. Another bullet tore through his trouser leg, drawing blood, but only scraping the surface, and embedded itself in the ground. George cried out in pain but was more scared of not opening the door than facing Nathaniel or whatever might be behind it. Ignoring his bleeding leg, he dragged the heavy door handle with all the strength he could muster, disregarding the banging noises inside. The door slid open, disappearing into a crevice in the wall.

"No!"

Now it was Nathaniel's turn to freeze. The gun in his hand hung limply by his side as he forgot all notion of capturing or killing the boy. George ran down the corridor and turned the corner out of sight. From the mortuary's freezer stumbled the first zombie: Father Thomas' sister. Nathaniel stared with a mixture of revulsion and fascination. Her body had been preserved perfectly and retained a lot of its strength. She moved jerkily and her eyes had glassed over, but otherwise, it looked like the same woman he had raped and strangled yesterday before dumping her inside. The milky eyes locked on Nathaniel and she snarled. Her advancing form filled the narrow corridor as she walked uneasily toward him, like a child learning to walk for the first time.

Nathaniel raised the gun as more dead bodies filed out after her. Fresh cadavers, born again from the depths of hell, stumbled out into the cramped corridor, all headed for him. He fired a shot, hitting the Father's sister in the head. Her right cheek blew open, jawbone shattering, exposing broken jagged teeth, and obliterating her right eye. Half her face had been blown away and she didn't even flinch. Still, she kept coming. With only a few feet between them, Nathaniel turned on his feet and ran back toward the house, almost tripping over his own feet in his eagerness to escape. Back through the cellar he ran, unable to stop the zombies behind him.

* * * *

Lily heard the gunshots and the sharp noise snapped her out of her wretchedness and misery. She watched the Father run out of the room, forgetting all about his perversions. Tottering on unsure feet, she took a shirt from the floor and put it on. It was one of the Father's and way too big for her. It went down almost to her knees. In his rush, the Father has forgotten to tie Lily up again and she followed him down the steps, keeping a short distance between them. She had no memory of when or how she had gotten here. She just walked on, knowing it was away from that despicable room she had been used and abused in. She passed through an old bedroom full of junk and jumble. She picked up an old doll, black eyes looking back at her, unblinking, from a round plain face. She threw it with all her might against the wall, breaking the china doll into pieces.

Stumbling out into the hallway, she saw Nathaniel run out of a room and stop at the top of the stairs. He fired the gun and then ran down. She didn't feel scared. She didn't feel elated that she had got this far without the Father touching her. She felt nothing. Lily carried on her morose journey down the stairs not knowing or caring where she was headed. Her head span as she walked down the stairs, spots of light floating in her vision.

Hearing the gunshots and commotion, Amane, Joe, and Evan were getting more and more worried about what was happening. They had no idea what was going on upstairs. Joe called out for help but got no reply. Evan hopped his chair over to the study door. It was difficult but he made it, the rope painfully digging into his wrists every time he moved. A pitter-patter of feet ran past. Evan gripped his teeth around the door handle and levered it down, managing to open the door. Though it was only open an inch, he saw Nathaniel fly past to the cellar door and disappear inside, hearing him call out.

"Hey, boy, get back here! You little fucker."

More footsteps on the stairs, but this time, slower, more controlled. Through the balustrade, Evan saw Lily float down the stairs in no hurry at all.

"Lily!"

He called out to her quietly, unsure if it was safe or not. At the base of the stairs, she turned around and smiled. His heart broke when he looked upon her. She could barely see through purple swollen eyes. Her smile showed bloody teeth and her nose looked slightly crooked. The Father had battered her, leaving deep welts, cuts and bruises all over. Fresh blood was seeping through the shirt she wore, down her legs.

"Oh, Lily."

Her smile dropped like a stone, and ignoring him, she continued on her sloth-like way into the vestibule. She limped along, wobbling on her feet unsteadily. Evan realised she was heading for the front door.

"Lily! No, come back!" he shouted at her, unafraid of the consequences or who might hear him. He didn't know if she hadn't heard him or was just choosing not to listen, but she entered the vestibule and the door swung loosely behind her. She turned the key in the lock, and with a click, the front door opened and she stepped outside into glorious sunshine. The warmth hit her instantly. Looking up through half-closed eyes, she saw the sunlight amid branches of tall green trees waving in the breeze. Her head felt lighter now and she forgot the incredible pain coursing through her frail body. She was back home, snuggled up on the sofa with her mum. It was warm and cosy here. She wrapped her arms around herself as her mum hugged her.

"Bedtime, honey."

Her mum kissed her on the forehead and Lily felt happy. Her mind felt nothing but peace and her body felt like it was floating on the wind. She was home.

The crowd of zombies swarmed over her, killing her instantly. What little was left of her body was crushed and mangled beneath the weight of hundreds of zombies. When the first had tasted the blood it craved, it continued, unable to go anywhere else but further into the house through the welcoming, open door, followed by a hungry horde.

* * * *

"We have to get the hell out of here and now!" shouted Evan. He shoved the door shut and propped his chair against it.

"What's happening?" screamed Amane. "Where's Lily and George?" She pulled at her ties only succeeding in making them tighter.

"I don't know what is going on up there, but it is not good. George just ran down into the cellar and Nathaniel was following. He's the one shooting."

"And Lily?"

"I'm sorry, Amane." Evan looked at her feeling impotent. "Whatever they did to her...she looked out of it. She's gone."

"What?" said Amane.

"She's gone. I'm sorry, Amane. She just walked out the door. Whatever the Father did to her..."

Amane screwed her face up and shook her head. "No. I can't believe it. That bastard. That fucking mongrel is going to pay."

"What else?" said Joe. Despite events unfolding around them he was calm and in control. He aimed to size the situation up and deal with it. He had been in scrapes before and always got out of them. This was no different; think logically and put your emotions away for another time.

"In about ten seconds, there's going to be several hundred zombies in this house," said Evan.

They were all silent. The sombre mood was broken by faint gunshots and a few crashing noises from upstairs. No one spoke for a minute.

"I don't think that door is going to hold them back, do you?" said Joe, breaking the silence.

"Fuck!" exclaimed Evan. He felt utterly powerless. His children were slipping out of his reach. The closer he tried to get, the further away they got.

"Ten seconds, eh? Evan, stay against that door as long as you can. Put your weight against it," said Joe, beginning to hop his chair up and down.

"Why? What are you thinking?" said Evan, leaning back so the chair jammed itself under the door-handle.

"I'm not thinking, I'm doing," grunted Joe. His chair neared the fireplace and Evan got wind of his plan.

"No, Joe, don't. We'll find another way."

"We both know there is no other way." Joe nodded at them both, grim-faced, and then toppled his chair backwards as best he could into the fire. The top of the chair stuck on the fireplace and his back and hands hung over the flames. He gritted his teeth as the fire licked at his hands, and crucially, the ropes holding them. He was aware that Evan and Amane were shouting at him to get out, but their imploring cries were drowned out by the whooshing sound in his head. He howled as the pain grew more intense. Screaming, the flesh on his fingers caught afire and his skin began to melt. As he felt the white-hot pain searing into his brain forever, he forced himself to stay the course. He pulled his wrists apart as the burning rope finally snapped. With burning hands, he reached down and quickly untied the binding on his feet.

Tears and smoke stinging his eyes, he stood up and rushed over to the dining table, knocking over his burning chair. He poured a solitary bottle of water over his hands, dousing the fire. Shaking uncontrollably, he slumped to the floor holding his black smouldering hands out in front of him. The distant yet insistent shouting voices of Amane and Evan stopped him from slipping into unconsciousness. He opened his eyes and looked up at them.

The door was jumping in its frame, rocking Evan back and forth in the chair. Joe took a deep breath and stood up. He let the dizziness subside and focused on doing one thing at a time. Looking around, there was nothing he could see of use. He needed a knife or something to cut with, but he couldn't go searching through the drawers now, there was no time.

He swayed over to Amane, and agonisingly slowly, started on the rope holding her wrists. His charred fingers were practically useless but he knew he had to get the ties undone. Ignoring the intense, excruciating pain, he finally released her and collapsed to the floor. Amane untied her feet and raced over to Evan, freeing him from his bonds. Evan pushed back on the door, holding it in place for now, blocking out the groaning sounds from the other side.

"Oh God, Joe," Amane tenderly picked him up. His hands were a mess. Where once strong hands had been, were now blackened stumps, measly strips of flesh where fingers had been. His breathing was slow and laboured. His shirt had turned a brown crisp shade and his back was red and blistered. Amane looked over to Evan.

"What are we going to do?"

"We go that way." Evan looked through the windows into the empty courtyard. The house flanked it on three sides, a tall fence completing the fourth. It was a redundant abandoned space full of dead leaves and pools of dirty water.

"How? To where?"

"Wrap Joe's hands in those napkins over there. Then open the window and get outside. There's an ivy climbing up that wall so there's probably a trellis we can use to climb up. We get onto the roof, over the fence, and take it from there."

"And if there's another hundred zombies on the other side?" asked Amane.

"Then we're no worse off than we are now." Evan pushed harder against the door as the weight against it increased. He heard the wood cracking and sweat was dripping annoyingly down his nose and forehead, stinging his eyes.

Amane sat Joe down in a chair, and using the cloth napkins on the table, wrapped them around his burnt hands. He winced the whole time she was touching him, but never complained once. She pulled up the window and helped Joe through. He rested against the outside wall, shattered. Amane followed and stood outside beside Joe.

"You're right, there's a framework here we can climb. Come on, Evan." Amane beckoned him through the window.

"When I let go, they are going to pour right in here. We have to get up those walls fast. I'll get up and pull you up, then Joe. Okay?"

"Okay, let's just hurry."

Evan scanned the room. Joe's chair was now well alight, the rug was smouldering and the painting of the last supper was melting in its frame. Soon, he mused, the whole room would be alight. The thought of this palace of sin being burnt to the ground pleased him. He hoped Father Thomas would burn with it. He let go of the door and sprinted to the window, diving through. He scrambled up the ivy-clad trelliswork onto a flat roof. As the zombies swamped the burning room, he leant down and offered his hand to Amane. She was halfway up and he grabbed her, helping her up onto the felt roof.

"Come on, Joe!"

A zombie appeared at the window, arms reaching through desperately. Joe looked up at Evan and put his feet on the trellis. Wrapping one arm through it, he hauled himself up about a foot off the ground. The exertion was too much for him and he fell back down onto the ground.

"Joe, fucking move it, mate. Or I'm coming back down to get you!" said Evan, shouting at his friend. The zombie at the window was joined by others, pressing on it until the first zombie fell through.

"I can't do this. Go get your kids, Evan. Find George, and go." Joe was sapped of all energy and looked up at Evan and Amane on the roof, stepping back away from the wall. He stepped back as the first zombie through got to its feet and began its sloping walk toward Joe.

"We'll get George together. Joe! Joe!" Evan watched as Joe walked backwards into the furthest corner, ignoring his friend. The zombies poured into the courtyard like a tidal wave directed straight for him. Not once did Evan hear Joe scream out or cry. He went down fighting, throwing punches that must have hurt him as much as the recipients. Eventually, Evan couldn't see Joe anymore. He was overcome.

Amane pulled Evan back from the edge and embraced him. "We need to keep moving," she said softly against the backdrop of the carnivorous horde, locking eyes with him. They had both lost someone dear to them and no words could express how they felt. Evan kissed her and took her hand. He looked around at where they were and wondered how they were going to get the hell out of dodge.

* * * *

Slamming the cellar-door behind him, Nathaniel heaved at the huge wine-rack, only just managing to topple it over, blocking the doorway as the zombies reached it. They clawed and hammered at the door but there was no way through. Red and white wine poured out together over the floor from broken bottles, spooling around in circles, tracing looping lines erratically through the dirt floor.

Up the cellar steps, he ran breathlessly, flinging the door open only to come face to face with an old woman. Her face had been shorn of its flesh and she looked more like a walking skeleton, only wiry hair protruding from flaps of skin left hanging on its scalp. In the corridor behind her, he saw more moving corpses and yanked the door shut, trapping the woman's hand. Unable to get the door firmly closed, he pulled on the handle until he heard the bones in her wrist snap. He heaved the door with all his strength, severing tendons and fingers, slowly bludgeoning through skin and bone until the door clicked shut. He kicked the pathetic dismembered limb down the stairs in frustration.

Rummaging in his pockets, he found the keys. He locked the door and trudged down into the cold cellar as the zombies piled up against both cellar doors, banging on them furiously. He was trapped in this hellhole: a cold cellar, smelling of wine, bloodthirsty zombies on both sides.

Nathaniel slumped against a damp wall as the single bulb overhead swayed gently whilst the ceiling vibrated from the hundreds of feet above. How could this be? Nathaniel realised he was not going to get out of this one. There was no way he could fight his way through so many up there and the corridor to the funeral home was only just wide enough for one person. Add a dozen zombies and it was a death trap. He picked up a bottle rolling around his feet and wiped the label: pinot noir. He unscrewed the cap and drank. Deep crimson spilled down his chin, matting the curly hairs of his beard together.

The thought of being eaten alive, torn limb from limb whilst still conscious, wouldn't leave him. No fucking way was he going down like that. He gulped down more wine, polishing off half a bottle in barely a minute. He took the pistol from his pocket and put the barrel in his mouth. He thought that he should try to think of a loved one before he bowed out. He briefly thought of his parents, but they had died when he was young so they'd never been close. The only notable woman in his life hadn't been around long and that was thirty years ago. The Father was his only real friend. He was a pompous prick though, always bossing him around. Fuck it, Nathaniel thought, and pulled the trigger.

The pistol clicked empty. Shocked, Nathaniel unlocked the chamber and stared at it. It was completely empty. His last bullet had gone into the corridor, taking off the face of that bitch who was currently trying to batter down the door to eat him. He knew he didn't have any more ammo on him, it was all upstairs. Nathaniel felt sick. He was going to die in this poky, cold cellar, shitting and pissing in the corner, until his body finally gave up on him.

He flung the useless gun against the wall and picked up the wine again. He stood up shakily, drinking until the acid rose up his throat and bile began to stir in his stomach. He idly scratched his groin and flung the bottle against the wall, sending smashed pieces of glass flying.

"Fuck off! Just fucking fuck off!" He screamed at the top of his voice, terrified, his words bouncing around aimlessly. The zombies neither heard nor comprehended them. They just continued their ceaseless assault on the cellar. Nathaniel gripped his dizzy head. That fucking little shit's mother, Karyn, it was all her fault. He roughly scratched his groin again, feeling the itch spreading down one leg. His alcohol-addled brain stalled. She had turned into one of them *after* he had screwed her. So she must have been infected *before* he screwed her. He finally put two and two together.

Nathaniel's roaring laughter echoed off the walls as he realised he was wrong. He wasn't going to be torn limb from limb, but he wasn't going to wither away down here, drooling and wallowing in his own excrement and self-pity. He was infected and soon he would be dead. Before long, he would be undead, reanimated and hungry for living flesh. He supposed he could open the door now and be savaged, dying in a relatively quick way, suffering only brief pain. Or he could bounce around these four walls for eternity, just one of the millions of zombies walking the world. He laughed again, a laugh of nervousness, fear and utter despair. It ricocheted back to him, reminding him that he was certainly going to die. He was going to die alone. Very alone.

* * * *

Father Thomas was old, overweight, and angry. He packed a powerful punch and kept Karyn at bay with sharp jabs at her growingly disfigured face. Nathaniel had the gun and the only other one was upstairs. He thought he would easily dispatch of this tiresome woman, but it was proving to be harder than he thought. Every time he pushed her away, she would spring back. He managed to corner her with a chair like a lion tamer. Pinned against the wall he looked at Karyn, fascinated. What was she thinking? Was there anything left of the mother inside her? Had she seen the Almighty in her brief death? If He had sent her back, what was her purpose? It didn't make sense to Father Thomas. He was a righteous man, why would God want him dead? He surmised that Karyn had not passed through the pearly gates but had more likely lived a life of sin and had a one way invite to Hell. Maybe the Devil had sent her back, along with the rest of the damned human race, to seek vengeance on God's miserable creatures. A shiver ran down Father Thomas's back. If that were the case, he was going to need more help.

Each time he stepped back, she pushed against the chair to follow him. If she got on top of him, it would be hard to shift her. Breaking her neck wouldn't stop her. He struggled and pulled a small penknife from his back pocket. Holding the chair with the weight of his body, he jammed the tiny blade into her neck and began to saw. If she knew what he was doing, she didn't show it; there was no reaction at all. He gripped the knife and sawed into her neck, congealing blood dribbling out and trickling down his arm. When he was halfway through her neck, he had to pause and rest. Her head was leaning to one side now, but still she tried to reach him. If anything, her desire to bite him seemed to be increasing. Her jaw was moving up and down slicing through the air, teeth clacking together.

He continued his slow kill. Father Thomas sawed through her neck and her face slumped forward. Her head was still attached to her body by the spinal cord that he couldn't reach. Karyn followed the Father as he dropped the chair and backed away, but, with her head dropping forward over her chest, could not see him. He whipped behind her, grabbing her hair with his left hand, yanking her head backwards. He pushed her forward so she fell onto the floor. She thrashed around on the floor, blood spilling over the floorboards as he stood on her back. With both hands holding her head he pulled it upward forcefully, bone's cracking as her spine slowly ripped out of her back. With the head now severed, trailing her spine with it like a tail, he watched her twitching hands and feet cease. He turned the head around to look at her and laughed as her eyes locked on him. Her jaw kept moving up and down like clockwork. He spat and wiped his sweaty brow.

"Is this what you wanted? Immortality? Was it worth a life of degradation and sin?" Father Thomas flung Karyn's decapitated head into the corner of the room and left her to suffer an eternity of frustration. Her jaw moved up and down and her eyes followed him as he left the room.

Out in the hallway he heard the stairs creaking, and moaning sounds emanating from below. He saw the flood of zombies in the corridor, many of them climbing up the stairs. Seeing him, they increased their speed: girls, boys, parents, all together in a deadly pursuit.

"No. No, this can't be." Father Thomas took a few steps backward in horror and realising he had nowhere else to run, turned and fled into the furthest bedroom. No sooner had he shut the door behind him than the barrage of bangs on the door began. He could smell decay and death on the other side of the door, eager to get in. He was trapped in the room with nothing but dolls for company and sat down on the bed. His gun was upstairs in the attic and Nathaniel had disappeared. Who the hell had let them in? For the first time in a long time, the Father was afraid.

CHAPTER TEN

Evan peered over the edge of the roof, the courtyard now full of moaning, shuffling zombies. Buried beneath them all was Joe. Evan prayed his friend was truly dead.

The zombies were pulling at the ivy and trellis, scrabbling at the wall, unable to work out how to get up there. More still were pouring in through the broken window, piling on top of one another. Eventually, Evan thought, the pile might be so big that they would simply be able to climb over one another to the roof. Pouring through the window was smoke. The room was alight along with many careless, carefree zombies who staggered about, unaware that they were burning. Amane was reminded of November fifth, of a guy lit up on a bonfire: limbs burning and a hideous face melting. Evan looked through the trees and saw the outline of the funeral home.

"We're going to have to jump for it. That tree there is close enough and big enough for us to get hold of. If we climb down a few more feet, we can drop to the ground. I think we'll land in the funeral home driveway so we should be clear." All the noise was coming from below and beside them; the grounds looked quiet.

"Assuming we don't break our legs falling out of a tree," said Amane, hands on hips, "then what? If George made it out, he might be over there you know? We have to look for him."

"Yeah, he's probably there right now. He seemed to have a good head start on Nathaniel, so I hope he got away. I'm not leaving without him either." Evan prepared himself to jump when he heard breaking glass overhead.

"Wait! Help!" called the Father.

"You have got to be joking," said Amane to Evan. "Let's go." She looked up to see smoke drifting out of the window where the Father was calling from. Evan nodded and ignored Father Thomas' pleas.

"Wait, please! You can't leave me here!" Coughing and spluttering, gasping for air, smoke was curling around him, squeezing its way past his fat body, which filled the framework of the window.

"Burn in hell!" screamed Amane.

"Please, I can help you. I have a boat. It's really close by. I can take you anywhere!" His face was red and sweaty. Amane thought he was going to die right there and then as he coughed up dirty black phlegm and dribbled it down his greasy chin.

"Where's Karyn?" said Evan.

"They got her. I'm sorry, I tried to save her but it was too late. Please, you must help me. Won't you have mercy?"

Evan turned to face him. He could feel the heat of the flames that were now leaping out of the window and across a sea of bobbing zombies' heads below. If the zombies didn't reach them first, the flames soon would.

"You're going to have to jump, Father." Evan shouted over the crackling noise of the fire and the cackling of the undead. Father Thomas crawled out onto the ledge and sat there coughing, chubby legs dangling.

"Please, there's a ladder next door, Nathaniel keeps one in the garage. If you can..."

"No, now, or we leave you to burn, there's no time, Father," shouted Evan, angrily.

"Seriously? After everything he's done?" said Amane to Evan, incredulous that Evan was going to actually save this man.

"For now, yes. We can use him, Amane. I've no interest in saving his worthless life, but do you have a boat? Do we even know how to sail one? Unfortunately, right now we need him."

Father Thomas looked down at the roof that looked a long way away, struggling to bring himself to jump. He imagined breaking his legs, or worse. Suddenly the banging on the bedroom door stopped and he heard a massive thud as the door gave way and the zombies scurried in toward him.

"God help me," he whispered, and closing his eyes, pushed himself off the ledge. He held his breath as he fell, waiting for the inevitable hard roof rushing up to meet him. Amane and Evan watched as he plummeted down and landed with a tremendous thump. The roof shook when he landed, sending vibrations through them all.

"Aaargh!" screamed the Father in agony, clutching his arm. His left arm was broken and twisted, his fingers bent at ridiculous angles. Evan picked him up by his collar and dragged him over to the roof edge. Holding him precariously balanced over the courtyard, the Father's feet were barely touching the roof. He looked down, snivelling and sobbing.

"What are you doing? Oh God, please!" Each time he kicked out, the baying mob below became more agitated. Swaying beneath him, the burning zombies reached for him. Wide-eyed with panic and pain the Father clutched onto Evan's arms.

"God isn't going to save you, Father, *I* am. From now on, you do what I say or I swear I will drop you. Understood?"

"Yes, please, just don't. Please!"

Evan swung the Father back onto the roof and he fell to his knees, crying.

"Amane go find George. Get to the garage and see if there's a car in there. I'll bring him," Evan said pointing to the Father. The heat was making them uncomfortably hot and Evan rolled up his shirtsleeves. Amane looked over to the trees and took the longest run up she could manage. She leapt through the air and crashed into leaves and branches, grabbing the tree and sliding down until she came to rest on a large solid branch. Rough bark splintered her hands and sharp twigs scratched her face. Wasting no time, she swung down and dropped onto the soft ground below.

"I'm over!" she called back to Evan, sprinting to the funeral home. Evan grabbed Father Thomas' arm and hauled him to his feet.

"Stop crying and move."

"I can't, it's too..." whined the Father before Evan punched him. Father Thomas tasted blood in his mouth as he recoiled.

"I don't give a shit!" shouted Evan advancing on him. Evan grabbed the Father and punched him again. He rolled over toward the edge of the roof and Evan kicked him in the back.

"Do it or stay here and die. Now jump to that tree just like Amane did. That's our way out of here. I'll be right behind you." Evan picked the snivelling Father up and shoved him forward.

Father Thomas stood on the edge of the roof staring at the tree before him. He launched himself forward, arms flapping at branches before he crashed through the tree, his weight breaking everything in his path. He fell short of any substantial branch and ended up on the ground not having slowed his fall at all. As he landed, his broken arm shot blinding pain to his brain and he passed out.

Evan watched him fall and could not summon up any sympathy. This man was responsible for the death of Joe and Lily: probably Karyn too. Evan wiped his sweaty brow and ran off the roof. Barring a few minor scratches, he got down with relative ease and dropped onto the ground beside the unconscious Father. He took hold of the Father's chubby legs and began pulling him to the driveway. Through the gravel, he ploughed a lone furrow with the Father. A few zombies out on the road, on the other side of the gates, watched, but most were drawn to the burning vicarage and paid little attention.

* * * *

George slammed the kitchen door behind him. He grabbed a table leg and pulled the big wooden table over the floor, propping it against the door. He wasn't sure how many zombies had gone after Nathaniel and how many were following him. Opening drawers and cupboards, he finally found a large knife and clutched it to his chest.

Into the lounge he went, and he spied their bags still lying in the middle of the room where they'd left them. The funeral home had lost its homely feel and George felt the quietness around him. The little house was morbid and unwelcoming. The family photos on the wall all seemed to be staring at him as if questioning why he was intruding into their home.

Slinging one of the bags onto his back, he ventured into the dim corridor, unsure of what to do next. If ravenous zombies didn't burst through the kitchen door in a minute, then surely Nathaniel would. What of Evan, Amane, Lily, and Joe? Were they dead like his mother? Why had Nathaniel shot at her? Was she really a zombie? His bottom lip trembled and tears began to fall as he remembered her. He only got told off when he was naughty. When he was good, mum always gave him a kiss and a hug. Lucy too. He sighed and felt very alone.

George decided he would go home and try to call the police. His father had taught him how to make the call. He would just stay at home until Joe came back. He went to the front door but it was locked, and so he tried another door just off to the side. It pushed open easily and he stared out into the dark garage. The only light came in through the door behind him and it illuminated a long black car, sleek and shiny. George stepped into the bare garage with trepidation. He held the knife out in front of him as he walked and felt along the wall for a light switch. His fingers scraped along smooth, clean walls. A loud bang from within the house made him jump as he realised the kitchen door had given way.

Blindly he carried on along to the garage door and put his hand on the handle. Pensively, he gripped it ready to open it, but suddenly he heard gravel crunching underfoot outside. Stones scattered and chinked off the metal door. He held the knife out and stood his ground, ready to defend himself from his unseen attackers.

* * * *

Amane tried the front door to the funeral home but it was locked shut and she couldn't force it. She jogged to the garage door hoping it wasn't locked too. Their luck had to change sometime. Turning the handle, the garage door lifted up and flew back with the faintest creak. A figure charged at her from the darkness and she shrieked.

"George!" she exclaimed in surprise.

"Amane!" George dropped the knife and hugged her as she swept him up into her arms.

"Oh, George, we were so worried about you. Are you okay?"

Amane examined him as she put him back down but saw no injuries. Hearing noises behind him, George didn't answer. A zombie stumbled into the garage from the house, a thin, naked man with scars and stitching covering his body. The sunlight appeared to dazzle it momentarily, giving them just enough time to move.

"Into the car, quick!" said Amane. Thankfully, it was unlocked and they bolted inside the hearse, locking the doors. The zombie threw itself against the side, pressing against the glass where George sat looking back in wonder. The stitches in the man's chest were coming loose, exposing his gruesome internal organs.

"Amane, we need to go now," George whispered, wishing he hadn't dropped the knife outside. He dropped the backpack at his feet and Amane searched desperately for the keys. They were not in the ignition or on the dashboard. She dropped the sun visor down expecting them to drop into her lap but nothing fell. She felt her fingers around in the foot-well and they brushed over a lone black key.

"Thank, God," she sighed, relieved, putting the key into the ignition. The hearse purred into life instantly and she put it into drive.

"George, listen, Evan is out there with Father Thomas. They're coming with us." Amane pulled out onto the driveway slowly whilst the jigsaw man loped along behind. Another zombie appeared through the doorway into the beaming sunlight.

"What about Lily? And Joe?" asked George.

"I'm sorry, no. They didn't make it."

"But the fat man did?" George didn't burst out in tears or scream. He was finished with crying. He clenched his fists and stared straight ahead.

"I'm sorry, George. Joe saved us. If it wasn't for him, we'd be dead. I wish things were different but..." There was nothing more she could offer him. She knew that there were no words she could offer in consolation. Amane pulled the car over by Evan who was waiting on the side of the drive with the Father. He pulled open the back door and bundled the Father in.

"Hurry!" said Amane, watching the zombies in her rear view mirror grow closer. Evan jumped in the other side and Amane pulled the car away, showering the zombies behind with a flurry of gravel and stones.

"Evan, the gate's shut!" cried Amane.

"Just floor it!" shouted Evan. Amane sped up and crashed into the iron gates. They flew open and the hearse careened through, pulling the smashed gates off their hinges and flattening the zombies ahead of it like mere bugs. Brains splattered onto the sidewalk as the wheels ran over diseased, deceased, fragile skulls.

"I'm sorry, George," began Amane, but she couldn't continue her sentence as the cumbersome hearse struggled to swerve around the truck they had crashed into previously. More zombies appeared on the road around them and bounced off the sides as Amane heaved the wheel with difficulty from side to side. Every time one bounced off the bonnet, she cringed.

"Where to, Evan?" she said, trying to keep the car on the road. Navigating zombies was easier than the abandoned vehicles and she frequently hit other cars, ruining their car's polished sleek bodywork.

"Just drive, anywhere you can. If you can stop, fine, we'll switch, but we have company outside so just drive as fast as you can. We need to get away from here."

Father Thomas was awake and holding his broken arm. He was amazed at what he saw. He hadn't been out of the vicarage since it had all begun. He had always sent Nathaniel out on his little errands.

"My, God. Look at it. Never did I imagine the end of the world would look like this."

They passed another army checkpoint. Grotesque charred bodies with twisted hands and arms reached up imploringly from gruesome piles of men, women, and children along the side of the road. Tents and marquees stood idle: canvas doors flapping in the breeze, exposing their contents. Dozens and dozens of zombies emerged into glorious sunshine, smelling the car fumes and hearing the sound of the living so tantalisingly close. Reanimated corpses of soldiers and citizens stumbled alongside each other toward the passing hearse.

Feral faces flashed past his window, snarling and sneering, evil eyes locking onto him with some kind of fury. He saw a once proud community devastated, now reduced to a forest of undead, foraging for flesh. Children and toddlers stumbled toward the car, arms permanently horizontal, reaching for their ungodly feast, now nothing more than primitive predators. He saw babies with no legs crawling over broken glass, young eyes devoid of life. He saw young men and women murdered in their prime, caked in blood, soaked in blood and vomit, emitting such primeval sounds that he had not heard before, that they could not be of this Earth.

As one, they followed behind the hearse, decaying corpses walking side by side like a bizarre funeral procession. At first, just a handful followed; then it was a dozen, fifty, and a hundred. All stayed true to the hearse's path, their sole goal ahead of them in a black box on wheels.

He saw shops and houses burning, flames leaping from roof to roof; fire spreading endlessly with no one to stop it. Front steps and gardens were flooded in deep dirty water as there was no one to turn the taps off now either. A small block of shops and flats had banners and signs draped out of every window, words crudely fashioned with paint, bleach, anything that had been to hand: Help, Trapped, Survivors. Father Thomas saw no one left alive. Their souls had long since departed, but to where, he was no longer sure.

On the horizon, he noticed a haze of smoke. Occasional plumes of fire would shoot up into the sky as something on the ground exploded, reminding him of those blurry images on television from the endless war in the Middle East. He saw no birds or animals. The grass, the plants, the flowers and trees: all passed by looking lifeless and fading under a sun, which seemed hotter and brighter than ever before. Brown crisp leaves littered the road, skittering and crunching under the car tyres sounding like gunfire.

He was jolted out of his sombre reverie as the car suddenly pitched forward and he was thrown against the front seat, his tingling arm stinging painfully back into life.

"Hold on!" grunted Amane, as the hearse slipped down a steep embankment toward the river. The wheels slid on the muddy plain as Amane slowed the car and spun it sideways. Mindful of the river only feet away, she took the car along the edge of the river.

"The roads are blocked, there's no way I can get through. This should take us a little way to the city." In the mirror, she saw the swarming crowd of zombies follow but there was an increasing distance between them. They drove for a good twenty minutes, leaving the shambling zombies in the distance, but eventually could not get any further. Four or five cars had blocked an access road to the river and there was no way round. Amane stopped the car and peered out. The cars had smashed into one another creating a metal snake that curved up the embankment.

"You think it's safe?" she said.

"I don't know," said Evan. "George, you got anything in that backpack we can use as a weapon?" He rustled around and came out empty-handed.

"No."

"I'll go out and check around," said Evan. "If we're going on foot from here, I'd better see how the land lies. You two keep an eye on him. If he moves, throw him in the river."

Evan got out of the car and the overhead sun beat down on him. The air was hot and dry. George turned around in his seat and stared at the demoralised Father who was slumped back in his seat, head pounding. He did not intend to go anywhere. Amane watched as Evan walked to the front of the hearse.

He surveyed the crash; the car doors were open and every car was blackened and burnt out. It was silent, save the gentle lapping of the water against the riverbank. He approached the nearest car and picked up a piece of wood, no more than a foot long. Evan banged the stick on the car door, the harsh clanging sound sounding abnormal in this stultifying atmosphere. Nothing happened. No zombies raced out. No soldiers came over the hill, shooting guns and mouthing off. No rescue came.

Evan trod cautiously. He was acutely aware of their unnatural and potentially lethal surroundings. He walked toward the river where one car was partially submerged, its trailer sunken into the riverbed. The car was empty and he climbed into the drivers' seat. As there was no way round, he decided to take the direct route and go through.

On the other side, he stepped out onto soggy ground. The embankment ahead was clear but what interested him more, was the small wooden pier with a boat tethered to it. Evan looked around again and called out.

"Anyone here?"

The sound of silence filled his ears. The pier went all the way to the rivers' edge and he walked over to the steps, out onto the pier toward the little boat. It was not much bigger than the hearse, but it would do. A propeller was at the back and a small cabin that would shield them from the sun. Looking down at the sluggish water, he saw two bodies floating face down and bloated, a woman and child. He could see bullet holes in the back of their heads and the little girls' blonde hair was tangled in the reeds. He squatted, and leaning over the side of the pier, prodded the mother with the wood. No response. Whoever they were, they were dead. As dead as dead can be, he thought.

Evan went back to the hearse and explained to Amane what he had found. They agreed it was a good idea to stick to the river. As far as they knew, the zombies could not swim and it should prove easier than driving the congested streets attracting unwanted attention. Amane and George headed through the burnt car to the boat whilst Evan helped Father Thomas.

"I hope you weren't lying, Father. If you can steer this boat down the river, then you have a chance of a future. But if you try anything at all, then I will have no hesitation in leaving you behind for them." Evan pointed back down the river where they had come from. A massive crowd of zombies was in sight now, heading their way. Some of them splashed into the riverbed and disappeared under the water, not to return. Most though, kept their footing and would not be deterred or distracted.

The Father disconsolately nodded and limped alongside Evan to the boat. When they reached the pier, George was on board in the cabin investigating, whilst Amane began untying the rope so they could cast off. Evan shoved the Father on and told him to get on with it. He sat down, monitoring the Father closely as the priest started the engine, moaning and cursing under his breath. Evan thought about Charlie and Anna. It really felt like he was getting somewhere now. Maybe this time tomorrow he would find them. He was sure his father's boat was much bigger than this, equipped much better with a far larger cabin.

"I'm scared, I'm scared." The words haunted Evan, day and night.

Amane's unexpected terrifying scream pierced the air, shocking everyone. The dead girl floating in the river had burst out of the brown sludge and grabbed Amane's arm whilst she was untying the boat.

"Help!" Amane couldn't shake her off. She struggled but she was losing her balance. The girl's hands were hooked around Amane's and her sodden weight was pulling them both to the water. Amane looked into the girl's face. It had been shattered by a bullet and her eye sockets were soggy and dark red. The girl no longer had eyes and she splashed about in the shallow water like a dying fish. Amane began to topple overboard, cold water splashing her face as she headed down to the river and the zombie's clutches.

CHAPTER ELEVEN

Amane braced herself, waiting for the icy water to suck her down, or the zombie's teeth to sink into her arms. A flash in front of her eyes and the girl was knocked sideways, her neck broken. George struck again with the oar and the girls face fell apart. He cleaved the girl's head off exposing dead brain and the zombie lost its grip, plunging back beneath the river's surface. Amane fell backwards and Evan grabbed her. George stood by the side of the boat looking at the zombie beneath the rippling water. He chucked the oar down onto the deck and threw the last of the rope off.

"What are you waiting for, let's move it!" he shouted at the Father who was looking on in amazement. The Father turned back to the wheel and slowly the boat drew away from the pier. George sat down, a mean, serious, look on his face. He scanned the riverbank looking for problems or solutions, whichever presented itself first. He knew that one would come soon enough, as sure as the sun would set.

"You okay, Amane?" Evan held her on the deck where they had fallen. She was shaking and glad he was holding her.

"Yeah," she said holding onto Evan's arms. She felt reassured he was there.

"I wasn't paying attention. I thought we were safe, you know? Stupid really."

"It's not your fault. We all have to be more careful. I should've checked properly first." Evan stood up and brushed himself down. The boat was chugging down the centre of the river now, away from the pier. The zombies were at the burnt out cars, trying to climb over, through and under, any way they could. A few struggled through, but the obstacle was proving difficult and they couldn't keep up with the boat as it headed toward the city.

Amane stood letting the sun dry her and standing close to Evan, spoke in a hushed voice so that only he could hear her.

"I'm worried about George. I've never seen him like this. I mean, it's great that he can handle himself but it's like he's not bothered by it all now. Remember when we met him? I thought he was a bit of a mummy's boy. He's changing. When I told him about Joe, he just clammed up. We need to keep an eye on him."

"True," said Evan, "we owe it to Joe at least. I think in George's defence, he's getting stronger which is a good thing. Look, I'm going to watch Father Thomas. Firstly, to make sure he knows where he's going and isn't trying anything funny, but secondly, because I want to know how to steer a boat. I'd hoped that being on deck like this might bring back some memories of my father's boat but I've got nothing. Maybe I never learnt? I seem to remember dropping the kids off for the holidays, so maybe I didn't actually sail anywhere with them? I just can't remember. If anything happens to the Father, we need to be able to handle ourselves." Evan put his hand on Amane's shoulder, looking at the sunshine reflect off her pale skin.

"Can you talk to George? Keep him company. Don't try anything heavy; just get him to open up if you can. Try and bring a bit of normality back into his life, even if just for a few minutes?"

Amane nodded. As Evan left her, she felt an urge to kiss him but swallowed it down. He had a family to find; thoughts like that would only cause them both problems. She watched as Evan walked up to the Father and began talking to him. She wondered how he did it. She couldn't talk to him like that, not knowing what he had done to Lily; how he had pretended to take them in and kept them captive whilst he plotted their demise. Amane wondered if he really was a priest. Maybe he was an imposter? Perhaps he had killed the real priest and took his place, took his house, took everything and perverted it for his own evil ends. She walked over to George.

"How're you doing, mate?" He had his hands in his pockets and was watching the embankment closely. He just shrugged and ignored her. Amane sat down beside him on the warm wooden deck.

"George, thank you for helping me, if you hadn't..."

He turned, finally, to look at her.

"Then you'd be dead."

"Well, yeah. Are you okay about what happened back there?" Amane had to shield her eyes from the sun as she talked to him.

"Why wouldn't I be? I'm not stupid you know." George sat down beside Amane, apparently satisfied that nothing was going to jump out at them for the time being.

"Sometimes dad used to go away for work: Hong Kong, Singapore, places like that. When he went, he used to say to me, 'you're the man of the house now, son. Look after your mother and sister for me.' I didn't really get that until now. I didn't do a very good job either. Mum's dead. Lucy's dead. There's only me left." He idly kicked at a piece of frayed rope lying on the deck.

"Well, I think your dad would be proud of you, George. What happened to your mum and Lucy was out of your control. But you helped me, didn't you? You've got to think about the future, George. You can't help them now. But you can help me and Evan. And you can help yourself."

"Mmm." George picked up the frayed rope and looked around. He couldn't see much over the riverbank. Occasionally, a tall building would peek over, and he could see smoke, but that was all. In another time, this would have been a beautiful day to cruise down the river. Today, he felt as if someone had opened the gates from another world and unleashed hell. Today was the first day he was able to see things for what they were. Evan and Amane were nice but they couldn't help him. They couldn't protect him. Amane was right. He had to think about the future now.

"How did Lily die?" he asked. "She was pretty cool. I liked her."

Amane let out a huge sigh. "I don't really know, George, and I don't want to know. All I know is that *he* is responsible for it." She looked at the Father with hatred.

"Lily was my friend. I wish we could have protected her but...sometimes things don't go as you planned. We talked a lot. She asked about you. She thought maybe you were my son!"

George laughed. "No offence, but do I look like you?"

"Not very much," laughed Amane. "She missed her family as well you know. She was a bit like you I thought. I miss her."

George let the silence hang in the air for a minute, the water splashing by the boat and the sun beating down refreshing him. He found the heat invigorating.

"What happened to her family?" he asked.

"Well, she lost her mother. When all this started, her mum went out and just never came back." Amane didn't feel the need to give George all the details.

"And her dad too?" George threw the useless frayed rope into the river.

"Not quite. Her dad was a politician. He was, or is, in Canberra. She actually believed he might still be alive, even after all this. She said they built a bunker there. I don't know if it's true. Sounds plausible I suppose. What do you think?"

George mulled it over before answering. "I believe her. Why would she lie? It's a good idea. We've got a safe room back home and it's got enough food and water to last six months. If my dad thought of that for us, then imagine what they'd do at parliament."

Amane was glad George was talking, sounding more like his old self. She had to get him to focus on the future and not dwell on the past.

"She told me something else too; something that I haven't told anyone else." Amane lowered her voice, noting that Evan and the Father were still out of earshot over at the tiller. "Can you keep a secret, George?"

He nodded enthusiastically.

"Well, she told me that before we lost power, you know, all the mobile phones, and TV's and everything, that she had a phone call at home. Before we picked her up, her dad called her from Canberra. It was very brief and she couldn't hear well: too much background noise at both ends. She told me that her dad had said there was a plan. They had an idea how to deal with all the zombies. It was something about burning them. He'd said, 'From the centre we'll start a fire and burn them all out.' I'm not sure what that means exactly. She was confused too. Her dad got cut off and that was the last she heard from him. She didn't get to find out where he is or what was going on. The next day, we picked her up and that was that."

"Wow," said George. "I think we should definitely go to Canberra. Think about it, Amane, if there *is* a bunker there, then they'll be safe: Lily's dad and all the policemen. We can hide with them and when the zombies have gone, we'll come out and we can go back to normal again."

"I'll tell you what I told Lily, that *maybe*, we'll go there, but only after we've found Evan's kids. We're better off sticking together right now. If we start splitting up, we'll get nowhere. Once we get to Tasmania, we can regroup and work out a plan, okay? Right now, there's too many of them, and too few of us to get anywhere. Do you understand, George?" Amane put her arms around him.

"Yeah, I guess so." He stood up, shrugging off Amane's arm. "I'm going to keep watch. I'm okay. I just want to make sure the coast is clear. If you know what I mean."

"Okay, mate." Amane stood up and gave him a reassuring smile. "Shout if you see anything or need anything, yeah?"

George didn't answer. He had plenty to think about and wanted to be on his own. Amane walked up to Evan who was steering the boat. Father Thomas was slumped down in the cabin, next to George's backpack, sheltering from the blistering sun, holding his arm.

"How's it going, sailor?" she said smiling at Evan, mock-saluting him.

"Not bad actually," he said, concentrating on the river's path ahead. "He showed me how to work the engine, how to steer. I think I've got the hang of it. It might be a bit early to put me behind the wheel of an ocean liner though."

They slipped under a low bridge, the shadow cooling them instantly, before sending them back on their way into the heat of the day.

"How's Father Thomas doing?" Amane stood beside Evan, watching how he handled the wheel.

"Don't ask. Physically, he's banged up, but he'll live. Mentally..?" Evan shook his head. "He's on a different planet. I had to make him go inside, he was doing my head in. He kept telling me how the kingdom of heaven was lost to mankind. He said we are being punished for our sins so the angels won't let us into heaven anymore. That's why when we die we're still walking the Earth, *apparently*. I think he was trying to inspire awe in me. Put the fear of God into me. All he inspired was the desire to throw him overboard."

"So what's the plan now? We can't take him with us. Well we could, but we're not going to, right?" Amane looked up at Evan earnestly.

"You're right, we're not. But can you just leave him here? Could you really throw him into the lion's den? I was full of big plans about how I was going to kill him, but now? If we do, we're stooping to his level. We can't take him to the police: there aren't any. I say, when we reach the city, we find a bigger and better boat that will get you, George, and me, to Tasmania. We'll leave him there and he can fend for himself, do whatever he likes."

"I suppose." Amane leant her head against Evan's strong shoulders. "How long do you think 'til we reach the city?"

"At this speed, about an hour. There are plenty of marina's where, if there are any left, we should be able to find a boat. He says the owners sometimes leave keys in the harbour master's hut. Keep your finger's crossed is all I can say."

Evan paused, feeling Amane's head on his shoulder. It felt normal. It was the first time since he had woken up at the airport that anything had felt remotely normal. In that moment, he was eternally pleased he had met her; doing this alone would be horrific. With her at his side, he felt stronger, more courageous and purposeful. He could talk to her as if he'd known her his whole life. It was difficult to grieve for his wife. However, the many years they had spent together were all condensed into the briefest of memories.

Time passed slowly as they wound their way down the river. The embankment began to flatten out and they chugged through more and more built-up areas. They could see more buildings and roads now. The bridges overhead grew bigger and were full of dead traffic and dead drivers. The odd zombie appeared at the sides of the bridges and stared at them, but could not threaten them from so far away. The boat glided past tantalisingly out of reach.

Finally, nearing the city, Evan spied a marina and the masts of yachts. As they drew closer, he saw that there were indeed some boats still around. The harbour itself appeared deserted, but beyond it, the streets were, as usual, clogged with cars and dead bodies, some animated, some not. Buildings burnt alongside perfectly preserved shops and blood-splattered high-rises. He slowed the boat down and turned off the engine so they could drift a little closer without making any noise.

"What do you think?" asked Amane. George was putting their only backpack on, whilst the incongruous Father staggered to his feet to look at the city.

"I think I don't know what the hell we are doing," said Evan. "Look for the harbour masters hut if you can. I'd say our best bet is if only one of us goes ashore. We grab as many keys as possible and try the yachts until we get lucky. If we don't, then we carry on. If we do, then we go now. No point hanging around."

They scanned the harbour looking at the boats standing tall and proud. Sails flapped briskly in the wind and the whole city seemed remarkably quiet. They sailed closer, keeping a keen eye out for danger. Twenty feet from the dock, Evan saw a hut.

"That it?" he said to the Father pointing it out.

"Yep. Come on, let's hurry, I'm sick of being cooped up on this shitty thing," said Father Thomas nursing his arm.

"You're not going anywhere. Amane and George are going to wait here with you while I go find what we need," said Evan.

Amane stood behind George who picked up the oar and pointed it at the Father.

"Sit down," said George. Father Thomas knew better than to argue and sat down obediently. The boat came up beside the pier and Evan threw the rope over the mooring, tying it up tight.

"I don't know how long I'm going to be," Evan said to Amane. "Just keep watch and stay with George okay? Any trouble from the Father here and don't even hesitate. If anyone or anything else comes down this pier other than me, cast off and leave."

"We're not going anywhere without you, Evan. Just take care." Amane gave him a hug.

"Look after her while I'm gone, eh, George?" said Evan, clambering onto the pier. George just nodded back at him, stony-faced. Evan bent low and headed off down the pier toward the city. It looked quiet but they had been caught out like that before. He skirted low past a couple of ships. The decks were awash with blood. He didn't pause to look any further but kept on jogging to the hut where he hoped they would find keys to a bigger boat with a more powerful engine, one that could cope with an ocean rather than a river. Truth was, he had no idea what he would find. He just hoped it didn't have teeth.

CHAPTER TWELVE

"Quite the happy family isn't it?" said Father Thomas from his seat in the cabin. Amane looked up at him but said nothing. She was too tired to argue. She could tell he was stirring. George said nothing and stood steadfast, swamped by scorching sunshine, the oar gripped in both hands. The backpack stuck to his sweaty back and he could feel beads of sweat dripping down his armpits.

"Do you know, George, I was going to help you: you and your mother. Honestly. If you'd followed in my footsteps you could have led a great life, one of devout worship to the Almighty, of purity and peace: of sacrifice. I had plans you know. Once your eyes are opened to Him, they cannot be closed. What you see around you, George, is the effect of the opposite of that. These zombies, these 'people,' were not believers. They are suffering now for their sins.

"Once all have been judged, the dead will be consumed in a lake of fire and sulphur. That day is coming my child. I heard what you and Amane talked about, the burning fire. If mankind starts it, it will take on a holy quest and burn the Earth. Cleanse it, and wipe it clean forever. That day will be joyous. The only place for redemption will be in Jerusalem. We must build a wall around it, fortify it. It is the most sacred place on Earth and it can be our Eden again. Only the pure, who show faith to God, may enter the city of salvation.

"George, it is not too late. You can still join me on my quest. Do not be fooled by these sinners. Evan and Amane will leave you to rot, given the chance."

"All right, that's enough," said Amane. George hadn't moved a muscle, but Amane was agitated. She walked over to the Father.

"Who do you think you are? You're nothing. You're lucky Evan is such a nice guy or you'd have been left to burn back there."

"Evan? A 'nice guy?' Who are you kidding?" Father Thomas got to his feet. "It is people like him who have lost us this bountiful paradise that the Lord gave us, and turned it into a Godless world where whores are celebrated and men of the cloth are pariahs. I am but a lamb in His service, but Evan...George, did I tell you how your mother died?"

George stepped closer to the Father. "I assumed Nathaniel shot her? What does it matter now, anyway? She's dead," he said.

"Well, Nathaniel certainly did try to shoot her, but he never was a very good shot. You see, George, I tried to save your mother. Evan left her you see. Before we found you, I saw what he did. Your poor mother was left behind on purpose, surrounded by zombies, whilst he ran like a coward. She was alive when we found her, but I'm afraid it was too late."

"What do you mean?" George was puzzled.

"Shut up, you hear me, just shut up," said Amane. Father Thomas ignored her and went on.

"She was infected, son. She was dying, probably bitten by one of those creatures whilst she lay there, unprotected, and unable to defend herself. Probably while Evan was relaxing with a nice glass of wine in my house I would say." He flashed Amane a sinister smile and went on.

"Shut up or I swear...," said Amane. The Father ignored her.

"I had to put her out of her misery. I hacked her head off. Took a bit of effort, I tell you. She didn't stop kicking the whole time. When I was through, she *still* wouldn't die. It's quite impressive if you think about it. She's still there now, back at the vicarage. I chopped her head off but it's still there, biting away at nothing, trapped in hell forever." The Father sniggered callously as George digested the information.

"I think she was trying to speak too. I swear she kept saying, 'no,' when I was sawing away at her face. Weird eh?"

Amane shook her head. "It's not true, George, don't listen to him." George looked up at her with glistening eyes. "Ignore him, George, he's crazy. These are the ramblings of an insane man."

"I think you know perfectly well what is true, George," said the Father. "I think the fresh ones, the ones who have only just died; somehow they retain some of their bodily functions. Don't ask me how it works. I'm a preacher not a doctor. If you want to see your mother again, you can. Just come back with me and I'll show you her rotting corpse.

"Do you know what I did to Lily before she died, Amane? I had a great time I have to say. I fucked the *shit* out of her." He laughed. His booming laugh echoed across the water.

"Amen to that. Ha!"

George let out a scream and swung the oar, which was just what the Father had been waiting for. He ducked and the oar hit Amane in the chest, sending her reeling backwards. Father Thomas grabbed the oar from George's hand and charged at Amane. He pushed the oar like a battering ram toward her and she skidded backward over the side of the boat, splashing into the cold water.

"No!" cried George. The Father spun round and held the oar menacingly above George, ready to strike.

"Hold it right there, son." Father Thomas' eyes were wild but he spoke with clarity.

"I was going to offer you a last chance to come with me but do you know what? You're stupid. Just like your fucking mother. It must be in the genes. Now get off my fucking boat."

George was so shocked he didn't know what to do. He could hear Amane splashing and spluttering over in the water. The Father drew the oar back.

"Now! Or I'll take your fucking head off like I did your cunt of a mother."

George jumped up onto the pier as Amane pulled herself up the ladder from the freezing cold water to join him, dripping wet. She was coughing and retching from the seawater she had swallowed. George knelt down beside her, his hands clasped in front of him as if in prayer.

"I'm sorry, Amane. I'm sorry."

The boat roared into life and George saw Father Thomas untie the mooring. The small boat slipped away from the pier as the Father took it back in the direction they had come from. The engine stopped suddenly and George's hopes were raised. Maybe he would come back for them? He wouldn't just leave them here would he?

Father Thomas disappeared into the cabin and moments later came out with what looked like a gun. He smiled and raised it into the air like a starting pistol.

"I found this when we got on board," he shouted. "Sorry, forgot to mention it. Oh well. Good luck." The Father laughed and fired the flare gun twice, red beacons sparkling in the sky above George and Amane. There was no doubt that they would be seen for miles around. Then Father Thomas restarted the little boat, pulling away and abandoning them as they had intended to do to him. He didn't look back.

"Amane, I'm sorry. Are you okay?" She lay on her back, panting.

"Yeah, I'm okay," she said sitting up, grimacing with pain and rubbing her chest where the oar had struck her. "It's not your fault, George. Shit, I should have seen what he was doing. We shouldn't have listened to him."

She spat a mouthful of salty saliva onto the deck, shivered, and swept her wet hair behind her ears.

"We're going to have to find Evan and get out of here. That bastard. It wasn't enough to take the boat. He had to ring the fucking dinner bell as well."

Amane stood up. Already in the distance, she saw movement: two, three, four zombies, shuffling in their direction. Behind them, she saw shadows, as more would surely follow.

* * * *

Evan had made it to the hut untroubled. The door was unlocked and he ventured inside. The small office was a mess. It looked as if it had been ransacked. There were papers everywhere and the key rack on the wall was empty. He began rifling through the papers on the floor, sifting through rubbish, desperately hoping to find something useful. Casting aside coffee cups and binders, he came across a set of keys. There was a rubber duck attached to the key ring and a plain piece of paper attached that read 'Johanna.' He rummaged around further but found no more keys.

"God, please let me find this boat." Evan pulled the door aside to head back to the others when he heard a knock on the other side of the office. He held his breath and froze. Again, he heard a knocking sound coming from outside and he held the door steady to stop it from creaking. Crouched down on the floor he glanced up at the small window. Silhouetted against the blue sky was a zombie. A bald man shuffled past the office, knocking against the walls. It paused by the open door and Evan looked it up and down. The man had little apparent physical injuries. He wore a suit and shoes and Evan wondered for a moment if he was wrong. What if this man just needed help? Evan kept perfectly still as the figure continued on its wayward journey. He noticed the bullet holes in the man's back and thanked God he had not offered to help him. It would have been the last thing he'd done.

Waiting a few minutes for it to wander off, Evan put the keys in his pocket and sat patiently. Finally, he pulled the door open again and peered outside. He could not see where the man had gone to and the area seemed quiet. He heard a faint engine sound and hesitated. Surely, that wasn't Amane? The marina was safe. There was no reason for her to move the boat, was there? Evan crept back toward the pier and heard two gunshots. Red flares rocketed up into the sky.

"Fuck me, what now?" he said to himself. Evan stood up and jogged past a listing yacht to where he could see where they had moored up. The boat was leaving and there were two lone figures on the pier.

"Amane? George!" he called out. The flares had attracted enough attention that there was no need to be creeping around now. Amane and George ran toward him. He felt a hand on his shoulder and whirled round to find the bullet-riddled bald man about to strike. Evan tripped backward and pushed the man away. The bald man kept coming and this time there was no weapon Evan could use but his own fists. He punched the bald zombie repeatedly, raining blows down on its head until it was forced into submission. Unable to see clearly, the zombie lurched around unsteadily and Evan, seizing his chance, barrelled into it, shoving it over the edge of the pier into the water.

"Evan, did you find a key?" Amane and George caught up with him as the zombie fell, leaving Evan breathing heavily but unhurt.

"Yeah, but no boat yet. What happened?" He was bent double, getting his breath back. He had to be more alert; he had been an inch away from being killed.

"Father Thomas happened. He jumped us. Sorry," said George. "Shit, we have to go now. Look!" They looked at the approaching zombies. From all directions they came, walking and running out of the shadows and the buildings, monsters of all shapes and sizes: hollow soul-less creatures, all brought by the flares.

"We're going to have to find the boat later. We stay out here shopping, we're sitting ducks. Over there, into the precinct. Let's go," said Evan.

Evan pointed at a small shopping precinct. They ran, beating the zombies to it. The doors were stuck open and Evan could not pull them closed. Inside smelt like death. Bodies littered the tiled floor, clothes and glass lying between them where the shops had been looted. The first of many zombies appeared at the doorway behind them.

"Upstairs, look for another exit!" They ran up a motionless escalator, jumping over the prostrate body of a half-eaten security guard lying in the middle. At the top, Amane scanned the upper floor for an exit.

"I don't see anything, Evan!" she said, frustrated. "George, come on." He was tugging at something by the security guard's feet. More zombies piled in through the doorway, and seeing George, began the approach up the escalator. George pulled the baton free and ran upstairs.

"Help! Wait!" Suddenly a woman came running to them, appearing from out of a café. She instantly rushed straight up to Evan.

"Oh God, you don't know how glad I am to find someone else alive!" She held on to Evan a little too long making him feel uncomfortable. Amane sized her up, young, slim, blonde and wearing very little other than some sneakers, a pair of white skimpy shorts and an eye-catchingly revealing vest.

"Get back here! Bloody idiot." A man appeared out of the café too.

"Hey," he said cautiously to Evan. "I'm Rob. This is..."

"...Sasha," finished the blonde, holding her hand out to Evan who shook it, not wanting to be rude. "We heard the gunshots and thought we'd better see what was going on. We've been stuck here and..."

"Rob, Sasha, pleased to meet you and all that stuff, but we can't stick around. Time for talk is later." Evan pointed to the escalator and the advancing zombies.

Rob muttered a cluster of swear words under his breath. He was thick-set and muscly. He also looked like he had walked straight out of a gym: shorts, tight, black top. Shame about the thinning thatch on top thought Amane.

"I'm not going back in there," said Sasha, looking at the café.

"No offence, both of you, but we're leaving right now. There's no time to discuss this. Come with us or stay, up to you. Amane, George, move it."

Evan jogged around the top of the shopping precinct and paused, looking down at the amassing horde below. They were streaming in now. It was as if half the city had seen the flares. Weaker zombies were crushed as ones that are more agile pushed past them to get upstairs. The noise increased dramatically in the small building as hundreds of wailing, moaning zombies filed in, their requiem echoing around the vaulted ceilings of the building.

Amane was shivering, partly through fear, partly through cold. Evan saw her clothes were still wet from her ocean plunge earlier, and inside where the sun couldn't reach, it was cool. Reaching through a smashed shop façade, he grabbed a jumper from a mannequin and handed it to her.

"Put it on. That'll have to do for now." Evan picked up a plastic leg from a broken mannequin and gripped it firmly. Better than nothing, he thought. Amane pulled the woolly cardigan on. It was three sizes too big for her, but was at least dry.

"We're going to get out of here, okay?" Evan spotted a sign for the car park and they followed him down the bare tiled corridor, past a ticket machine to a set of double doors. Sasha and Rob followed close behind, evidently agreeing that their temporary home was no longer safe.

The doors swung open into a multi-storey car park. No sooner had they run through than they heard the doors swing open again and zombies began spewing through. George ran up a ramp to the next floor.

"It's harder for them to go up than down," he shouted.

They all followed him. There were no vehicles in the car-park. Evan kept looking about but he couldn't see a single one. Just their luck, he thought. He could hear Rob muttering something but ignored him. Evan didn't care if those two were married, strangers, half dead or half alive; he couldn't keep babysitting people. After what had happened to Lily, he didn't want to anymore. They ran up another floor to the roof, listening to the zombies beneath them.

"What now?" said Amane, out of breath. With the exertion of running in heavy, soggy clothes and where the oar had hit her earlier, her chest felt as if it was on fire. Up on the roof, the sun was beating down again. It was mid-afternoon but she felt as if they had been running for hours.

"We keep going," said Evan. "Those things are not going to stop and neither are we." He took her hand.

"Thanks for ruining our hiding place, mate. We were doing fine back there." Rob was looking around, working out where he could go now to hide.

"No we weren't, you idiot," said Sasha. "We'd barricaded ourselves in and were living off stale bread. It was smelly, dirty, and horrible."

Her explanation was directed at everyone, but she only looked at Evan when she spoke. She even shed a few tears. It was obvious to Amane that Sasha was looking for a new hero. Rob clearly didn't size up. Ignoring them, Evan asked George if he was all right.

"Look over there." George used the baton to point to the edge of the car park. There was a door leading to an overhead walkway. A glass funnel crisscrossed by girders and metal, leading to the next building. It was some sort of office building Evan guessed. There were grey blinds and computer terminals in the windows.

Evan pulled Amane by the hand and they jogged over to the edge of the roof. They could see that the glass walkway was empty inside. In the mid-section stray bullets had hit the glass and shattered the central panes. They were intact but cracked. They would have to step very carefully over the metal girders holding it together.

The street below looked like a war zone. Evan counted at least six army trucks and one tank. There were a few soldiers shuffling about, obviously dead. Whatever dead means now, he thought. There were more people piled up against the vehicles who looked as though they may have been shot, executed even. Several zombies were hitting the brick wall of the car park, looking up. Fingernails broke off as they clawed at the walls. They knew someone alive was up there but had no way up.

Evan opened the door and they all went through onto the glass walkway. It was unnerving. Down below them the zombies stared up, following their every movement. Should the glass break, if the fall did not kill them, the zombies undoubtedly would. Amane focused on Evan's back and took it one step at a time whilst George trotted behind. He was not unduly worried. In fact, he seemed to be relishing a newfound sense of freedom. As Evan and Amane made it to the far end of the walkway safely, George looked behind at Rob reaching to take Sasha's hand. She brushed him away.

"I don't need your help, Rob."

"'Course you don't," he said sarcastically, as he crossed safely to the end of the glass walkway. Sasha tiptoed across and stood on the middle pane.

"It's not that hard," she said. "See?"

The glass shattered beneath her and she fell down, hands clutching at thin air. She shrieked in terror and reached out for something to grab onto, trying to stop her fall. She managed to grab onto a metal pole in the flooring and she swung back and forth over the zombies below like a fish on a line.

Evan raced to help her whilst Amane held George back from doing the same. Rob stood still, watching in morbid fascination.

Sasha was crying tears of terror as Evan pulled her up and dragged her back into the safety of the glass cage. Her hands were cut from broken glass and Evan carefully picked out the larger pieces that he could. He helped her back to the end of the corridor where Amane took over, brushing away shards of glass.

"Should've stayed where we were," said Rob dryly, offering no help at all.

Evan squared up to him. "Yeah, maybe *you* should."

"Whatever. You gonna start on me, prick?" said Rob, flexing his muscles, edging closer to Evan.

"No, he's not," said Amane. "Right now is not the time, boys." George looked on bemused. Amane picked up the weeping Sasha. The crowd below them was growing bigger, as was the crowd of zombies watching from on the roof where they had come from.

Evan stepped back and rubbed his face with his hands.

"I don't know what we're going to find in there," he said. "Hopefully nothing, but..."

"We're behind you, Evan. Whatever we find in there we face it together," said Amane. Evan looked back through the glass and saw the zombies on the roof. No going back. Evan pushed open the door and they entered a dark stairwell.

"What do you say we go down now, mate?" asked Evan to George who merely nodded in agreement. The stairwell was lit by emergency lights. Fluorescent wall lights brightened the grey steps. Evan went first, walking softly, listening for any noises that might suggest they weren't alone. At the next floor down, they ignored the sign inviting them to come in for a check-up with a friendly dentist, and carried on down to the ground floor. Evan stepped out into the foyer of the office complex. Tall plastic green plants brushed against him as he walked out onto the marbled floor. There was a desk to his left, another door, and a revolving glass door to his right that led to the street. He tried the other door but it was locked. Not wanting to risk going back outside, Evan led them to the desk and they all crouched down behind it. They sat on the floor pondering their next move.

Evan could sense Amane's discomfort. Her body was cold and stiff, and her clammy hand was clutching his tightly. Sasha was still weeping, holding her bloodied hands out in front of her; they needed looking at. Rob and George were quiet and composed respectively. For a young child, Evan thought, George had a remarkably cool head on his shoulders. Evan spoke quietly.

"Guys, I don't think we should keep running. If we run, we're just going to go further into the city and end up in a dead end eventually. We need to eat and drink. We haven't got the energy for this. My head is splitting and I'm guessing yours is the same. We need to get Sasha's hands seen to."

They didn't answer. He was right. They were tired, fed up and scared.

"Amane, we need to get you some dry clothes or you're going to get sick."

"Sorry, Evan, my credit card's maxed out." Evan smiled and put his arm around her shivering shoulders.

"We can't stay in here, it's far too dangerous. Who knows what's up there. It's much too risky to try and bolt ourselves in here. There are too many doors and hiding places. There are a few zombies outside but not many; they haven't figured out where we are yet. They're spread out and we can dodge them if we're fast. I noticed there's a tall building over the road where they're building some apartments or flats or something."

"It's true," said Sasha, sniffing, "Luxury flats for the rich and famous. My boss was going to buy one. They're not finished though."

"What, that building site? It's just a shell, Evan, I saw the cranes and scaffolding from the roof of the car park. What's the point of going there?" said Amane, wondering where this was going.

"That's exactly why we're going there; *because* it's not finished. I would say that building is empty. If we're unlucky, there may be a couple of workmen? There should be a showroom or at least an office we can rest up in. I'd say the building is likely to be deserted. The foyer looked smart and there was a small shop in the front. We can get supplies and hold up there. It'll be dark soon and with any luck the zombies will piss off when they can't find us."

It made a strange sort of sense to Amane, although she had no idea how they would get there.

"Only one problem," Rob said. "The moment we step out those doors, we're going to attract hundreds of those things."

"He's right," said Amane, "They aren't going to let us go. I don't know what sort of chance we have to be honest."

"Losing hope is easy," said George. Amane was taken aback by the statement. It sounded precocious coming from someone so young.

"I heard it somewhere," he said, answering an unasked question. "You'll get in fine. I saw it too, Evan. The doors are open. As long as you can get them shut and locked behind you, it's a good idea."

"Er thanks, George, but, when you say '*you'll* get in fine,' you mean 'we'," said Evan, looking at the boy. "All right?"

A sick feeling was rising in Evan's stomach and it was not from lack of food. George took the sweat-drenched backpack off and gave it to Evan.

"I'm not coming with you," he said, and cradled the baton in his hands.

CHAPTER THIRTEEN

"George, don't be stupid," said Amane.

"Me, be stupid? How many times have I saved your life today, Amane?" George stared at her. There was no malice, but his penetrating gaze disconcerted her.

"You can't protect me. Father Thomas was insane, I'll agree with you, but he was right about one thing. I'm better off on my own. I'm going to Canberra." Amane closed her eyes and regretted ever mentioning it.

Evan was dumbfounded. Rob and Sasha listened, interested in this dysfunctional family that they had come across and how a ten-year old boy could be so brave.

"George, what are you talking about?" Evan shuffled around to face George. "Why would you go there? You're far too young to be out there on your own. This is a difficult time for all of us, mate, but if we stick together..."

"Evan, do you know how my mother died? Lily? I know you mean well but...this is impossible. I've been thinking about it for a while. I'm younger and fitter than you and I can run fast. I can squeeze into smaller spaces. I can hide in smaller places. I am determined and I *will* make it." Such was the confidence in this little man's voice, that neither of them actually doubted him.

"When you get into that building, try and rest. Eat, sleep, whatever. If I were you, I'd wait 'til the morning before you go looking for that boat you've got the keys for. There's far too much activity going on out there now. Even if the street clears, there are hundreds of them around the harbour. You try to find that boat now and you're dead meat." George let out a long sigh. "I hope you find your children, Evan."

"Thanks, George, but I still think you should stick with us. I know I've let you down. I let Lily down. But Canberra? That's a long way to run, Georgie." said Evan.

"Don't call me Georgie! I'm not a kid anymore. And I *know* how far Canberra is. Amane can tell you why I'm going there. I know you think I'm just a little kid and maybe a few days ago I was. I've seen a lot in the last few days and I'll be *fucked* if I'm going to waste any more time running." George stood up holding the baton in his hand.

"George, sit down, this is madness!" said Amane.

Evan sighed, stood up, and held out his hand to George. "There's no stopping you is there? I suppose if I tied you up you'd still sneak out when my back was turned and run away, wouldn't you."

"Yep." George shook Evan's hand.

"Promise me, George, when you get there, you'll wait for us. Wherever it is you're going, whatever you find in Canberra, wait. We'll come for you, I swear."

George nodded. He didn't smile; he just kept looking back at Evan. He had such a serious face for one so young.

"Here's what's going to happen." George looked at Amane to make sure she was listening. "We're going to run out of these doors all together. You four run into the building opposite and shut those doors after you. Make sure they're secure coz I don't know how long I can draw them away. I'm going to run down the street and I'll be yelling and shouting. That should draw most of the zombies away from you. At least it'll give you enough time to get in and block the doors."

Evan looked at them all. Rob and Sasha seemed prepared to go along with them for now. He looked at Amane who shrugged her shoulders and nodded. Annoyingly, George had a good plan.

"Where will you go?"

"I've been to the city a lot, Evan. I know all the little alleys and back streets. I'll dodge, duck, hide, and run. The long and short of it is; I'll be fine."

Amane stood up and hugged George. He swallowed the lump in his throat, ignoring the guilty feeling that was enveloping him. He almost felt as if he was abandoning them.

"Well, no time like the present. Good luck." George let go of Evan's hand and ran to the revolving door.

"Last one out is a loser!"

He smiled and waved, then disappeared outside. Evan picked up the backpack and he and Amane sprinted after him, Rob and Sasha right behind, through the revolving doors. Evan swung the mannequin's leg at a small dead child that was running toward them, landing a powerful blow to its head. He cringed as the small girl went flying. Grabbing Amane's hand, they ran over to the building site, through the big front doors, past the hoarding offering unrivalled views of the ocean for just a small deposit, and shoved the doors shut when Rob and Sasha were in. Evan bolted the doors shut and dragged a heavy table in front of them. Rob pushed some tall plastic plants in front of the doors too, providing more cover and disguising the doors to the brain dead zombies. A tear rolled down Amane's cheek as she watched George flee down the street, evading clawing hands and biting teeth, turning the corner, and running out of sight.

* * * *

A lone zombie repeatedly stumbled into the glass door to the building site like a dazed fly, whilst all the others followed George. Evan and Rob found a large sofa in the foyer and dragged it in front of the door. They were finally satisfied that they were secure and pretty much out of sight of the road. The door was invisible now to anyone who didn't already know it was there. Evan pulled Amane back from the window and took her down a corridor. The shop next door was enticing, with its fully stocked shelves of food, drink, and warm clothes. It was also impossibly out of reach. The only way in was from the outside. Another time, Evan thought.

"Come on," he said to Amane, taking her by the hand again. From the foyer, there had been two doors. One was locked and the other opened out into a long corridor. It was lined with grey doors. Holding the mannequin leg ready, he got Amane to push them open, ready to hit anything that moved. Sasha trailed at the back whilst Rob followed nonchalantly. He was not interested in helping and Evan knew it; he was only looking out for number one. Every door was the same though, opening out onto a completely plain bare room: concrete floor and plastered walls, no furniture of any sort. After the ninth door, Evan was becoming increasingly irritated.

"Fucking hell, there's got to be something."

"Hey, it's okay," said Amane through chattering teeth. Evan's sweat-stained, ripped jacket would offer no warmth to her and he vowed to carry on or she would get really ill.

"Hey, what's that?" said Sasha. There was a notice on the wall by some stairs. It read:

Showroom upstairs - Room 17.

Evan cautiously led the way up the stairs. The building sounded quiet and the zombies outside were fading into the distance. The first floor looked exactly the same as the ground. Evan reached room 17 and they followed the usual drill. Amane pushed the handle and Evan steadied himself, raising the model leg like a bat, as if he were stepping up to face a pitcher.

The door swung open and revealed a luxurious room with a king-size bed replete with sheets and duvet, a large television, dresser, wardrobe, table, chairs, double-lined curtains, bedside lamps and a thick chestnut carpet. Nothing had been spared in the effort to get indulgent city workers and the pin-stripes to part with their easy earned cash. They went in and closed the door behind them.

Evan walked over to the window, slung the backpack down, and looked out at the scene below. He could see the street where George had run down. He really had drawn most of the zombies away, but to where, and for how long, who knew. To the far left, Evan could see the marina and boats. Somewhere out there was the 'Johanna.' It was their only ticket out of the city.

Evan's hot sweaty forehead pressed against the cold windowpane whilst the others explored the room. For an instant, the cool glass absorbed the horror of their new lives. The sounds, the screams, all silenced: just a vague unsettling echo at the back of his head. The bloody gore, the killing, the dead faces staring at him were all blanked out by the cold that spread momentarily from his head to his toes and back again. His breathing was shallow and measured, his eyes closed, relaxed. With Evan's mind cleared, it was as if a new wave of energy had come over him. He stepped back from the window. His mind dealt with the situation and he knew he could carry on. He had to carry on, for Charlie and Anna's sake.

"I think we're safe here for a while," he said. "They won't get in. I think we should get some rest. I don't know about you two, but it's been a while since we slept properly." Behind Evan, the sun sank beneath the building and the last glints of sunlight disappeared. The room was engulfed in shadows.

"Amane, we'll make a move first thing in the morning. They don't seem quite as alert then, so we've more chance. George was right."

Rob tried a door in the corner of the room and walked through into an adjoining room. Evan heard Rob's overly loud laugh, forced more for effect than from genuine mirth.

"Same set up in here." Rob came back into the bedroom. "Well if it's okay with you guys, me and Sasha can take that room and you can take this one. Happy days." Rob beamed.

"Fine," said Evan, still leaning against the window, "but do me a favour will you? Shut your fucking mouth. What are 'happy days' for you, are fucking miserable for the rest of us. I've dealt with far worse than you, but no, I'm not spoiling for a fight or an argument. I'm tired. We just need some peace, okay?"

"Your funeral." Rob sniffed, turned and walked into the other room, slamming the door behind him.

"Sasha, I'm sorry," said Evan.

"It's okay, I understand. He's a complete dick but he has helped keep me alive for the last couple of days. I don't *really* know him. When it happened, we were at the gym and somehow we ended up in that café together. We were running around and found ourselves in the shopping centre so we just locked ourselves in and thought we would wait it out. That was two days ago.

"Why hasn't the government done something? Have you heard anything? I used to live by my blackberry, now I haven't spoken to my friends or family for days. I hope my boss is keeping my job open for me."

Evan smiled. Work was the least of this young woman's problems. "We've been out there and we've seen no help at all. There isn't any, just chaos and death. We're not the last people alive on the planet though, I'm fairly sure of that. We met a man, a priest; he told us it was the end of the world."

A heavy silence descended upon the room. Sasha took in what Evan was saying. Deep down she expected it. If there was any help, they would have seen or heard about it by now. She felt oddly hollow. Her parents were old and she had no brothers or sisters. She had no boyfriend, just occasional lovers. Evan seemed nice though.

"Will you be okay in there with him?" said Evan, breaking the gloom. "We can't offer you much, but tomorrow we intend to get a boat and get the hell off this island. We're headed to Tasmania. You can come with us if you like? Up to you though."

"Maybe. I was kind of hoping to find my parents but...well let's face it, they're probably dead. I don't know. Can I sleep on it?"

Evan nodded and Sasha gave him a peck on the cheek whilst Amane looked on amused.

"Just don't shoot off in the morning without me, okay?" said Sasha.

"Of course not," said Amane. "All right, let me look at your hands before you go, come on." They went into the bathroom together, chatting. Evan felt drained.

"I'm just going to make sure we're safe and secure. I'll pull that sofa in front of the door. Put your clothes over the handrails, Amane, let them dry out."

Evan dragged a purple two-seater sofa in front of the door and then the dresser. If anyone tried to get in, they would know about it. He was sure the building was empty but it still felt safer knowing the door was blocked.

He sat on the sofa and kicked off his shoes. His clothes stank of death. The room was surprisingly warm considering there was no heating. He stared out of the window at the sky. Thank God, they weren't on the ground floor. Up here, in this room, it felt as if they had escaped the real world. He could still hear the groaning of the dead below but they were faint. He wondered how Charlie and Anna were: if they would still be on the boat. He hoped his father was taking good care of them, if the same thing was happening there as with the rest of the world, then logical thinking suggested that Tom's boat was actually the safest place to be. His son had said it was dark though and they were trapped in the cabin. What if something had happened that had forced them to barricade themselves into the cabin below the deck? Evan reckoned there would be food and water for a few days but not much more. And Anna? If his daughter was not moving, that did not bode well. What if she was ill or had been bitten by one of those creatures. Evan needed to distract himself from the perilous dark thoughts entering his mind.

He walked over to the bed and tried the radio on the nightstand. He went through both AM and FM but got nothing but static. He flicked on the television but it was just static too on every channel.

"A hundred channels and there's still nothing on," he muttered to himself.

Amane came out of the bathroom, Sasha following.

"You gonna be okay?" said Evan, seeing Sasha's hands wrapped in a loose cloth.

"They hurt like hell and I might need help tying my shoelaces, but yeah, I'll be fine. They'll heal. Well I'd better go see what he's up to. I'll tell him about the boat and see what he thinks if that's all right by you?"

Evan nodded.

"I guess I can stand it for one more night. If you need anything just knock, I'm not far away! Thanks, Amane. Good night, Evan," she said, and disappeared into the adjoining room.

Amane sat down on the edge of the bed, taking off her shoes, relishing in the freedom her feet felt. She let out a satisfied sigh and massaged her aching feet.

"I hope George is all right," she said to Evan.

"Me too. You know I think he'll be okay. We underestimated him. He'll make it."

"And our new friends?"

"I have no idea. They seem okay. Well Sasha does. Rob could be trouble if you ask me. If he puts us in danger, I'll have to cut him loose. No one else is going to hold us back," said Evan, missing what Amane was really fishing for.

"You think the shower works?" he asked, hopefully, nodding to the bathroom.

"There's hot water in the tap so I guess so. I'm not sure which is more inviting: a hot shower or this bed," she said, looking at Evan.

"Go on, you first," he replied, "We don't know how long the hot water will last. You need to get warm and out of those damp clothes."

Amane practically ran to the bathroom, exclaiming her thanks as she did so. She stripped off her filthy sodden clothes she'd been wearing the last few days, hung them out on a towel rack to dry, and jumped into the shower. Bracing cold water hit her face first and she took a few mouthfuls, thirsty for the taste of clean water. Seconds later, beautiful hot water sprung out gushing over her body. She was in raptures. They hadn't washed in days.

"Feels amazing!" she called out. Evan smiled thinking about how good she must feel now.

* * * *

Sasha and Rob did much the same, taking it in turns to wash, but without the convivial atmosphere. She made it quite clear that just because they now had a bed, it was not for sharing. Rob had a choice of the floor or the bathtub. They chatted idly for a while whilst the sun set, but had little to say to each other; they'd spent the last forty-eight hours cooped up in the same room and had exhausted everything there was to talk about.

"I'm beat," said Sasha. "It's surprising how doing nothing can make you feel so tired."

"This whole end of the world shit is fucking boring if you ask me," said Rob from the floor. He had made himself a bed out of a couple of towels and the dressing gowns. "What do you make of them? Evan's got a big mouth. Who does he think he is, bossing me about?"

"Oh come on, he's all right," said Sasha. "He reminds me of someone I used to...well anyway, I think he's nice. Amane is too, you should talk to her tomorrow. If you stop acting like such a dickhead all the time, you might find you like her and maybe she'll like you." Sasha yawned and hunkered down under the bed covers.

"Hm, maybe. She did look quite trim. I think I saw her checking me out," he said lying down in the darkness.

Sasha rolled her eyes and rolled over. "I think I'm going to go with them tomorrow on that boat and get out of here. I can't see much point in hanging round. Did you see what it's like out there? I couldn't believe it. They've been on the streets the last few days. They said there is no police or army. It's all gone."

Rob just grunted. "Whatever. I'm going to get some shut eye. Try not to snore."

Sasha gave up trying to make a decent conversation and let herself fall asleep. Rob considered sneaking into bed with her, but decided it was too soon. If it was the end of the world, she wasn't going to get much attention and he'd be first in line. Rob fell soundly asleep quickly and slept well, undisturbed by anything.

* * * *

Amane finally came back into the room wrapped in a huge, clean towel.

"Evan, that is bliss. Go!" she said. Her slick, damp hair draped lushly around her bare shoulders.

"Scrub my back?" he said, as he walked past her to the bathroom, taking off his shirt.

"You wish," she shouted after him. Evan drank from the sink tap greedily. His throat was dry and rough. After gorging himself, he jumped into the hot shower and scrubbed himself clean. Amane opened the wardrobe and found two dressing gowns. She dropped the towel on the floor and slipped one on. The first clean thing she had put on for days.

"Did you try the radio? Is there any news?" she called out through the open door.

"I tried it, but nothing. Just dead air."

He instantly regretted saying it: 'dead.' It reminded him of the dead world they were now living in that, momentarily, he had forgotten. He cleaned his body as he cleansed his mind. He caught sight of himself in the reflection of the shower's glass partition. The bruising on his face had subsided. A few scratches and scars remained, but nothing permanent. A week ago, he had probably looked at himself in the mirror and thought nothing of it. Maybe he had kissed his wife and kids goodbye and joined the rat race to work with everyone else? One week later, he was in a strange city, in a strange room with a relative stranger. He knew his wife was dead, his children were lost, and the world was full of zombies. He barely knew himself. Evan dried himself off and put dark thoughts to one side. If he kept thinking like this, he would go insane.

He wrapped the white towel around his waist and went back into the bedroom to find Amane sitting on the bed.

"So, beans or beans," she asked, holding a tin in each hand.

"Don't suppose there was anything in the minibar? I could do with a cold beer right now."

"No such luck. Here." Amane held out a tin for him. "I did, however, find this in the bottom of the rucksack, lovingly wrapped in a protective blanket. I assume Joe packed this bag." She whipped out a bottle of vodka from behind her.

Evan grabbed two plastic cups from the sideboard, put on the second gown and then dropped his damp towel on the floor before sitting back down on the bed. Amane poured a generous helping in each.

"Cheers," said Evan holding his little white plastic cup out. "To lost friends." They kept eye contact whilst toasting. Amane coughed.

"To lost friends," she agreed.

"We should probably share," said Evan, staring at the vodka and food.

"Yeah, right," said Amane, topping up their cups. They both knew that, stale bread or not, this was their time.

They sat on the bed together and polished off a tin of beans each. When they'd finished, Amane lay back on the bed, threw the tin into the far corner and stifled a yawn. Evan lay back.

"What else did you find?" he asked.

"Not much I'm afraid: a torch, a blanket, this vodka and a packet of cigarettes. That about sums it up. There are two tins left. I hope you're looking forward to beans for breakfast."

Evan smiled but was worried.

"We need to find more food, Amane. In the morning, when we leave, we should try to grab something from that shop down there."

"Yeah. And more importantly, some coke to go with this vodka!"

Evan laughed and knocked back his cup, holding it out for Amane to top him up.

"You think Sasha will be all right in there?"

"Evan, stop worrying about everyone else. She'll be fine. She's fended off the big guy for the last few days, I'm sure she can cope tonight too."

"Look," said Evan, "you can take the bed tonight. I'll be fine on the floor with that blanket." He threw his tin into the corner too.

"I trust you, Evan," said Amane looking at him. "Let's not waste this opportunity for us both to get a good rest. This bed is big enough for the both of us. Can you even remember when you last had a good night's sleep?"

"No. I actually don't think I can move. This bed is *so* comfy." Evan bounced up and down a couple of times before settling back with his hands behind his head. He was secretly grateful he didn't have to spend the night on the floor as he suspected Rob was going to have to do.

There was silence. Both lost in their own thoughts, content enough not to feel as if they had to talk. They polished off their cups. Evan was grateful they even had it, it took the edge off. Amane broke the peace first.

"Those fucking zombies just don't stop do they? Day or night. They quieten down at night but you *know* they're still there. Jesus, I can't take much more of this. I hope we can find that boat tomorrow out there. I'm sick of running like this. I'm sick of this fucking island."

"They're still a bit like us, I guess. We don't give up do we? Doesn't matter how bad it gets or fucked up things look, we keep going. You've got to. I don't want to fight or run every day but there's no other choice right now. I think it's the same for them. There's no call-centres or MTV anymore. What else are they going to do?"

He paused, images of the dead people he'd despatched over the last couple of days whirring past his eyes: old, young, male and female.

"You realise we're headed to another island," he continued. "It's just a lot...smaller."

Amane smiled. "Amen to that. Smaller means fewer people. And that means fewer zombies unless the whole island's dead." Her attempt at a joke fell flat as she suddenly remembered that Charlie and Anna were on that smaller island they were talking about. She put her hand on his leg and looked up apologetically at him.

"I mean I'm sure your kids are all right though. Oh shit, Evan, sorry I didn't mean..."

"It's okay, don't worry. I try not to think about it, but it's virtually impossible not to really. I fear for Anna, what with Charlie saying she wasn't moving. But he's old enough to have his wits about him; he'll take care of her. And they're with my father, right? The more I think about the last time I heard Charlie's voice though...

"I keep picturing them stuck on the boat, locked away down there in the cabin. What if they'd cast off and something happened to my dad? Maybe that's why they're trapped."

Evan sighed deeply and stared at the blank television screen opposite the bed.

"It's just so..."

Amane squeezed his leg tenderly. She poured out another cupful of vodka each. Evan guzzled it down.

"We'll find them safe and sound. We will." She thought how she could take his mind off them. Otherwise, they'd go mental bouncing around negativity in this room.

"Look, I know you want to get to Charlie and Anna as soon as possible, but I'm kind of glad we found this room, you know? Even if it's only for a few hours, I need a break from this shit. We're close, Evan."

"It's going to be difficult tomorrow," he said. "It's probably going to be hard getting out to the marina unless George is leading those zombies a merry dance all the way to Canberra. Then we have to find the boat. We have a long trip ahead of us too. I only know a little about sailing from what Father Thomas taught me, not much. I hope I can figure it out." He swallowed the last of his vodka. "You're right, we need this break. I'm shattered." Evan yawned loudly.

They lay together for some time as the sky outside turned jet-black, the room darkening with each passing minute. Amane curled up and yawned once more, longer this time, as the moon rose.

"Thish vodka is fucking great," laughed Amane. Was she slurring or was it Evan's imagination?

"Cheers to that," said Evan, not sure now if he was slurring too. Amane poured out the last of the vodka. Between them, they had managed to polish off a whole bottle on a stomach of cold beans.

Before long, Amane fell asleep, too tired even to get under the covers. Evan found sleep harder to come by, his mind racing a million miles an hour. His mouth was dry and his arm around Amane had pins and needles. He extricated himself without waking her and went to the bathroom where he gulped down more cold water from the tap. It was chilly as he slipped back into the bedroom quietly. A luminous moon had risen and was casting a faint light into the room through a crack in the curtains. As he lay back down on the bed, Amane stirred.

"You okay?" she murmured.

"Sorry," he whispered, "didn't mean to wake you. You warm enough?"

She rolled over to him as he lay down beside her, her gown casually falling open exposing her flesh. Goosebumps scattered down her arms. She moaned and her arm draped across his stomach. He took her hand and squeezed it reassuringly. The vodka still hadn't worn off and he felt a little woozy. Amane fumbled for the opening of his gown and felt her way inside to his warm body. She moaned again and slowly rubbed his stomach. Her hand stroked his skin and began to move downward.

Evan rolled over so his face was only an inch away from hers. He could feel her warm breath and make out her outline from the glow of the moon. He felt inside her gown and ran his hand down the length of her back. She giggled and he brought his hand across her waist up to her firm breasts. Her hand inside his gown had found what she wanted and was toying with him, gently caressing him as he grew harder. She pulled him closer. Subconsciously, they wanted an escape from the life they had come to know, and hate, side by side, these last few days.

Evan tenderly stroked her breasts as he kissed her passionately, and Amane, already halfway out of her gown, slipped it off, exposing her whole body to him. Evan looked down at her slender body and long slim legs. She slid over on top of him and pushed his gown back so she could see the full length of his body. She tenderly kissed his neck and chest, taking her time as she slowly wound her way down his taut body. She found his burgeoning erection and eagerly enveloped it with her warm mouth. Evan's heart beat faster as she moved up and down his length, steadily increasing speed. Releasing him, she sat astride his thighs, grasping his throbbing penis in her hand and Evan looked at her beautiful face smiling back at him.

She whispered something quietly, in Japanese. Her breasts moved up and down gently in the moonlight as she breathed heavily, and their eyes locked together. She guided his hardness into her, gasping when he penetrated her. Her hips rose as he held her waist firmly and he slid in as smooth as silk. They revelled in each other.

Evan grabbed her hands and their fingers entwined. He sat up, nuzzling her neck, her perfect breasts, fondling her pointed nipples, his tongue tasting her soft skin as he rhythmically glided in and out of her. Tenderly he withdrew, and instinctively, she turned over, clambering onto the bed and lay herself before him. With Evan kneeling between her legs, Amane eagerly spread herself further apart for him. He grabbed her small waist, drawing her closer and his erection briefly teased her, hesitating momentarily, before she reached down to guide him in, encouraging him to enter her. Unable to contain himself any longer, he thrust long and hard inside her. She cried out his name as his substantial penis reached deep inside her. She moaned and whimpered in pleasure as he repeatedly slid himself in and out of her. His hands grabbed her hips roughly so he could control his measured, powerful thrusts.

Evan became more insistent, urgently slamming himself into Amane, over and over, faster and faster. She encouraged his wild lunges and finally she came. Arching her back, she climaxed, crying out his name. Her knees quivered and her body shuddered in ecstasy as her orgasm washed over her, overwhelming her. Her body trembled and her cries echoed around the room until, unable to control himself anymore, he thrust into her with one final surge and Evan came, deep inside her. Amane felt Evan's huge erection stay long inside her until slowly, it began to ebb away.

He carefully slid out of her and they collapsed onto the bed panting. As they lay side by side, Amane reached for Evan and pulled him closer. She traced her finger over his lips and kissed him ardently.

Evan saw her heavily flushed chest rising and falling. His eyelids felt heavy now as the two exhausted lovers lay side by side. Before they slept, Amane lifted the duvet and they got into the bed, burying them both in the clean cotton sheets. It was not long before sleep took them both. This time Evan slept a long time, his sleep untarnished by the disturbing dreams that had wracked him so recently.

CHAPTER FOURTEEN

Evan woke and instantly new Amane wasn't next to him. It was dawn and the sunlight was cascading gently around the room. Evan got out of bed, and pulling on his dirty clothes from yesterday, pulled back a curtain, peering out of the window. The sun was barely over the horizon. The sky was filled with billowing, ominous dark clouds. Down on the street below, nothing was moving. There were no birds twittering, not even a wind rustling through the trees. Crucially, he could see no zombies, not one. Amane came out of the bathroom.

"Shame we don't have any clean clothes to put on, eh?" She sat on the bed and put on her shoes. "There's no hot water either I'm afraid. We must have used what little was left in the tank last night."

Evan rubbed his sleepy eyes and prepared himself for a cold shower. "Have you looked outside? It's deserted. We should be able get to the harbour and find the 'Johanna' easier than I thought." He was going to see his children later today if things went as planned. He had to concentrate on his objective and think logically.

"Yeah. I hate to be the harbinger of doom but it almost looks too good to be true," replied Amane. She pulled open the last tin of food they had and began eating.

"I'll get showered and wake myself up. You can wake the neighbours up if you're ready?" said Evan trudging off to the bathroom. He was so used to looking out for the group that it felt strange now, just the two of them. He had almost forgotten about

Sasha and Rob. The cold water invigorated him and he washed away the cobwebs. Today was the day. He just knew he was going to meet his kids again soon. There was just the small matter of finding a boat and navigating it to Tasmania, easy.

He towelled dry and put his clothes back on. They were starchy and smelly but there was nothing he could do about it. This was the new reality.

Back in the bedroom, Evan wolfed down a tin of beans whilst Amane slung the backpack over her shoulder and stood up, stretching.

"They're just getting dressed, should be here in a minute." She yawned. It was still early and they needed more than one night's sleep to make up for the energy they had been using lately. A tin of beans would only get you so far.

"Amane, last night," began Evan. He wasn't quite sure what to say to her.

"It's okay, Evan, you don't have to say anything." Amane fussed herself with the backpack, fidgeting with it until the adjustable compression straps had clicked together.

The door opened and Rob and Sasha came in, stopping the conversation in its tracks. Rob was rubbing his neck and frowning.

"How's your back, mate? Did you take the floor or the bathtub? I'm thinking I should've tried the bath. The floor is bloody hard eh?" he said to Evan.

"Yeah, yeah, it was really hard." Rob didn't notice Evan blush as he stretched his back, pretending it hurt. Amane stifled a smile and said nothing.

"Ready when you are, guys," said Sasha. Her hands were cut, blistered and sore, but otherwise, she looked immaculate. Amane didn't know how she did it, given the circumstances.

"Right," said Evan, "if you're coming with us let's keep this simple. We go as quickly, but as quietly of course, as we can. We'll go straight over the road to the harbour. We need to find the 'Johanna.' There's only half a dozen boats out there, so it shouldn't take us too long. Don't talk unless you have to, okay?"

He began sliding the furniture from the doorway.

"You coming too, then Rob?" said Amane, wishing he wasn't.

"Hell yeah, and leave you alone? Two's company and three's a crowd. Oh, you know what four is? A party!" He nudged Sasha and winked, as she rolled her eyes and ignored him.

Evan heard the exchange and silently cursed that Rob was coming with them. Still, he couldn't exactly tell him not to. As long as he kept quiet and did what he was told, there would be no problem.

Evan opened the door, inch by inch, careful not to make a sound. The corridor was empty and they trod softly down the stairwell. Nothing stirred when they went down the stairs and into the foyer. Evan and Rob cleared the door, dragging the tables and desks out of the way, whilst Amane and Sasha pulled the large plastic plants to one side. Outside was like a ghost town. Evan stepped out first, into the cold street, drawing in a lungful of fresh air. The sun was still low, looping inauspicious shadows over the street. Litter lined the pavements and ash and dust covered the empty cars.

Evan opened his mouth to tell them that it was safe, when he stopped. A zombie appeared by the corner of the building between him and the marina. There was an aberrant noise made by something out of sight that was intensifying. The zombie, an old woman, just seemed to stare at Evan, strangely making no effort to move.

Rob pushed past Evan and pulled at the nearest car door of the row of parked cars outside the building. When it didn't open, he moved to the next one.

"What are you doing?" said Evan, quietly.

"Getting us some transport, what do you think?" replied Rob. He pulled at the door to a silver BMW and it snapped open.

"Come on girls!" Rob shouted, grinning madly.

"Stop, you idiot! We don't need a car, that'll just attract too much attention. I told you, we can make it on foot from here. Bloody fig-jam," said Evan, approaching the BMW, annoyed by the posturing bravado displayed by Rob so early on in the day.

"Whatever, pussy," said Rob, shaking his head and slamming the door shut. The keys were hanging in the ignition and the engine started immediately. He positioned the mirror so he could admire himself; his strong jaw and blue eyes had served him well so far. It wouldn't be long before he got in Sasha's pants. Or Amane's, he thought.

Rob gawped in disbelief and his daydreams evaporated when a hooded figure rose up from the back seat. A blanket slipped off the figure's head revealing a young girl. Her dead eyes locked on Rob's in the mirror and the zombie lunged forward, clawed fingers puncturing his neck as it snapped its rotten teeth into his handsome face.

Rob's body went rigid as he fought valiantly against the zombie ripping his throat out. His hands gripped the wheel and his foot slammed down on the accelerator as he screamed. The BMW sped forward quickly, speeding up and bearing down on the entrance to the building. Evan jumped out of the way, hitting the pavement, whilst Amane and Sasha, half-in and half-out of the door, scurried back inside. The BMW smashed through the glass doors and crashed to a halt, embedding itself into the wall. Amane and Sasha got out of the way just in time but were showered with glass fragments.

Evan looked up and saw a thousand zombies suddenly appear from around the corner and rush headlong toward him.

Evan scrambled through the foyer, crunching glass underfoot, and picked Amane up.

"You two okay?" he said, looking from one to the other. They nodded and then Sasha screamed.

The driver's door opened and Rob got out of the car, blood pouring down his neck and chest. He reached out to them, pirouetted, and fell onto the floor, lying still. The hooded girl, who proceeded to tear greedily into the back of Rob's neck, chewing flesh and tissue, slobbering bright red blood down her face, immediately followed him.

"We need a new plan," whispered Amane, watching in disbelief. Sasha bent over and retched. If she had eaten anything, it would have been all over the floor.

"Back inside, hurry!" Evan pushed the two girls ahead of him, into the corridor they had just left. The swarming zombies outside broke through the mangled frontage of the building easily, just feet behind the trio running back into the corridor. Evan threw the mannequin leg at them in vain and it was instantly swallowed up by the advancing horde. He was not going to be able to beat a thousand zombies to death with it.

They ran up the stairwell, headed toward their room, headed anywhere away from the ghouls chasing them. As they ran up the stairs two at a time, they could hear the footsteps echoing behind them. Evan heard George's words in his head: 'It's harder for them to go up, than down.'

"Keep going up!" he shouted to Amane at the front. "The room's a dead-end, we'd be trapped!" They ran for their lives.

* * * *

Seven, eight, nine, ten... Evan counted the floors as they ascended each one. Their pace slowed as they climbed. A lack of decent food and dehydration meant they were running out of energy fast. On the tenth floor, which otherwise looked exactly the same as the others, there was a newly installed fire hose. Evan pulled it and laid it out, curling it across the steps. It wouldn't stop the following zombies but it might slow them down and buy some valuable time. They had no energy for talking and climbed further when Evan was done.

On the fifteenth floor, they paused, unable to carry on. All three sat down, breathless, listening. The zombies were slow but still coming.

"One minute," said Evan wheezing. He spoke with a rasping voice, his throat sore. Amane and Sasha sat down on the floor, getting their breath back, whilst Evan quickly skirted up and down the corridor. All the rooms were empty. There was no other stairwell or fire escape. He tried the lift but there was nothing installed yet. He pulled apart plywood doors revealing smooth walls and a bottomless pit. There was no other way down. Evan punched a door in frustration.

"We have to keep going."

Their brief respite over, they carried on. On the next floor, Evan was confronted with a ghoulish sight. Lying on the top step was a woman, curled up in a ball, her back to them. She was dressed in a blue skirt, navy stockings, heels, and a blood-soaked white blouse. Evan could see scratch marks on her arms plus deep chunks of skin missing where something had taken several bites out of her.

He stepped over her cautiously and told the others to follow him quickly. She had a badge still pinned to her front that read:

"Stacy – here to help"

"She must have worked here," said Amane, peering over Evan's shoulder. Amane felt guilty but she couldn't help but be disgusted. The woman's face had been turned inside out. From the blood on her clothes and the stairs, it looked as if she had died painfully and slowly, probably bleeding to death. Upon closer inspection, Amane could see that Stacey's head was actually separated from her body. Whatever had killed her had ripped her head off and discarded it.

"Be careful," said Evan. "There aren't any blood trails leading up the stairs. So whatever killed her might still be here."

Sasha shivered, turned, and looked up the stairs. "Look's clear."

"Let me go first," said Evan, and Sasha stepped aside; relieved she didn't have to go up first. Evan had taken no more than one-step when he heard it: a grumbling sound from above somewhere, getting louder, echoing down the stairwell. Evan heard slow footsteps that slipped and scuffed erratically down the stairs. He took a step back.

"Get back," he said.

Amane and Sasha stepped back into the corridor nervously, as a young man appeared on the stairs in front of Evan. He looked like a builder or tradesman of some sort in scruffy trousers and shirt, once stained with paint, now stained crimson. The zombie was still wearing a yellow hard hat. The man's face was smeared with blood and when he opened his mouth, he showed off sharp, dark red teeth. The zombie practically threw itself down onto Evan who grabbed it as it fell on top of him and they skidded across the floor. Ignoring the girls' screams, he pushed it up and off him.

Evan picked it up by the shoulders and rammed the man into the concrete wall head first. He did it twice more and the hard hat fell off. Evan rammed the head again and again into the wall until he succeeded in breaking the man's skull. The zombie continued to struggle and its arms caught hold of Evan's legs. Evan kicked out and the zombie lost its hold of him. He kicked the zombie in the face, feeling its nose break on his foot. The head slammed back down onto the plain concrete floor and Evan knelt down. Grabbing the zombie by the hair, he smashed its head over and over and over until its skull finally caved in, spraying the walls with blood. Brain oozed out of the split skull. Whilst it lay there twitching, Evan stood up and brought his boot down hard on its throat, snapping the zombie's neck. It lay still.

"Come on, let's move." Evan glanced at Amane and Sasha, cowering in a doorway. The zombie dismantled, they stepped over the putrid corpse and followed Evan up the stairs.

* * * *

Another few floors up and they reached the final level. The doors opened out onto the roof. It was surrounded by scaffolding and tarpaulin blowing in the wind. The air was bitter and foul up here. The breeze blew but only brought them more air full of smoke and burning chemicals. They were exhausted. They had gone up about twenty flights. The zombies were slower but they did not run short of breath; they climbed steadily and surely, aware only that they must keep going. Their muscles did not ache and they had no concept of time. Onward and upward, the dead climbed.

Evan looked for something to barricade the door, but there was very little. There was a small cart full of tools that Evan dragged over and pushed in front of the door. He rushed from one edge of the building to the other looking for an escape route. The scaffolding did not reach the ground as it was only on the last few top floors. There was a fire escape but it stopped a few floors short of the roof, as it was incomplete. There was no way of reaching it. They were stuck.

"Oh, God, Evan, what are we going to do? We're going to die." Sasha sobbed into her hands, salty tears stinging her cuts.

"Sasha, can you just hold that cart against the door. I need to think for a minute." If he kept her preoccupied it might keep her quiet, he thought. Evan looked at Amane, hoping for answers. He felt helpless. He had led them into a trap. This was the dead end he had hoped to avoid and his heart sank as he realised they weren't going to make it.

Amane picked up a piece of scaffolding and walked over to Evan. She handed it to Evan and looked him in the eyes.

"If we're going down, we're going down fighting." He weighed up the metal pole in his hands.

"Right." He embraced her and they kissed passionately. Sasha noticed them and left the cart.

"So what, I have to do the hard work while you two make out? Do you even care about me? Or what happened to Rob? Jesus Christ." Sasha looked accusingly at Evan.

"I'm not even getting into this with you. Here." Evan thrust the metal pole into Sasha's hands who winced when she took hold of it.

"You're going to need it. We're in this together, okay?" Sasha just grunted.

Amane avoided looking at Sasha and looked around for more spare poles they could use. She picked one up, small enough for her to handle whilst Evan did the same.

The door suddenly banged against the cart and a single startled seagull flew up into the air from a walkway adjoining the scaffolding.

"Shame we can't fly too," said Sasha, and through bloodshot eyes, prepared herself to face the mass of zombies now pushing against the door to the roof.

Evan looked at the walkway and jogged over to it. Amane hesitated and then ran over to Evan. The wooden walkway extended over the edge of the roof onto a small platform. She walked over carefully, looking out over the city from a much greater height than she wanted to. Up here, exposed, she felt very uneasy.

"What are you doing, Evan?" she said looking at him. He was staring out into the open air and for a second it crossed her mind he might be thinking about jumping.

Looking over her shoulder, he considered the tower crane. It was the same one that Amane had seen yesterday. From the mast was a long horizontal jib, from which a large hook was dangling.

"That's it," he said, pointing past the platform, over a gap of about fifty feet to the crane. The towering column stuck out awkwardly against the blue sky. From where they stood, the mast went up another twenty feet or so to the operator's cab. The worker's arm jutted out, an Australian flag fluttering strongly in the wind. Amane felt sick.

"You're not serious."

"I can do it." Evan continued staring at the crane, sizing it up, working the plan through his mind. "If I take a long enough run up, I can make it. I'll climb up to the cab and as long as it's got power, I'll figure out what I need to. I'll swing the hook around to you and Sasha then back over to the car park. It'll reach. We go back the way we came, Amane. The zombies won't be able to follow us and the few left on the ground we can get past. This is a workable plan. This is our only plan."

"A workable plan, are you insane? Have you grown wings in the last five minutes?" Said Amane, mad. "Do you see how far it is? If you even make it to the crane, you have to hold onto that thing when you hit it." She held his arm worried he might go through with it.

"They're coming!" screamed Sasha, as the cart toppled over and the first of the zombies burst through the doorway onto the rooftop.

"Be ready," said Evan as he jogged to the far end of the walkway. Amane's head spun as she realised Evan was going to jump. Sasha's screams faded into the background as Amane watched Evan sprint past her and launch himself into the air. He glided silently, shirt flapping as the wind whistled past him and he dropped over the edge of the building out of sight. Amane raced down to the roof in shock to help Sasha fight the advancing zombies. Her metal pole connected with soft skulls and bloated stomachs. One after another, they were sent flying, only to be replaced by more. They kept on pouring in through the open door. Amane stood next to Sasha and whirled the pole above her head, smacking it into anything that came close enough.

"When I tell you to go, run up to that walkway as fast as you can, okay?" said Amane.

"What?" said Sasha, brutally bashing a man's head in, ignoring the pain from her hands that were now dripping with blood: her own blood. "Where's Evan?"

"He's gone to get help. Look, just be ready, okay." They spoke no more and tried to hold back the unstoppable horde.

Amane couldn't believe what Evan was attempting, but she had to admit it was the only way off this building. Every step forward they took to hit a zombie they took two back. They were gradually being repelled backwards and would finally be cornered with nowhere else to run.

What if Evan didn't make the jump? What if he did, but couldn't hold on to the crane? Amane felt queasy. The rotting guts falling at her feet she could handle, the thought of Evan plummeting to his death she could not. Gripping the metal pole firmly, she continued hitting the zombies beside Sasha, praying Evan would make it: for all their sakes.

CHAPTER FIFTEEN

Evan hurtled into the tower crane with a resounding crash. A metal bar struck his chest and winded him. As he clawed for breath, he wrapped his arms desperately around the crane trying to stop his fall. His body banged painfully into the metal mast and he half expected to go bouncing back off, down to the ground where he would be breakfast for several hundred zombies.

Instead, his momentum took him so fast and hard into the crane that it almost carried him past it. He managed to hold on, and trying to catch his breath, focused on the metal latticework before his eyes. As he regained control of his breathing, he gripped tightly onto the metal frame and looked down. He watched as two hundred feet below him, the zombies attacked the building, looking like tiny ants scurrying into their nest. All the way back to the marina at one end, and a junction at the other, the street was full of zombies, swarming toward them. Over the azure ocean, he saw the clear blue sky stretching toward Tasmania.

Carefully, he reached into the mast and took good hold of a metal bar, intending to use the latticework as a ladder to climb up. The metal was cold and slippery. He ascended the sturdy framework steadily and eventually reached the control booth. He flung open the door and sat down in the chair, sighing as pain in his arms and legs sent throbbing waves through his body. He felt dizzy but he could not stop; Amane and Sasha were relying on him. Charlie and Anna were relying on him.

"I'm scared, I'm scared."

Looking down to the roof, he saw Amane and Sasha battling against an escalating tide of zombies. They were slicing through the rotting bodies but when one went down another two came through the door to replace it. He noticed they were gradually being forced back to the walkway. He hit every button and lever on the controls in front of him and the crane juddered to life. The gears and motors hummed, and Evan crudely jostled the levers around until he worked out how to make the jib swing and he could lower and raise the hook. Swinging it to the roof, he pushed back the cab door and called out.

"Amane! Sasha!"

He didn't have to shout to get their attention, as they were by now already standing up on the walkway, fending off the zombies, waiting for him. The rooftop was full of the dead and the walkway was weakening. Amane could hear it straining and threatening to give way as it was jostled and leant on by so many bodies. Evan stopped the jib above them and lowered the huge hook. Once it was within reach, Amane grabbed it and hauled herself on. The metal was icy cold to the touch. She sat astride it with the backpack resting against the chains that attached the hook to the jib. She pulled Sasha up quickly and they threw the metal poles down, gripping the dirty hook as Evan lifted it up and away from the roof. The zombies stared, still trying to grab them, although impossible, as the two women were lifted away and out of their reach.

Sasha sat hugging Amane, her arms wrapped around her as her lacerated hands bled. Yesterday's wounds had opened and she could barely close her palms, so she gripped Amane with her arms. Amane shut her eyes and clung onto Sasha tightly. The flag ruffled her hair annoyingly and the cold hook sent chills down her spine.

"Oh God. Oh Jesus, this is crazy," said Sasha. Despite the sun, she was freezing. The cold air whipped at her svelte bare legs and she struggled to keep a grip around Amane as Evan swung them out over the street toward the marina's car park roof.

"Just keep still, Sasha," said Amane, quietly, keeping her eyes firmly closed. Sasha looked down at the street below teeming with zombies.

"Oh, my, God."

Swinging over the street, she began to panic. The pain in her hands was excruciating. They felt numb and she shifted her weight to get a better grip. Sasha slipped, losing her hold on Amane. She screamed and flapped her arms uselessly. Amane had to open her eyes and reached out in desperation as Sasha flew away from her. Sasha's bloodied hands managed to grab onto one of the backpack's straps and she screamed in pain. Both women were pulled sideways over the hook. Amane grabbed the huge hook and held on with both hands as Sasha clung onto the backpack, legs kicking wildly, pointlessly, searching for a ground that was not there.

"Help, Amane, I can't hold on!"

Sasha dangled from Amane's back who, with all the weight, was struggling to hold on. Evan saw them and stopped the jib abruptly, which only caused the hook to swing more.

"Please help me, don't let me fall!" Tears streamed down Sasha's cheeks as she pleaded for her life.

"Stop moving around! You're too heavy, I can't hold on!" said Amane, trying to wrap her arms tighter around the hook.

Evan saw they were struggling to hold on and there was no way they would be able to climb back up on to the hook now. He began to manoeuvre the crane's arm again, hoping they could hold on until he got it over the roof and lowered them down, safely.

"Sasha, can you climb up me?" Amane could feel her grip weakening whilst Sasha wriggled around below. Any longer like this, and they would both fall.

"No!" Sasha gripped the backpack fiercely. Blood was trickling down her wrists, dripping onto her face.

Amane tried to pull herself up but with so much weight on her back, she couldn't do it. Her grip was loosening and her arms slipped. She only kept a tenuous hold on the hook by her hands and the roof looked a million miles away. She began crying. There was only one way she was going to make it.

She inched her hand over to the backpack strap and clicked the quick release on her left shoulder. The backpack slipped down her arm and swung wildly. Sasha lost her hold but managed to cling on with one hand to the remaining strap that clung to Amane's right shoulder precariously. Sasha's free arm grabbed Amane's leg.

"No, Amane, no, please!"

Amane looked down at Sasha's face, freckled with blood and tears, utter terror in her eyes.

"I'm sorry," said Amane, quietly. She sobbed as her hand crept toward the other strap.

"I'm sorry," she repeated. Amane clicked the other strap and the backpack slid off her back. She watched as Sasha fell away. She would never forget that abject look of terror in Sasha's eyes, the knowledge that she had seconds to live.

In Amane's ears, Sasha's final blood-curdling scream lasted for an eternity. She tumbled through the air, dropping to the ground fast. From the cab, Evan watched in horror as Sasha fell, cartwheeling over and over. Her long blonde hair hid her terrified face from him. He heard the scream though and it sent a shiver down his spine. It was a scream that would haunt him until his dying day. The zombies below seemed to bellow as one, as she sped toward them.

Amane watched and shuddered as Sasha hit the ground, crashing through a field of zombies, smacking into the road with a loud, sickening thud. Her bones shattered and her internal organs exploded, spraying fresh blood from her body over the zombies, waves of excitement spreading through them like ripples in a pond. A circle of nightmarish creatures descended upon her mangled body to feast. At the moment of impact, her spine snapped in half causing her head to spin around as if she was looking at her own back legs. Her arms and legs were twisted cruelly, pulled from their sockets, her warm blood drenching those zombies closest to her.

Amane, with the weight off her back, pulled herself up onto the hook, cradling it. Her crying continued unabated whilst Evan continued sending the hook over to the car park, and when he was sure it was safely over the centre, he lowered the hook until it reached the surface. He saw Amane get off and fall to the floor. Leaving the safety of the cab, Evan began his tricky journey to Amane. Climbing out of the cab, he climbed up the metal mast and clambered stealthily over the jib, ignoring the zombies below, inch by inch, out to the point where the trolley held the hook in place.

Wrapping his suit jacket around his hands, he lowered himself through the arm into the chains and started to slide down toward Amane and safety. Once he started sliding down, it was hard to stop. The first few feet were reasonable but he soon began to lose his grip and descend faster. He finally met the hook and rolled over painfully as he landed on the roof. He was dazed and lay on his back looking up into the never-ending turquoise sky.

Déjà vu, he thought, and forced himself to stand up, discarding his jacket, now torn to shreds. He held his hand to his head, trying to stop the spinning. Amane grabbed his shoulder and he instantly felt better.

"Hey," he said.

"Time to go," she said, emotionlessly. "Quietly."

"Yeah. Amane..." She strode off in the direction of the exit ramp. He jogged to catch up with her.

"Amane, wait."

Evan stood in front of her. "It was an accident, you know. It's not your fault."

"I know it's not *my* fault," she said, bluntly. "It's yours. Now stop talking and get walking. We probably have a five minute head start on those things before they find out where we are."

Leaving Evan standing there, astonished, she walked off down the ramp without him. He followed, walking six feet behind her, keeping her in sight but unsure of what to say. Was she right? He hadn't forced Sasha to come with them, but it was his plan. Maybe he was lucky they hadn't all been killed. He felt bad about it certainly, but, damn it, it was nobody's fault. If only she had been able to hold on. A storm cloud brewed in Evan's head.

As Amane approached the swing doors to the shopping centre, he called out to her to wait and she stopped with one hand on the door. He placed himself in front of the door, forcing her to look at him, waving his finger as if he was admonishing a naughty schoolgirl.

"Fine, blame me, whatever. But you go out there unfocused and you are going to wind up dead or worse."

"Fine," she sighed. "I hope at least you still have the key to the boat?"

Evan took it from his pocket and dangled it in front of her face briefly before putting it back. He was mad with her. He was mad with himself. But right now, they had to concentrate at the job in hand or they would both be very dead, very soon.

"Stick behind me. Move fast and quietly. There are only a few boats out there so we should be able to find it before *they* find us. If, God forbid, we don't find it, then..."

"Then what?" Amane folded her arms and looked at him expectantly.

"Then I don't fucking know! What do you want me to say?" Evan caught himself before his temper took hold and let out a long slow breath. He looked her up and down and pushed open the door. He didn't have time to argue now.

"Coming?" he asked, angrily.

She nodded and he went through. It looked the same as it had done yesterday. It was eerily silent. All the zombies had evidently given chase and left. A huge ornate clock hung over the doorway downstairs that Evan hadn't noticed before. A smiling koala and a kangaroo pointed to the time. It was 11.57 and they were running out of time. Another day was slipping away.

Evan retraced their steps from yesterday, which only served to remind him of George. He wondered where he had gotten to. The boy deserved a break and Evan truly hoped he was all right. Maybe they would meet up in Canberra one day soon. Evan promised himself that after he got Charlie and Anna that they would go and find George.

Amane stayed just behind Evan keeping an eye out for movement. She did not want anything to surprise them anymore. When you looked closely, there were hiding places everywhere. She tried not to look too hard into the darkest corners; her imagination went to places she did not want to go to. Sasha's face glared back at her from every shadow.

They skirted low down the first pier and had no luck. She read names that meant nothing to her, 'The Merri Rose,' 'Terrys,' 'Mangahoe.' She noticed a few zombies in the marina heading their way but decided they weren't worth telling Evan about, not yet anyway. They were too far away to need handling.

They had to go back down the pier and onto the next one, which was almost deserted. One ship was still moored up at the end. She heard Evan give a quiet exclamation and soon saw why. The 'Johanna' was there waiting for them. A joyful Evan ran up the gangway and turned around beaming.

"This is it, Amane!" He temporarily forgot the recent animosity between them and bounded across the deck up a flight of gleaming white steps to the bridge.

"Evan, wait!" Amane ran up to him. "Be careful. We don't know who, or what, could be on board."

"Of course, don't worry."

The last time someone had told them not to worry was Miguel, and his dead body was currently skulking around Melbourne. Evan's confidence reminded her of Rob. Too much of it could be a bad thing. Evan opened the door to the bridge and walked in. The ship's bridge was spotless. Whoever owned it kept it in mint condition. Looking around, he felt a little bamboozled by all the controls and reluctantly thought back to what the Father had said: 'Keep it simple.'

"Evan, look," said Amane pointing out the window. A couple of zombies were shambling up the pier toward them. Further back, hundreds more were entering the harbour.

"Shit. I'll get us going," said Evan, taking the key out of his pocket. "Can you cast off? Just untie those ropes over there."

She left the bridge and walked back down the steps to the deck where she began untying the ropes. The meaty rope was heavy but she got the job done. She heard the engine start and as soon as she had loosened the final rope, the 'Johanna' pulled away from the pier.

Shielding her eyes from the overhead sun, she looked at Evan through the crystal clear glass of the bridge. He was steering them away out to sea. His face was driven and focused. She wondered how he did it. How he could just switch off and focus like that? Had he forgotten Sasha already?

She looked back at the pier melting away as the approaching zombies fell into the ocean. Unable to swim, they splashed around momentarily before dipping below the surface. She wondered how long they would stay that way. Would they rot? Would they stay below the water forever? She stayed out on the deck watching the city recede whilst Evan drove them on.

Amane was enchanted. She had never seen the city skyline from this vantage point before and it was beguiling. Tall skyscrapers shot up into the sky, highlighting man's ingenuity, his ability to beat nature. Yet looking closer, she could see that man was now dead or dying; the city was burning and the last two people alive there were leaving.

She left the bow and walked carefully to the stern so she could watch Australia fade away. It was a peculiar feeling. She had made it her home in the last few years, yet she also felt as if she was a stranger here. Her true home was back in Tokyo. Her friends were there: people she had gone to school with, her first boyfriend, her relatives, aunts and uncles.

She sat back feeling the warmth of the sun and counted her blessings that she was alive. So many people had died, her parents, Lily, Joe, Rob, and Sasha. Back when she was fifteen, a close aunt had died. She hadn't told her parents or even Hakuba, her best friend, when she had visited the family's Kannushi in the temple.

"Where do you go when you die?" she had asked him. His wizened old face remained expressionless. After the old man had considered this, he had answered her.

"Where do *you* think?"

At the time, she hadn't known what to say and had blurted out something she had read in a magazine: something vague about heaven or hell. Amane had left the Shinto shrine and ran home. She replayed the conversation in her head.

"Heaven or hell," she said out loud. "Except when Hell is full, the scum get sent back to Earth until we're all wiped out."

"What's that?" said Evan, arriving behind her. He sat down beside her.

"What about the ship?" she said, worried.

"It'll be okay for a second. I just wanted to make sure you were all right."

"I'm fine."

He sat beside her for a moment while they watched the city retreat from view. The sea air was invigorating. Heading away from the mainland with the gentle ocean spray on his face, it almost felt as if their problems were disappearing along with the city skyline. Soon he would be reunited with his children. He had to believe they were there. They *must* be.

"Well I've got to get back to the bridge."

They stood up together and Evan walked away. "How long will it take? Until we get there I mean?" Amane asked him.

"All night I expect. We should be there by early morning. Why don't you take a look down below? There should be somewhere to rest up. Just take care, okay?" Evan trudged back up to the bridge leaving her alone.

Amane stayed a minute or two longer and then followed him. She found her way through the bridge, proceeded down below, and tried the doors one at a time. The first door led further down to the engines. The second was a galley. She wandered around opening cupboards admiring all the food and drink. She helped herself to a chocolate cupcake and carried on exploring the ship.

Amane paused in front of the third door. There was a rolling, banging sound inside, faint, but definitely there. Were they not alone on this ship? Evan was up on the bridge. Surely if there was anybody on board, they would've come out by now, unless they were incapacitated for some reason. She looked around for a weapon and drew a blank. She went back to the galley and grabbed a kitchen knife. She approached the door again slowly. The sound was still there and she turned the door handle slowly. When the lock clicked, she flung the door open brandishing the knife. A bottle of gin rolled up against the wall and she let out a sigh: spooked by a bottle. She picked up the unopened bottle, unscrewed it, and took a swig. The alcohol burnt her throat and she coughed before taking another, longer swig.

Venturing further into the room, she put the knife down on a small table. There was a bed, table and chairs, closet, television, even a music system and an iPod dock. A photo hung on the wall by the bed and Amane took it down. A cheerful family smiled at her: a mother, father, and a girl. She took another long swig from the bottle and lay down on the bed. With one hand on the gin and the other grasping the photo tightly, she wept until she fell asleep.

* * * *

Evan looked at the charts spread out before him. Much of it was gibberish but he had a good idea where they were headed. They were going to be at sea for hours bobbing up and down over the ocean. Father Thomas had told him about the Bass Strait, about the dangerous squalls and troughs. He also told him of the abundant marine life, the whales and sharks. It had been a couple of hours since Amane had gone downstairs and he heard her resurface, padding up the wooden steps to the bridge. He shuffled the charts away, not wanting to worry her.

"There's some sort of marine GPS thing on here, but damned if I can work it out," he said as she sat down next to him.

She looked out over the bow. The ocean was calm and peaceful. Occasional white crested waves broke the serene blue glassy sea reflecting the sky. She found it hard to tell where the ocean and the sky split. The horizon just merged them together. A large seagull flew down and landed on the deck, picking at its feathers, interrupting her thoughts.

"Do you think the animals know what's going on? I mean cats and dogs and that, well they're basically fucked, right? Either their owner ate them or they're stuck at home starving to death, probably contemplating eating their owner. What about the free animals that weren't caged or tied up. The ones we hadn't tamed yet: the birds, the insects, fish. It's just another day for them isn't it?"

"Well *he* certainly seems happy," said Evan, watching the gull watching him. It flapped its huge white wings and took off, soaring over the railings and swooping low over the waves, until it was out of sight.

"Amane, can I ask you something?"

He took her silence as a yes.

"What was George talking about? Why would he want to go to Canberra?" said Evan.

Amane shifted in her seat and swivelled the seat to look at Evan. He looked tired. He hadn't shaved in days now and he had bags under his eyes. If it was possible, he looked even thinner than when she had met him. It wasn't just the physical punishment, but the stress that was taking its toll: on them both.

"I told him about a conversation I had with Lily. I wish I hadn't, but you can't undo what's done. And that's a fact."

Amane turned the seat back to the window and for a minute, Evan wondered if she was going to carry on or just stare out the window.

"You remember she said her father works there? Well, he was quite the VIP apparently, so what he told her is probably true. There's a bunker beneath parliament. They built it a few years ago in secret, in case of a terrorist attack. After what happened to Hong Kong a couple of years ago, they weren't taking any chances so they built it deep. Like *really* deep. Lily said it was stocked with food and water in case of a nuclear attack so they could survive down there for years."

"So that's where George is going? Good God."

"There's nothing good about Him," snorted Amane. "Anyway, you think George will make it? Or you think Lily was making it up, trying to impress us?"

"I don't doubt her word. Will George find it and find a way in? That's another question. I bloody hope so. He's a brave kid and he deserves a break. He's lost his entire family in the space of a week. I'm not convinced the people in charge, whoever or wherever that is, have a clue what they're dealing with though."

"Evan there's something else. Lily told me about a plan. She spoke to her father briefly before we met her and he told her something. The line was bad and she only half caught it before they got cut off, but if she's right..."

"What plan?" he asked. Amane looked pale.

"They're going to burn it: all of it. They think they can burn them out. Burn the country and the zombies will burn with it. Disintegrate, turn to ash and Australia will spring back up as it always does."

"Burn it? That's ridiculous. You can't burn a whole country!"

"That's what I said, but Lily was adamant that's what he'd said."

"Well, whatever genius came up with that idea probably hasn't got the ability to go through with it anyway. For starters, they're buried below ground, so how do they even know what's going on up here? Don't tell me they're using the cameras. The cities are on fire, Amane. Half the cameras don't work and the other half are going to show you nothing but vast plumes of smoke.

"Anyway, the zombies aren't scared of fire. If they were, they would've left already, but they haven't. If anything, they seem more concentrated the further you go *into* the cities. There are millions of them and a fucking bonfire is not going to wipe them out. Shit I don't know. My head hurts trying to think about it all."

Evan was exasperated. Amane looked at the beautiful blue ocean shimmering in the sun. It was hard to juxtapose the serenity of the sea against the scenes of death and devastation floating around her mind.

"I found a letter," he said, "pinned to the back of the door."

"What sort of letter?" she asked.

"From the owners of this boat I think. It was more of a note to one of their children, asking them to meet back at the hotel. They were worried as they had called their parents back in London and they'd said that England was overrun."

"Overrun?"

"By zombies I assume. Said they were going to try to get the train to Paris, but then they'd gotten cut off. Whatever's happening is happening everywhere, Amane. You know what your parents told you about your home? Do you think the idiots at Canberra know any better than anyone else? London, Tokyo...where does it end? I don't know. I don't know if it will end."

For a while, they just sat looking out the window. There was nothing either could say.

"Tell me about the ship," said Evan feeling disheartened, trying to lighten the mood. "Anything useful down there? I could use something to eat and drink. It's got to be getting on a bit by now."

Amane stood up. "Yes actually. There's a pretty well stocked kitchen down there. I was going to get us something but I fell asleep. I guess I needed a power nap. You want to come down with me and get something now?"

Evan powered down the engines. "No worries, just give me a minute, I'll see you there."

He busied himself at the controls whilst Amane went to the galley. She poked around and found plates and cutlery. In the fridge was a cold litre of unopened water. She took it out and placed it on the counter alongside various tubs and jars of chilled food she'd found: pasta, potato salad, relish, cheeses, tomatoes, even some fresh prawns. Whoever owned this boat was clearly never going to go hungry. Her stomach growled as she lay it all out and it was only then she realised she was hungry. It had been hours since they'd eaten last. As the engines died, she found some glasses and poured out the water as Evan came down the stairs.

"Wow," he said, standing in the galley doorway surveying the feast spread out before him. Amane passed him the water and dolloped a spoonful of pasta onto her plate.

"Tuck in," she said through a mouthful of food. They both began eating, stuffing themselves with food that, though simple, tasted like a slice of heaven.

"Are we still headed the right way?" said Amane, loading her plate with more food.

"Yeah, I just stopped while we eat. We don't want to go floating off in the wrong direction. There might be some sort of auto pilot thing but I don't know where. I wouldn't even know how to programme it." He opened the fridge and rummaged around until he found a bottle of beer wedged at the back beside a jar of pickles. He slammed the bottle on the bench, taking the top off and took a long gulp, polishing off half the bottle in one go.

"You want any?" he said, offering Amane the bottle.

"No thanks. I feel a bit off." What with the rolling of the ship, the events of the morning and a full stomach, she was beginning to feel jaded.

"I need some air. I think I might just go and sit out on the deck for a while. Okay?" She took a drink of water and pushed her plate away.

"Sure. Just be careful out there, it's slippery." He sensed there was still something on her mind but she clearly didn't want to talk about it.

"I'll get us on the move again," he said as she glided past him like a ghost. Out on the deck, the sea air instantly made her feel better. Events in the city pushed themselves to the back of her mind and she tried to look forward. You can't undo what's done, she thought. She said a prayer for Sasha and wished she could undo it. Amane listened to the hum of the engines as Evan sailed them onward to Tasmania. She sat down on the deck. They were on their way.

CHAPTER SIXTEEN

The hours dripped by lazily as Amane lay on the deck under the shade of the ship's bridge, occasionally nodding off, only to jerk awake when the dreams evolved into nightmares. Evan tried to keep his focus on navigating. Some of it seemed to be coming back to him from his previous life, whatever that was. The charts and compass felt familiar. Perhaps he had spent some time after all on his father's boat.

'Lemuria' was small, he recalled, much smaller than the ship they were on now. He tried to remember where his father, Tom, lived, but couldn't bring up anything specific. All he was sure of was that his father lived in a small, quiet village, not one of the major towns. As the glimmering ocean swept by, he tried picturing 'Lemuria' in a harbour, to try and think where exactly they should head for. Evan forced his mind to freeze the only image he had of it so he could go deeper, to scour his perforated memory for clues as to where they should go.

The boats moored around his fathers were quite small, as was the harbour itself. The piers, as they were, were made of stones and bricks. There was no giant wharf jutting out to sea or a yacht club, no shopping centre like there had been in Melbourne. Beyond the harbour were a few small buildings, houses or shops dotted by a small road, flanked by green hills. One building stood out more than the rest. It was a shop of some sort made of red brick with a sign above the door. Evan tried to read the shop's sign but the fuzzy image was out of focus.

He ransacked the cupboard where he had found the charts until he found a large map of Tasmania. Examining the coastline, he read the names hoping one would jog a memory, starting with Devonport and working out, Burnie, Bridport, and Wynyard. They may as well have been on the moon. He traced his finger across the map and finally stopped over a place called Stanley.

"Stanley," he said aloud. That was it! He remembered his children running up to him and his wife. The dream he'd had at the airport hangar burst vividly back to life: Charlie, and Anna in that red dress running up to him. They had come from the red brick building and the sign above the door suddenly came into focus:

'Tom's Place'

It wasn't a shop, it was his father's home! Evan picked up a bottle of water and drank down the last droplets inside. If his children were still trapped in the cabin, then he would free them soon. If, by some chance, they had gotten out and off the boat, he knew they wouldn't go far. Tom would keep them safe at home. Evan was relieved he wouldn't have to scour the island for them. He felt as if luck was turning his way once again and he smiled.

The sky outside was fast growing dark. Clouds were billowing up and the sun was sinking. It would be night soon. Evan was keen to push on, especially knowing they were so close, but he also knew his own limitations and was not enthusiastic about sailing at night. He didn't want to crash and drown them both in a pitch black, ice cold sea. He slowed the engines and thought for a few minutes on what to do. Ultimately, he decided to stop the ship completely and Amane came inside, shivering.

"What's up, why have we stopped?" she said.

"I hate to say it, but I think we have to. I'm not confident of doing this at night."

"Okay, well fair enough. Sorry I can't help." She walked over to Evan and leant her head on his shoulder. "I'm sorry, but I needed some space earlier."

"That's okay," said Evan putting his arm around her. "What do you say I secure the ship and we try and relax for a bit? There's not much else we can do until the sun comes up. If I could click my fingers and make it happen, we'd be there right now and

Charlie and Anna would be here with me, but I'm no good to them dead. If I try to keep going, we're going to end up as fish food or so far off course we'll end up in the bloody Antarctic. Let's eat, sleep, and be ready for tomorrow. The sun will be up early and we should be too. I don't like to think how long my kids have been out there now without me."

"I'll see what I can rustle up to eat. Don't beat yourself up, Evan. They'll be okay."

Evan watched her go down the stairs. Amane felt better as she went back into the galley. Her head felt lighter as she raided the cupboards for more food. She loaded up plates and bowls and carried it through to the bedroom, putting it on a small table. Evan appeared a few minutes later and helped her with the last of it.

"All sorted upstairs," he said. Amane sat down on a chair and started slicing some meat whilst Evan poked around the room. He had not had a chance to look around earlier.

"Bathroom's next door," she said, whilst he investigated a drawer full of jewellery and trinkets. "Found some toothpaste but no toothbrushes. Better than nothing though."

Evan swung open a wardrobe and examined the clothes hanging up: bland shirts and boring skirts gave precious little information away about the ship's owners, other than that they had very little adventure regarding fashion. Another cupboard revealed a stack of well read books. Romance novels stacked next to staid historical biographies. A photo lay on crumpled bed sheets and he picked it up. The family looked happy and he wondered if the child in the photo was Johanna. He set it back down and opened a cupboard above the bed.

"Jackpot." Smiling, Evan turned to Amane who was munching on some crisps, and he held out two bottles.

"Red or white?" he said, cheerfully.

"Ha! I'll go find some wine glasses," she said. "I think I saw some in the galley somewhere. We are not drinking out of plastic tumblers tonight."

As they ate and sipped wine, they talked. They skirted around the big issues. They'd both had enough of serious talk. Amane asked Evan about his children, sport, anything that might jolt a memory and help him. Mostly though, Evan let Amane do the talking. She told him about her life growing up in Japan, what Tokyo was like, why she hated sushi and loved steaks, why she lived in Australia now and how she was planning on studying before settling down. Evan didn't once mention what happened back at the city. Eventually, Amane did.

The porthole in the bedroom showed a distant moon glimmering over the ocean and Amane sighed wistfully.

"She didn't deserve it you know," she said out of the blue. Evan knew exactly what Amane was talking about but said nothing. He listened. Amane talked slowly.

"I shouldn't be sitting here. When I shut my eyes, I keep seeing Sasha's face. I've never seen such fear in a person's eyes before, or contempt." Amane rubbed her eyes.

"Amane, it was an accident. Truly, it was. If anything, you were right, it was my fault. It was my stupid idea."

"No, she didn't fall, Evan. I had to do it. She was dragging me down with her. I had to let her go."

"What do you mean? I saw her fall. With her hands cut up like that, I'm not surprised she couldn't hold on," Evan said.

"I cut her down. The straps on the backpack, I... She wouldn't stop thrashing around and I couldn't hold her up as well as myself. I..." Amane's throat tightened up and she couldn't continue.

"Well for what it's worth, I think I would've done the same," said Evan. "I'm sorry you were in that position and I'm sorry that Sasha isn't here right now, but there's no point looking back. You did what you had to do to survive, Amane. I don't mean to sound callous, but I'm bloody glad you did."

Amane sniffed and cleared her throat. "You're right, I survived. Would I do it again? I don't know. But I have to live with her death every day. Her face when she fell... Fuck, Evan, what's the world come to? What about Lily? It's not fair. Why am I sitting here and they're not?"

"Fate, God, natural selection, sod's-fucking-law? You have to figure that one out for yourself. I don't think there is an answer. I think what happens, happens. There's no rhyme or reason to it."

Amane sipped her wine and they sat in pensive silence. Eventually Amane moved to sit next to Evan on the bed and poured out some more wine.

"It's late. We should get some rest. Up early tomorrow, remember."

They talked a little more whilst they finished their wine. Amane went to the bathroom and when Evan took a turn and came back, he found her tucked up in bed. He climbed in beside her and they held each other in the warmth as they drifted to sleep. Evan felt guilty. Shouldn't they be powering through the sea right now to his children? He couldn't do it. His useless brain could only get them so far. Evan fell asleep praying for their safety. He prayed that Tom was keeping them safe on his boat.

Across the sea, Australia lay silent. Skyscrapers smouldered in devastated cities, whilst the ravaged countryside tried to hide its secrets of housing estates, shops, garages, farms, offices, all destroyed. Smaller communities suffered destruction as much as the larger urban areas. The afflicted roamed freely, encountering little resistance. The foolish and the foolhardy fell as easily as the other. One by one they died, reawakening to join their flesh-eating brothers and sisters.

Further away, the rapacious destruction of civilisation continued unabated and uninterrupted. Man was powerless to intervene as The Petronas Towers crumbled to a pathetic pile of rubble and the refineries of the Middle East burnt unattended. Unobserved chemical plants around the world exploded, sending acrid smoke over the once green fields of South America and Europe unchecked.

Worldwide they rose in their millions from the slums: from Brazil, India, America, and Eastern Europe, the zombies rose up to kill, to destroy, and to take vengeance on the living.

Resistance around the globe was small and disorganised. Bands of men and women here and there struck where they could, holding their ground wherever they had taken cover. The rich and famous cowered in their paper palaces until they were forced out to scavenge for help or food. They rarely returned home. The world had become a circus: a House of the Dead, the Damned, and the Dying.

* * * *

With a little help from a full belly and plenty of red wine, Evan slept contentedly, at least for a few hours. In the night he was awoken as the wind rocketed around outside and waves rocked the ship back and forth. He left Amane sleeping and went up to the bridge. The 'Johanna' listed from side to side and Evan hoped the storm didn't grow any worse. The ocean seemed hungry now. Huge waves broke over the bow and lashed salty water against the window. Evan slumped down in the captain's chair and sat watching the storm, listening to the howling of the wind. He was reminded of Sasha, the roaring noise of the zombies surrounding her as she had fallen echoing in his head like the wind outside. He shuddered and peered into the night sky. Random stars shone through gaps in the clouds and the half-moon cast a weak lustre over the sheen of the ocean. Evan stayed in the chair until; at last, he fell asleep again.

A loud bump against the ship's hull jolted him awake and he sat up, instantly alert. He heard Amane call out to him.

"Evan, come quick!"

Faint sunlight splayed down through dissipating storm clouds. Out on the deck, Evan saw that Amane was dressed and standing by the railing, looking over at something in the water. Evidently, he had slept in the chair for the rest of the night. He stretched and rolled his shoulders before going outside to find out what was happening.

"Sorry. I wasn't going to wake you but it's amazing. I've never seen anything like it!" Evan looked to where she was pointing at the water excitedly and looked over the scaly, barnacle-encrusted body of a whale. As it slipped through the water, it nudged the ship again and Evan grabbed the railing.

"Do you know what it is?" said Amane scanning the surface as the whale sunk silently into the murky depths.

"A whale?" came Evan's sardonic reply.

"Very funny," said Amane groaning.

"Beyond that, I can't help you," said Evan. "A big whale?"

"You're useless, you know that?" Amane replied. The whale had gone out of sight for good and they went back inside to the warmth of the cabin.

"You missed the storm last night," said Evan walking down to the galley with Amane following.

"What can I say, I'm a heavy sleeper." She took some yoghurt from the fridge and dug into it.

"I wouldn't say I slept very well, but who cares," Evan said. "In a few hours, we'll be in Tassie with my kids and my dad. I can feel it, Amane, it's going to be...awesome!"

Evan grabbed a bottle of water and bounded like a child out of the galley. He dressed, pulled up the anchor and put the engines into motion. He checked the charts and headed, full throttle, to Tom, Charlie and Anna. Amane tidied up and hoped that Evan's prayers would be answered today.

* * * *

Amane stayed in the bridge with Evan as they approached land a few hours later. It was cool outside and the sun was unsuccessfully trying to edge its way over Tasmania slowly. The clouds had reappeared, blocking it out, and it had begun drizzling. The rain was constant and fine: enough to soak the skin.

"Do you know where we are?" she said.

"I think so. Over to the right there is Robbins Island, which means, according to the map that over there is Perkins Bay. Stanley is just past it. We're very close now." Evan pulled the ship around the headland and slowed the engines.

As they headed closer toward land, Evan began trembling. He was both excited and apprehensive about seeing his children again. When he saw them, would he remember them? Would holding them bring back his memory? Would they reminisce about the past? Darker thoughts gripped him too. What would he tell them had happened to their mother? What should he tell them about himself? How much did they know of what was happening in the world? He would confront it as and when he needed to, he decided.

As they approached the harbour, Evan was sure that he'd found the right one. He saw the red brick building and it looked exactly as he remembered. Evan pulled the boat up slowly and as they reached the first stony pier, there was a horrible cracking noise and the ship lurched to a sudden halt.

"Shit," said Evan. "It's too shallow. I think we hit the bottom."

Amane raced outside and looked down at the hull. "Evan, we've hit something, there's a huge gash in the side of the ship!"

"Okay, let's go," he said, "we can make it down onto the pier from here. I hope my father's boat is in better condition than this one."

He lowered a rope ladder over the railings and they scrambled onto the pier, splashing over dark coloured stones as the 'Johanna' began taking on water.

Evan shielded his eyes from the constant drizzle and scanned the harbour. It was devoid of life and sound. It seemed as if the whole island was. Beyond the harbour were a few houses, then verdant bush. Evan saw his father's home. Bare, sickly trees dripped in the rain beside it.

He saw a yacht listing side to side in the water, holes perforating its sails. They looked ominously like bullet holes. Beyond the yacht, he spied what he was looking for: the 'Lemuria.' His heart began pounding in his chest.

"There," he said to Amane pointing toward the boat, "they're still here! We have to go past my father's house, over there, to get to it. You see that brick building? I'm going to look inside, just in case they're in the house."

They ran carefully over the slippery, smooth, stone lined piers. Reaching Tom's home, Evan tried the front door and slammed it open. Inside the little house, it was cold and quiet. Evan recognised a few things, the grandfather clock, the fishing poles over the fireplace, and the faded brown rug in the middle of the room. As Amane looked around, he ran through the small building, calling out, but finding nothing.

"They're not here," he said to Amane, breathless. "It's empty. The kid's things aren't here. There are no clothes or toys or anything, so they must still be on the boat!"

He was charging around like a bull after a red rag. He pushed past her and ran out into the rain with Amane struggling to keep up. "Evan, wait!"

The closer he got to his father's boat, the more nervous he became. He wasn't expecting a welcoming party but the oppressive sky and the lack of lights on board, suggested little evidence of life at all. He stopped beside the boat and looked it over as Amane caught up.

"They might be inside you know? You said they were stuck in the cabin didn't you?" said Amane. "It's probably safer in there without the lights on too, so as not to attract *them*."

Evan peered grimly at Amane through squinting eyes, raindrops cascading down his face. He didn't know whether to feel elated or deflated.

"I'm going in. Come on."

He jumped down onto the deck and helped Amane on. The boat was tethered to the pier as normal, anchor down. There was no sign of a struggle. Or bullet-holes, thought Evan thankfully.

"Charlie? Anna? It's me, dad," he called out loudly. Amane stood shivering behind him in silence in the rain.

As he ran toward the cabin door, Amane called to him. "Hey, wait, I heard something."

They listened and Evan heard it too. A faint knocking was coming from beneath their feet. Evan dashed through the cabin door and down the stairs below deck, calling out constantly.

"Charlie! Anna! I'm here!"

"Be careful!" shouted Amane, lagging behind, battling to stay on her feet in the slippery, wet conditions. When she got to the bottom of the stairs, she saw Evan standing in front of a wooden door.

"It won't open," he grunted, pulling the door handle frantically. The knocks and bangs on the other side were getting louder. Amane put her hands over Evan's and looked him in the eyes.

"Evan, if it's them, why haven't they answered you?" she asked softly. Evan's eyes locked on hers and she saw the fire in him burning brightly.

"They could be hurt, Amane. I've got to get in there!"

He yanked the handle violently, knocking Amane backwards, who slipped over on the damp floorboards and landed painfully on her back. The door flew open and Evan came face to face with his father. Tom had been dead for some time. His stomach was bloated and his face was pale and blotchy, purple patches contrasting horribly against pallid, loose skin. Tom's grisly corpse lunged at Evan and they fell to the floor together in a heap. Amane screamed.

"Evan!"

She watched the two men grappling, Evan barely holding his father away, jaws snapping inches away from his face. Amane looked around the dim corridor and saw nothing she could use to help Evan. She scrambled back up the stairs to the cabin. Flinging aside fishing rods, tarpaulin, buckets and nets, she finally got lucky and found a rusty, yet solid, harpoon. She jumped down the steps two at a time.

"Evan!" Amane cried out, raising the harpoon above her head with both hands. As he turned to look at her so did his father. Amane looked into the dead eyes and hesitated.

"Youuuu."

The word dripped slowly out of the dead man's mouth, striking dread and despair into Amane's heart. Had he really spoken or had she imagined it? She stopped thinking and thrust the harpoon straight at him. Entering through one eye, it sliced through his head and embedded itself in the wall behind. Evan slipped out from beneath his father and watched as Tom writhed like a worm on a hook. Clammy dead hands reached up to the harpoon and started trying to pull it out.

Leaving Amane trembling where she stood, Evan disappeared upstairs to the bridge and came back quickly with a large knife.

"I used to gut fish with this," he said absently, turning it over in his hands.

He approached his still struggling father and watched as Tom struggled to get up.

"I'm sorry, Dad."

He jammed it into his father's neck and began sawing. Coagulated blood flecked the knife as Evan used all his might to cut through muscle and bone. As he finally severed the head from the body, he stepped back. The body sank to the floor unmoving. His father's head was stuck to the wall like a trophy and the mouth was still moving but making no sound. Evan rammed the knife through his fathers' remaining eye up to the hilt, and left it there. Eventually, the mouth stopped and Evan knew his father was truly dead at last. He turned and faced Amane who was in shock. He had to know what had happened here. Why was his father locked away? Where were his children?

"You okay?" he asked Amane. She nodded and followed him silently as he stepped over Tom's body into the room that had been locked. The first thing that struck them was the smell. Vomit and faeces dribbled down the walls, empty whisky bottles rolled around the floor dodging mouldy food trodden into mush. The room was a mess. The table and chairs were knocked over and torn books and paper littered the floor alongside cups, plates, broken glass and holes in the walls. Evan noticed the empty pill vials and chose to ignore them. He didn't want to think of his once strong father ending his life alone in this cramped, cruddy cabin. There was no sign of anyone else. Amane sat on the small bed, exhausted.

"Charlie? Anna?"

Evan called out forlornly, knowing in his heart he wasn't going to get an answer. He went back into the corridor and opened the remaining closed doors, but he knew he was going to find the rooms all empty. He returned to Amane and sat down beside her. He picked up a photo from the floor and straightened it out. It showed everyone on the boat smiling on a gloriously sunny day. His father must've taken the photo. Evan and his wife were hugging whilst Charlie and Anna were laughing, showing off a fish they'd caught. A picture perfect happy family, he thought.

Evan kicked the door in frustration and it slammed shut sending a sharp echo around the small room. He put his hands on his head. It had taken so much to get this far, yet what had he achieved? He had had to put down his own father. His children were not here. He punched the wall, adding yet another hole to the soft wood.

"Where are they, Amane? My dad's dead and they're not here. He was supposed to look after them. Where are they?" His face was burning with rage. This was not right. This was not supposed to happen.

"Evan, look."

He looked at Amane who was staring at the cabin door. There was an envelope pinned to it with Evan's name written on the front. He grabbed it, picked up one of the chairs from the floor, and plonked himself down heavily into it. Tearing open the envelope, he unfolded the letter inside and read aloud:

"Dear Evan, if you are reading this then I am surely dead. I only hope that I stay that way."

Evan paused and sighed, exhausted. He wiped his moist eyes and continued.

"Son, what has happened to us? The world was far from perfect but we didn't deserve this. I am starting to lose my faith. Is this some terrible vengeance from God? Or some hideous disease mankind has dreamt up? I have no answers. I pray that you are all safe and have escaped this horrible mess.

The island has been evacuated. I didn't want to go; I wanted to wait for you so I hid down here. I don't care if I get marooned here. This is my home. There are worse places to die.

I tried to reach you Evan but the phones stopped working. I waited for you, Alice and the kids but you never came."

Evan stopped reading and looked up at Amane, confused.

"That's not right," Evan said. "I'm sure we dropped the children off here. We did it every year. I can still picture it in my head. It's one of the few memories I still have."

Evan frowned and read on.

"Please, God, let you all stay safe and out of this mess. Your plane was supposed to land today and when you didn't arrive I asked the harbour master if he could check. He managed to radio someone and he said there was a lot of trouble on the mainland, especially in the cities. He said Sydney and Melbourne were overrun. I guess you probably never took off.

Son, look after your family. Stay at home, lock yourself in, and hope this thing passes. I am going to wait here for you. I have nowhere else to go and it's not safe out there. I heard gunfire today and shouting. I suspect I will be seeing your mother quite soon which gives me some solace.

Take care son, I love you."

Evan let the letter fall to the floor as a wave of nausea passed over him. He stood up feeling sick to the stomach, his head reeling.

"Amane."

Evan swayed, feeling dizzy, and collapsed to the floor. She raced to help him and cradled him like a mother holding her child. They sat on the floor together, surrounded by filth.

"Amane, we didn't make it here. My memories of leaving the kids here on the boat are just that: memories, but not from last week. They're from last month or last year, or God knows when! Oh Jesus..."

He tailed off, and through bleak, red-rimmed eyes, looked up at Amane.

"My kids. They never left Melbourne. Oh God, they were on that plane with me. Alice and I were bringing them here. So Charlie must've called me from the plane. What if they didn't get out before it exploded? I left them behind! Oh God, what have I done? Oh my God..."

He rocked back and forth, crying uncontrollably, as Amane held him.

"Evan," said Amane, choking back tears, "what if they did get out?"

EPILOGUE

As he slowly awoke, he found himself staring up into a cloudless blue sky. No. Not the sky, a ceiling. It was a sickly, pale blue ceiling. He yawned and looked around. The walls were the same depressing blue. His head hurt a bit and for a moment, he wasn't sure where he was.

"Dad? Mum?"

Charlie was cold. He blinked his eyes open and his sister, Anna, woke up too as he called out.

"Come on, Anna, I don't like it in here. We've got to get home and find mum and dad. They'll be waiting for us."

Clutching a rag doll, Anna reluctantly got up and rubbed her sleepy eyes. They had slept with the light on, too fearful to turn it off. The room was bare. There was a gurney with a wheelchair beside it and a first aid box on the wall, which had spilt its contents all over the floor.

"How's your arm?" said Charlie picking up plasters and stuffing them into his pockets.

"It still hurts. My whole arm hurts," replied Anna, kneading her arm, idly picking at the bandage her brother had crudely strapped on over the cuts last night.

"Come on then, let's go find mum and dad."

Anna stopped.

"What if there are more of those funny people out there?" she said timidly, wide eyed with fear.

"We'll be all right," her brother assured her, "we can run faster than them!" He gave her a wink and opened the door. His confidence was just an act for his sister. Deep down he was petrified.

They stepped outside into a murky new world. Shivering with cold, they walked out hand in hand. The meaty fog meant they couldn't see far in front of them. As they trudged onward, Charlie looked up as a giant metal behemoth loomed over them. Two black windows appeared like eyes, staring down at him, and a shiver ran down his spine. Nervously, he continued onward, saying nothing. Charlie tripped over something in the dismal dawn and stuttered to a halt.

"Maybe we should wait a bit?" he asked his sister. "When the sun comes up we'll be able to see a bit better."

He was worried about her. She was normally so full of life and now she was so quiet. It was as if she was still asleep. She looked so sad but he didn't know what to do to help her. All he knew was he had to look after his little sister.

"What's that noise?" Anna said, tilting her head to one side, frowning.

He heard it too but couldn't tell what direction it was coming from. It was just a faint rumbling sound. Muffled lights pierced the fog and Charlie realised it was a car. He began waving at it to stop.

Alice called out, "Help us, help, please!"

They watched in horror as a zombie bounced off the side of the car and headed in their direction attracted by Anna's voice. Charlie waved frantically as the car slipped out into the fog, red lights fading to a dull crimson then blinking into nothingness. Through the grey, the zombie gained speed as it saw them. Charlie ran back underneath the plane and crouched behind a huge wheel. It reminded him of the horrible crash yesterday. This was as close as he ever wanted to be to a plane again.

"Anna, come on!" Charlie looked back. Anna was rooted to the spot.

"No, it's okay, it's mum!"

Anna smiled and waved to Charlie then ran toward the zombie. He saw it was wearing a green top and had brown hair like their mother, but surely, it couldn't be her? As it came closer, he recognised his dead mother. Her clothes were charred from the explosion and her face was drawn. Her eyes were dead, yet deadly focused on Anna. He knew it was her. He flashed back to yesterday and the last time he'd seen his mother. They had all been so excited to be going to Tasmania, to see Granddad and his boat, except the plane had crashed on take-off. He'd tried phoning them but got no answer. He hadn't seen his parents since he'd woken up on the burning plane and dragged his sister off.

"Anna! No!"

Charlie froze in disbelief as his mother picked up Anna, who ran into welcoming open arms. Alice ripped her daughter apart. Anna screamed and fought: confused and tormented. Her dead mother had no hesitation in slicing Anna's throat open and Charlie's sister's screams turned to gurgles.

Charlie stood up, transfixed. He watched as his mother dropped his sister's limp body on the ground and fixed her eyes on him. As his mother started toward him, snarling lips smothered with blood, he ran.

"Dad! Dad! Where are you? Daaad!" he cried as he fled.

With his mother chasing after him, Charlie disappeared into the fog. Just as his mother caught up with him, he made it back to the medical room and slammed the door shut behind him. His dead mother beat furiously on the door, shaking it violently. Charlie curled into a ball in the corner of the room, away from the door, tears streaming down his face as he silently pleaded for his father to come take him home.

THE END

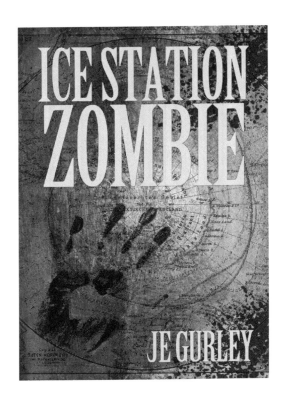

ICE STATION ZOMBIE
JE GURLEY

For most of the long, cold winter, Antarctica is a frozen wasteland. Now, the ice is melting and the zombies are thawing. Arctic explorers Val Marino and Elliot Anson race against time and death to reach Australia, but the Demise has preceded them and zombies stalk the streets of Adelaide and Coober Pedy.

www.severedpress.com

The Coalition

When the dead rose to destroy the living, Ron Cutter learned to survive. While so many others died, he thrived. His life is a constant battle against the living dead. As he casts his own bullets and packs his shotgun shells, his humanity slowly melts away.

Then he encounters a lost boy and a woman searching for a place of refuge. Can they help him recover the emotions he set aside to live? And if he does recover them, will those feelings be an asset in his struggles, or a danger to him?

THE STATE OF EXTINCTION: the first installment in the **COALITON OF THE LIVING** trilogy of Mankind's battle against the plague of the Living Dead. As recounted by author **Robert Mathis Kurtz.**

www.severedpress.com

RANCID

Nothing ever happens in the middle of nowhere or in Virginia for that matter. This is why Noel and her friends found themselves on cloud nine when one of their favorite hardcore bands happened to be playing a show in their small hometown. Between the meteor shower and the short trip to the cemetery outside of town after the show, this crazy group of friends instantly plummet from those clouds into a frenzied nightmare of putrefied horror.

Is this sudden nightmare related to the showering meteors or does this small town hold even darker secrets than the rotting corpses that are surfacing?

"Zombies in small town America, a corporate conspiracy, fast paced action and a satisfying body count- what's not to like? Just don't get too attached to any character; they may die or turn zombie soon enough!" - Mainak Dhar, bestselling author of Alice in Deadland and Zombiestan

www.severedpress.com

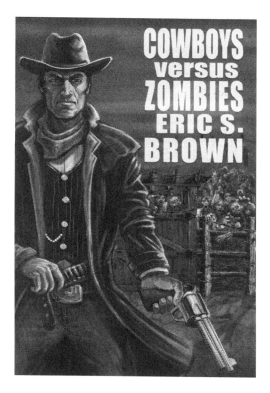

COWBOYS VS ZOMBIES

Dilouie is a killer. He's always made his way in life by the speed of his gun hand and the coldness of his remorseless heart. Life never meant much to him until the world fell apart and they awoke. Overnight, the dead stopped being dead. Hungry corpses rose from blood splattered streets and graves. Their numbers were unimaginable and their need for the flesh of the living insatiable.

The United States is no more. Washed away in a tide of gnashing teeth and rotting, clawing hands. Dilouie no longer kills for money and pleasure but to simply keep breathing and to see the sunrise of the next dawn. . . And he is beginning to wonder if even men like him can survive in a world that now belongs to the dead?

TIMOTHY
MARK TUFO

Timothy was not a good man in life and being undead did little to improve his disposition. Find out what a man trapped in his own mind will do to survive when he wakes up to find himself a zombie controlled by a self-aware virus.

Made in the USA
Lexington, KY
03 May 2013